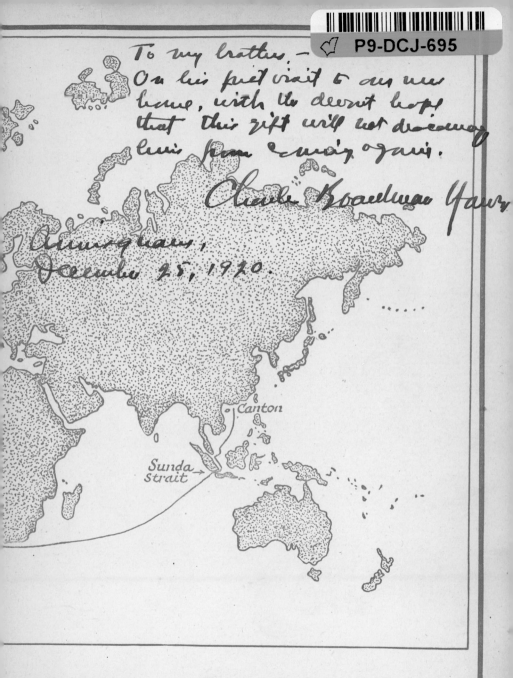

ISLAND PRINCESS

THE MUTINEERS

"At 'em, men! At 'em! Pull, you sons of the devil, pull!"

THE MUTINEERS

*A tale of old days at sea
and of adventures in the Far East as
Benjamin Lathrop set it down
some sixty years ago*

By CHARLES BOARDMAN HAWES

ILLUSTRATED

The ATLANTIC MONTHLY PRESS
BOSTON

To D. C. H.

TO PAY MY SHOT

TO master, mate, and men of the ship *Hunter*, whose voyage is the backbone of my story; to Captain David Woodard, English mariner, who more than a hundred and twenty years ago was wrecked on the island of Celebes; to Captain R. G. F. Candage of Brookline, Massachusetts, who was party to the original contract in melon seeds; and to certain blue-water skippers who have left sailing directions for eastern ports and seas, I am grateful for fascinating narratives and journals, and indebted for incidents in this tale of an earlier generation.

C. B. H.

CONTENTS

I

IN WHICH WE SAIL FOR CANTON, CHINA

II

IN WHICH WE ENCOUNTER AN ARAB SHIP

III

WHICH APPROACHES A CRISIS

IV

IN WHICH THE TIDE OF OUR FORTUNES EBBS

V

IN WHICH THE TIDE TURNS

VI

IN WHICH WE REACH THE PORT OF OUR DESTINATION

VII

OLD SCORES AND NEW AND A DOUBTFUL WELCOME

ILLUSTRATIONS

I

IN WHICH WE SAIL FOR CANTON, CHINA

THE MUTINEERS

CHAPTER I

MY FATHER AND I CALL ON
CAPTAIN WHIDDEN

My father's study, as I entered it on an April morning in 1809, to learn his decision regarding a matter that was to determine the course of all my life, was dim and spacious and far removed from the bustle and clamor of the harbor-side. It was a large room paneled with dark wood. There were books along the walls, and paintings of ships, and over the fireplace there stood a beautiful model of a Burmese junk, carved by some brown artist on the bank of the Irawadi.

My father sat by the open window and looked out into the warm sunshine, which was swiftly driving the last snow from the hollows under the shrubbery.

Already crocuses were blossoming in the grass of the year before, which was still green in patches, and the bright sun and the blue sky made the study seem to me, entering, dark and sombre. It was characteristic of my father, I thought with a flash of fancy, to sit there and look out into a warm, gay world where springtime was quickening the blood and sunshine lay warm on the flowers; he always had lived in old Salem, and as he wrote his sermons, he always had looked out through study windows on a world of commerce bright with adventure. For my own part, I was of no mind to play the spectator in so stirring a drama.

With a smile he turned at my step. "So, my son, you wish to ship before the mast," he said, in a repressed voice and manner that seemed in keeping with the dim, quiet room. "Pray what do you know of the sea?"

I thought the question idle, for all my life I had lived where I could look from my window out on the harbor. "Why, sir," I replied, "I know enough to realize that I want to follow the sea."

"To follow the sea?"

There was something in my father's eyes that I could not understand. He seemed to be dreaming, as if of voyages that he himself had made. Yet I knew he never had sailed blue water. "Well, why not?" he asked suddenly. "There was a time — "

I was too young to realize then what has come to me since: that my father's manner revealed a side of his nature that I never had known; that in his own heart was a love of adventure that he never had let me see. My sixteen years had given me a big, strong body, but no great insight, and I thought only of my own urgent desire of the moment.

"Many a boy of ten or twelve has gone to sea," I said, "and the Island Princess will sail in a fortnight. If you were to speak to Captain Whidden — "

My father sternly turned on me. "No son of mine shall climb through the cabin windows."

"But Captain Whidden — "

"I thought you desired to follow the sea — to ship before the mast."

"I do."

"Then say no more of Captain Whidden. If you wish to go to sea, well and good. I 'll not stand in your way. But we 'll seek no favoritism, you and I. You 'll ship as boy, but you 'll take your medicine like a man."

"Yes, sir," I said, trying perversely to conceal my joy.

"And as for Captain Whidden," my father added, "you'll find he cuts a very different figure aboard ship from that he shows in our drawing-room."

Then a smile twinkled through his severity, and he laid his hand firmly on my shoulder.

"Son, you have my permission ungrudgingly given. There was a time — well, your grandfather did n't see things as I did."

"But some day," I cried, "I'll have a counting-house of my own — some day — "

My father laughed kindly, and I, taken aback, blushed at my own eagerness.

"Anyway," I persisted, "Roger Hamlin is to go as supercargo."

"Roger — as supercargo?" exclaimed a low voice.

I turned and saw that my sister stood in the door.

"Where — when is he going?"

"To Canton on the Island Princess! And so am I," I cried.

"Oh!" she said. And she stood there, silent and a little pale.

"You'll not see much of Roger," my father remarked to me, still smiling. He had a way of enjoying a quiet joke at my expense, to him the more pleasing because I never was quite sure just wherein the humor lay.

"But I'm going," I cried. "I'm going — I'm going — I'm going!"

"At the end of the voyage," said my father, "we'll find out whether you still wish to follow the sea. After all, I'll go with you this evening, when supper is done, to see Joseph Whidden."

The lamps were lighted when we left the house, and long beams from the windows fell on the walk and on the road. We went down the street side by side, my father absently swinging his cane, I wondering if it were not beneath the dignity of a young man about to go to sea that his parent should accompany him on such an errand.

Just as we reached the corner, a man who had come up the street a little distance behind us turned in at our own front gate, and my father, seeing me look back when the gate slammed, smiled and said, "I 'll venture a guess, Bennie-my-lad, that some one named Roger is calling at our house this evening."

Afterwards — long, long afterwards — I remembered the incident.

When my father let the knocker fall against Captain Whidden's great front door, my heart, it seemed to me, echoed the sound and then danced away at a lively pace. A servant, whom I watched coming from somewhere behind the stairs, admitted us to the quiet hall; then another door opened silently, a brighter light shone out upon us, and a big, grave man appeared. He welcomed us with a few thoughtful words and, by a motion of his hand, sent us before him into the room where he had been sitting.

"And so," said Captain Whidden, when we had explained our errand, "I am to have this young man aboard my ship."

"If you will, sir," I cried eagerly, yet anxiously, too, for he did not seem nearly so well pleased as I had expected.

"Yes, Ben, you may come with us to Canton; but as your father says, you must fill your own boots and stand on your own two feet. And will you, friend Lathrop," — he turned to my father,— "hazard a venture on the voyage?"

My father smiled. "I think, Joe," he said, "that I 've placed a considerable venture in your hands already."

Captain Whidden nodded. "So you have, so you have. I 'll watch it as best I can, too, though of course I 'll see little of the boy. Let him go now. I 'll talk with you a while if I may."

My father glanced at me, and I got up.

Captain Whidden rose, too. "Come down in the morning," he said. "You can sign with us at the Websters' counting-house.— And good-bye, Ben," he added, extending his hand.

"Good-bye? You don't mean — that I 'm not to go with you?"

He smiled. "It 'll be a long time, Ben, before you and I meet again on quite such terms as these."

Then I saw what he meant, and shook his hand and walked away without looking back. Nor did I ever learn what he and my father talked about after I left them there together.

CHAPTER II

BILL HAYDEN

More than two-score years and ten have come and gone since that day when I, Benjamin Lathrop, put out from Salem harbor, a green hand on the ship Island Princess, and in them I have achieved, I think I can say with due modesty, a position of some importance in my own world. But although innumerable activities have crowded to the full each intervening year, neither the aspirations of youth nor the successes of maturity nor the dignities of later life have effaced from my memory the picture of myself, a boy on the deck of the Island Princess in April, 1809.

I thought myself very grand as the wind whipped my pantaloons against my ankles and flapped the ribbons of the sailor hat that I had pulled snugly down; and I imagined myself the hero of a thousand stirring adventures in the South Seas, which I should relate when I came back an able seaman at the very least. Never was sun so bright; never were seas so blue; never was ship so smart as the Island Princess.

On her black hull a nicely laid band of white ran sheer from stem to stern; her bows swelled to meet the seas in a gentle curve that hinted the swift lines of our clippers of more recent years. From mainmast heel to truck, from ensign halyard to tip of flying jib-boom, her well-proportioned masts and spars and taut rigging stood up so trimly in one splendidly coördinating structure, that the veriest lubber must have acknowledged her the finest handiwork of man.

It was like a play to watch the men sitting here and

there on deck, or talking idly around the forecastle, while Captain Whidden and the chief mate conferred together aft. I was so much taken with it all that I had no eyes for my own people who were there to see me off, until straight out from the crowded wharf there came a young man whom I knew well. His gray eyes, firm lips, square chin, and broad shoulders had been familiar to me ever since I could remember.

As he was rowed briskly to the ship, I waved to him and called out, "O Roger — ahoy!"

I thought, when he glanced up from the boat, that his gray eyes twinkled and that there was the flutter of a smile on his well-formed lips; but he looked at me and through me and seemed not to see me, and it came over me all at once that from the cabin to the forecastle was many, many times the length of the ship.

With a quick survey of the deck, as if to see who had spoken, yet seeming not to see me at all, Roger, who had lived all his life within a cable's length of the house where I was born, who had taught me to box the compass before I learned my ABC's, whose interest in my own sister had partly mystified, partly amused her younger brother — that very Roger climbed aboard the Island Princess and went on into the cabin without word or sign of recognition.

It was not the first time, of course, that I had realized what my chosen apprenticeship involved; but the incident brought it home to me more clearly than ever before. No longer was I to be known as the son of Thomas Lathrop. In my idle dreams I had been the hero of a thousand imaginary adventures; instead, in the strange experiences I am about to relate, I was to be only the ship's "boy" — the youngest and least important member of that little isolated community banded together for a journey to the other side of the world. But I was to see things happen such as most men have never dreamed of; and now, after fifty years, when the others are dead and gone, I may write the story.

When I saw that my father, who had watched Roger Hamlin with twinkling eyes ignore my greeting, was chuckling in great amusement, I bit my lip. What if Roger *was* supercargo, I thought: he need n't feel so big.

Now on the wharf there was a flutter of activity and a stir of color; now a louder hum of voices drifted across the intervening water. Captain Whidden lifted his hand in farewell to his invalid wife, who had come in her carriage to see him sail. The mate went forward on the forecastle and the second mate took his position in the waist.

"Now then, Mr. Thomas," Captain Whidden called in a deep voice, "is all clear forward?"

"All clear, sir," the mate replied; and then, with all eyes upon him, he took charge, as was the custom, and proceeded to work the ship.

While the men paid out the riding cable and tripped it, and hove in the slack of the other, I stood, carried away — foolish boy!—by the thought that here at last I was a seaman among seamen, until at my ear the second mate cried sharply, "Lay forward, there, and lend a hand to cat the anchor."

The sails flapped loose overhead; orders boomed back and forth; there was running and racing and hauling and swarming up the rigging; and from the windlass came the chanteyman's solo with its thunderous chorus:—

> "Pull one and all!
>   Hoy! Hoy! Cheery men.
> On this catfall!
>   Hoy! Hoy! Cheery men.
> Answer the call!

Hoy! Hoy! Cheery men.
Hoy! Haulee!
Hoy! Hoy!!!
Oh, cheery men!"

As the second anchor rose to the pull of the creaking windlass, we sheeted home the topsails, topgallantsails and royals and hoisted them up, braced head-yards aback and after-yards full for the port tack, hoisted the jib and put over the helm. Thus the Island Princess fell off by the head, as we catted and fished the anchor; then took the wind in her sails and slipped slowly out toward the open sea.

Aft, by the lee rail, I saw Roger Hamlin watching the group, a little apart from the others, where my own people had gathered. My father stood half a head above the crowd, and beside him were my mother and my sister. When I, too, looked back at them, my father waved his hat and I knew his eyes were following me; I saw the flutter of white from my mother's hand, and I knew that her heart was going out with me to the uttermost parts of the earth.

Then, almost timidly, my sister waved her handkerchief. But I saw that she was looking at the quarter-deck.

As land fell astern until it became a thin blue line on the western horizon, and as the Island Princess ran free with the wind full in her sails, I took occasion, while I jumped back and forth in response to the mate's quick orders, to study curiously my shipmates in our little kingdom. Now that we had no means of communication with that already distant shore, we were a city unto ourselves.

Yonder was the cook, a man as black as the bottom of his iron pot, whose frown, engraved deeply in his low forehead, might have marked him in my eyes as the vil-

lain of some melodrama of the sea, had I not known him
for many years to be one of the most generous darkies, so
far as hungry small boys were concerned, that ever ruled
a galley. The second mate, who was now in the waist,
I had never seen before — to tell the truth, I was glad
that he held no better berth, for I disliked the turn of his
too full lips. Captain Whidden and the chief mate, Mr.
Thomas, I had known a long time, and I had thought
myself on terms of friendship with them, even familiarity;
but so far as any outward sign was concerned, I might
now have been as great a stranger to either as to the
second mate.

We were twenty-two men all told: four in the cabin —
Captain Whidden, Mr. Thomas, Mr. Falk, and Roger,
whose duties included oversight of the cargo, supervision
of matters purely of business and trade in foreign ports,
and a deal of clerical work that Captain Whidden had no
mind to be bothered with; three in the steerage — the
cook (contrary, perhaps, to the more usual custom), the
steward, and the carpenter; and fourteen in the forecastle.

All in all I was well pleased with my prospects, and
promised myself that I would "show them a thing or
two," particularly Roger Hamlin. I 'd make a name for
myself aboard the Island Princess. I 'd let all the men
know that it would not take Benjamin Lathrop long to
become as smart a seaman as they 'd hope to see.

Silly lad that I was!

Within twenty minutes of that idle dream the chain of
circumstances had begun that was to bring every man
aboard the Island Princess face to face with death. Like
the small dark cloud that foreruns a typhoon, the first act
in the wild drama that came near to costing me my own
life was so slight, so insignificant relatively, that no man of
us then dreamed of the hidden forces that brought it to pass.

On the forecastle by the larboard rigging stood a big, broad-shouldered fellow, who nodded familiarly at the second mate, cast a bit of a leer at the captain as if to impress on the rest of us his own daring and independence, and gave me, when I caught his eye, a cold, noncommittal stare. His name, I shortly learned, was Kipping. Undeniably he was impudent; but he had, nevertheless, a mild face and a mild manner, and when I heard him talk, I discovered that he had a mild voice; I could find no place for him in the imaginary adventures that filled my mind — he was quite too mild a man.

I perceived that he was soldiering at his work, and almost at the same moment I saw the mate come striding down on him.

"You there," Mr. Thomas snapped out, "bear a hand! Do you think you're waiting for the cows to come home?"

"No-o-o, sir," the mild man drawled, starting to walk across the deck.

The slow reply, delivered with a mocking inflection, fanned to sudden laughter chuckles that the mate's words had caused.

Mr. Thomas reddened and, stepping out, thrust his face close to the other's. "You try any of your slick tricks on me, my man," he said slowly and significantly, "you try any of your slick tricks on me, and so help me, I'll show you."

"Ye-e-es, sir," the man replied with the same inflection, though not so pronounced this time.

Suddenly the deck became very still. The listeners checked their laughter. Behind me I heard some one mutter, "Hear that, will you?" Glancing around, I saw that Captain Whidden had gone below and that Mr. Thomas was in command. I was confident that the mild seaman was mocking the mate, yet so subtle was his challenge, you could not be sure that he actually was defiant.

Although Mr. Thomas obviously shared the opinion of the men, there was so little on which to base a charge of insubordination or affront that he momentarily hesitated.

"What is your name?" he suddenly demanded.

"Kipping, sir," the mild man replied.

This time there was only the faintest suggestion of the derisive inflection. After all, it might have been but a mannerism. The man had such a mild face and such a mild manner!

"Well, Kipping, you go about your work, and after this, let me warn you, keep busy and keep a civil tongue in your head. We'll have no slick tricks aboard this ship, and the sooner you men realize it, the easier it will be for all hands."

Turning, the mate went back to the quarter-deck and resumed his station by the weather rail.

While his back was toward us, however, and just as I myself, who had listened, all ears, to the exchange of words between them, was turning to the forecastle, I saw — or thought I saw — on Kipping's almost averted face just such a leer as I had seen him cast at the captain, followed, I could have taken my oath, by a shameless wink. When he noticed me gazing at him, open-mouthed, he gave me such another cold stare as he had given me before and, muttering something under his breath, walked away.

I looked aft to discover at whom he could have winked, but I saw only the second mate, who scowled at me angrily.

"Now what," thought I, "can all this mean?" Then, being unable to make anything of it, I forgot it and devoted myself industriously to my own affairs until the hoarse call of "All hands on deck" brought the men who were below tumbling up, to be summoned aft and addressed by the captain.

Apparently Captain Whidden was not aware that there was a soul on board ship except himself. With his eyes on the sea and his hands clasped behind him, he paced the deck, while we fidgeted and twisted and grew more and more impatient. At last, with a sort of a start, as if he had just seen that we were waiting, he stopped and surveyed us closely. He was a fine figure of a man and he affected the fashions of a somewhat earlier day. A beaver with sweeping brim surmounted his strong, smooth-shaven face, and a white stock, deftly folded, swathed his throat to his resolute chin. Trim waistcoat, ample coat, and calmly folded arms completed his picture as he stood there, grave yet not severe, waiting to address us.

What he said to us in his slow, even voice was the usual speech of a captain in those times; and except for a finer dignity than common, he did not deviate from the well-worn customary phrases until he had outlined the voyage that lay before us and had summed up the advantages of prompt, willing obedience and the penalties of any other course. His tone then suddenly changed. "If any man here thinks that he can give me slovenly work or back talk and arguing," he said, "it 'll be better for that man if he jumps overboard and swims for shore." I was certain — and I still am — that he glanced sharply at Kipping, who stood with a faint, nervous smile, looking at no one in particular. "Well, Mr. Thomas," he said at last, "we 'll divide the watches. Choose your first man."

When we went forward, I found myself, as the green hand of the voyage, one of six men in the starboard watch. I liked the arrangement little enough, for the second mate commanded us and Kipping was the first man he had chosen; but it was all in the day's work, so I went below to get my jacket before eight bells should strike.

The voices in the forecastle suddenly stopped when my feet sounded on the steps; but as soon as the men saw that it was only the boy, they resumed their discussion without restraint.

"I tell you," some one proclaimed from the darkest corner, "the second mate, he had it all planned to get the chief mate's berth this voyage, and the captain, he put him out no end because he would n't let him have it. Yes, sir. And he bears a grudge against the mate, he does, him and that sly friend of his, Kipping. Perhaps you did n't see Kipping wink at the second mate after he was called down. I did, and I says to myself then, says I, 'There's going to be troublous times ere this voyage is over.' Yes, sir."

"Right you are, Davie!" a higher, thinner voice proclaimed, "right you are. I was having my future told, I was, and the lady — "

A roar of laughter drowned the words of the luckless second speaker, and some one yelled vociferously, "Neddie the fortune-teller! Don't tell me he's shipped with us again!"

"But I tell you," Neddie persisted shrilly, "I tell you they hit it right, they do, often. And the lady, she says, 'Neddie Benson, don't you go reckless on this next voyage. There's trouble in store,' she says. 'There'll be a dark man and a light man, and a terrible danger.' And I paid the lady two dollars and I — "

Again laughter thundered in the forecastle.

"All the same," the deep-voiced Davie growled, "that sly, slippery — "

"Hist!" A man raised his hand against the light that came faintly from on deck.

Then a mild voice asked, "What are you men quidding about anyway? One of you 's sitting on my chest."

"Listen to them talk," some one close beside me whispered. "You 'd think this voyage was all of life, the way they run on about it. Now it don't mean so much to me. My name 's Bill Hayden, and I 've got a little wee girl, I have, over to Newburyport, that will be looking for her dad to come home. Two feet long she is, and cute as they make them."

Aware that the speaker was watching me closely, I perfunctorily nodded. At that he edged nearer. "Now I 'm glad we 're in the same watch," he said. "So many men just cut a fellow off with a curse."

I observed him more sharply, and saw that he was a stupid-looking but rather kindly soul whose hair was just turning gray.

"Now I wish you could see that little girl of mine," he continued. "Cute? there ain't no word to tell you how cute she is. All a-laughing and gurgling and as good as gold. Why, she ain't but a little old, and yet she can stand right up on her two little legs as cute as you please."

I listened with mild interest as he rambled on. He seemed such a friendly, homely soul that I could but regard him more kindly than I did some of our keener-witted fellow seamen.

Now we heard faintly the bell as it struck, *clang-clang*, *clang-clang*, *clang-clang*. Feet scuffled overhead, and some one called down the hatch, "Eight bells, starbowlines ahoy!"

Davie's deep voice replied sonorously, "Ay-ay!" And one after another we climbed out on deck, where the wind from the sea blew cool on our faces.

I had mounted the first rung of the ladder, and was regularly signed as a member of the crew of the Island Princess, bound for Canton with a cargo of woolen goods and ginseng. There was much that puzzled me aboardship — the discontent of the second mate, the perversity of the man Kipping (others besides myself had seen that wink), and a certain undercurrent of pessimism. But although I was separated a long, long way from my old friends in the cabin, I felt that in Bill Hayden I had found a friend of a sort; then, as I began my first real watch on deck at sea, I fell to thinking of my sister and Roger Hamlin.

CHAPTER III

THE MAN OUTSIDE THE GALLEY

STRANGE events happened in our first month at sea —
events so subtle as perhaps to seem an unimportant part
of this narrative of a strange voyage, yet really as necessary to the foundation of the story as the single bricks
and the single dabs of mortar at the base of a tall chimney
are necessary to the completed structure. I later had
cause to remember each trivial incident as if it had been
written in letters of fire.

In the first dog watch one afternoon, when we were a
few days out of port, I was sitting with my back against
the forward deck-house, practising splices and knots with
a bit of rope that I had saved for the purpose. I was
only a couple of feet from the corner, so of course I heard
what was going on just out of sight.

The voices were low but distinct.

"Now leave me alone!" It was Bill Hayden who
spoke. "I ain't never troubled you."

"Ah, so you ain't troubled me, have you, you whimper-
ing old dog?"

"No, I ain't troubled you."

"Oh, no! You was so glad to let me take your nice
dry boots, you was, when mine was filled with water."

The slow, mild, ostensibly patient voice could be none
other than Kipping's.

"I had to wear 'em myself."

"Oh, had to wear 'em yourself, did you?"

"Let go o' my arm!"

"So?"

"Let go, I tell you; let go or I 'll — I swear I 'll hammer you good."

"Oh, you 'll hammer me good, will you?"

"Let go!"

There was a sudden scuffle, then out from the corner of the deck-house danced Kipping with both hands pressed over his jaw.

"You bloody scoundrel!" he snarled, meek no longer. "You wait — I 'll get you. I 'll —" Seeing me sitting there with my bit of rope, he stopped short; then, with a sneer, he walked away.

Amazed at the sudden departure of his tormentor, Bill Hayden stuck his own head round the corner and in turn discovered me in my unintentional hiding-place.

Bill, however, instead of departing in chagrin, joined me with a puzzled expression on his kind, stupid face.

"I don't understand that Kipping," he said sadly. "I 've tried to use him right. I 've done everything I can to help him out and I 'm sure I don't want to quarrel with him, yet for all he goes around as meek as a cat that 's been in the cream, he 's always pecking at me and pestering me, till just now I was fair drove to give him a smart larrup."

Why, indeed, should Kipping or any one else molest good, dull old Bill Hayden?

"I 'm a family man, I am," Bill continued, "with a little girl at home. I ain't a-bothering no one. I 'm sure all I want is to be left alone."

For a time we sat in silence, watching the succession of blue waves through which the Island Princess cut her swift and almost silent passage. A man must have been a cowardly bully to annoy harmless old Bill. Yet even then, young though I was, I realized that sometimes there is no more dangerous man than a coward and a bully.

"He's great friends with the second mate," Bill remarked at last. "And the second mate has got no use at all for Mr. Thomas because he thought he was going to get Mr. Thomas's berth and did n't; and for the same reason he don't like the captain. Well, I'm glad he's only *second* mate. He ain't got his hands out of the tar-bucket yet, my boy."

"How do you know he expected to get the mate's berth?" I asked.

"It's common talk, my boy. The supercargo's the only man aft he's got any manner of use for, and cook says the steward says Mr. Hamlin ain't got no manner of use for him. There you are."

"No," I thought,— though I discreetly said nothing,— "Roger Hamlin is not the man to be on friendly terms with a fellow of the second mate's calibre."

And from that time on I watched Mr. Falk, the second mate, and the mild-voiced Kipping more closely than ever — so closely that one night I stumbled on a surprising discovery.

Ours was the middle watch, and Mr. Falk as usual was on the quarter-deck. By moonlight I saw him leaning on the weather rail as haughtily as if he were the master. His slim, slightly stooped figure, silhouetted against the moonlit sea, was unmistakable. But the winds were inconstant and drifting clouds occasionally obscured the moon. Watching, I saw him distinctly; then, as the moonlight darkened, the after part of the ship became as a single shadow against a sea almost as black. While I still watched, there came through a small fissure in the clouds a single moonbeam that swept from the sea across the quarter-deck and on over the sea again. By that momentary light I saw that Mr. Falk had left the weather rail.

Certainly it was a trifling thing to consider twice, but

you must remember, in the first place, that I was only a boy, with all a boy's curiosity about trifles, and in the second place that of the four men in the cabin no other derived such obvious satisfaction from the minor prerogatives of office as Mr. Falk. He fairly swelled like a frog in the sun as he basked in the prestige that he attributed to himself when, left in command, he occupied the captain's place at the weather rail.

Immediately I decided that under the cover of darkness I would see what had become of him. So I ran lightly along in the shelter of the lee bulwark, dodging past the galley, the scuttle-butt, and the cabin in turn. At the quarter-deck I hesitated, knowing well that a sound thrashing was the least I could expect if Mr. Falk discovered me trespassing on his own territory, yet lured by a curiosity that was the stronger for the vague rumors on which it had fed.

On hands and knees I stopped by the farther corner of the cabin. Clouds still hid the moon and low voices came to my ears. Very cautiously I peeked from my hiding-place, and saw that Mr. Falk and the helmsman had put their heads together and were talking earnestly.

While they talked, the helmsman suddenly laughed and prodded Mr. Falk in the ribs with his thumb. Like a flash it came over me that it was Kipping's trick at the wheel. Here was absolute proof that, when the second mate and the mild man thought no one was spying upon them, they were on uncommonly friendly terms. Yet I did not dream that I had stumbled on anything graver than to confirm one of those idle rumors that set tongues wagging in the forecastle, but that really are too trifling to be worth a second thought.

When the crew of a ship is cut off from all communication with the world at large, it is bound, for want of

greater interests, to find in the monotonous daily round
something about which to weave a pretty tale.

At that moment, to my consternation, the bell struck
four times. As the two dark figures separated, I started
back out of sight. Kipping's trick at the wheel was
over, and his relief would come immediately along the
very route that I had chosen; unless I got away at once
I should in all probability be discovered on the quarter-
deck and trounced within an inch of my life. Then suddenly, as if to punish my temerity, the cloud passed and
the moonlight streamed down on deck.

Darting lightly back to the companion-ladder, I slipped
down it and was on the point of escaping forward when
I heard slow steps. In terror lest the relief spy me and
reveal my presence by some exclamation that Kipping or
the second mate would overhear, I threw myself down
flat on the deck just forward of the scuttle-butt, where
the moon cast a shadow; and with the fervent hope that
I should appear to be only a heap of old sail, I lay without
moving a muscle.

The steps came slowly nearer. They had passed, I
thought, when a pause set my heart to jumping madly.
Then came a low, cautious whisper: —

"You boy, what you doin' dah?"

It was not the relief after all. It was the good old villainous-looking black cook, with a cup of coffee for Mr.
Falk.

"Put yo' head down dah," he whispered, "put yo'
head down, boy."

With a quick motion of his hand he jerked some canvas from the butt so that it concealed me, and went on,
followed by the quick steps of the real relief.

Now I heard voices, but the only words I could dis-
tinguish were in the cook's deep drawl.

"Yass, sah, yass, sah. Ah brought yo' coffee, sah. Yass, sah, Ah 'll wait fo' yo' cup, sah."

Next came Kipping's step — a mild step, if there is such a thing; even in his bullying the man was mild. Then came the slow, heavy tread of the returning African.

Flicking the canvas off me, he muttered, "All 's cleah fo' you to git away, boy. How you done come to git in dis yeh scrape sho' am excruciatin'. You just go 'long with you while dey 's a chanst."

So, carrying with me the very unimportant discovery that I had made, I ran cautiously forward, away from the place where I had no business to be.

When, in the morning, just before eight bells, I was sent to the galley with the empty kids, I found the worthy cook in a solemn mood.

"You boy," he said, fixing on me a stare, which his deeply graven frown rendered the more severe, "you boy, what you think you gwine do, prowlin' round all hours? Hey? You tell dis nigger dat. Heah Ah 's been and put you onto all de ropes and give you more infohmative disco'se about ships and how to behave on 'em dan eveh Ah give a green hand befo' in all de years Ah been gwine to sea, and heah you 's so tarnation foolish as go prowlin' round de quarter-deck whar you 's like to git skun alive if Mistah Falk ketches you."

I don't remember what I replied, but I am sure it was flippant; to the day of my death I shall never forget the stinging, good-natured cuff with which the cook knocked my head against the wall. "Sho' now," he growled, "go 'long!"

I was not yet ready to go. "Tell me, doctor," I said, "does the second mate get on well with the others in the cabin?"

The title mollified him somewhat, but he still felt that

he must uphold the dignity of his office. "Sho' now, what kind of a question is dat fo' a ship's boy to be askin' de cook?" He glanced at me suspiciously, then challenged me directly, "Who put dose idea' in yo' head?"

By the tone of the second question, which was quite too straightforward to be confused with the bantering that we usually exchanged, I knew that he was willing, if diplomatically coaxed, to talk frankly. I then said cautiously, "Every one thinks so, but you're the only man forward that's likely to know."

"Now ain't dat jest like de assumptivity of dem dah men in de forecastle. How'd Ah know dat kind of contraptiveness, tell me?"

Looking closely at me he began to rattle his pans at a great rate while I waited in silence. He was not accomplishing much; indeed, he really was throwing things into a state of general disorder. But I observed that he was working methodically round the galley toward where I stood, until at last he bumped into me and started as if he had n't known that I was there at all.

"You boy," he cried, "you still heah?" He scowled at me with a particularly savage intensity, then suddenly leaned over and tapped me on the shoulder. "You's right, boy," he whispered. "He ain't got no manner of use foh dem other gen'lems, and what's mo', dey ain't got no manner of use foh him. Ah's telling you, boy, it's darn lucky, you bet, dat Mistah Falk he eats at second table. Yass, sah. Hark! dah's de bell — eight bells! Yo' watch on deck, hey?" After a short pause, he whispered, "Boy, you come sneakin' round to-morrow night when dat yeh stew'd done gone to bed, an' Ah'll jest gadder you up a piece of pie f'om Cap'n's table — yass, sah! Eight bells is struck. Go 'long, you." And shoving me out of his little king-

dom, the villainous-looking darky sent after me a savage
scowl, which I translated rightly as a token of his high
regard and sincere friendship.

In my delight at the promised treat, and in my haste
to join the watch, I gave too little heed to where I was
going, and shot like a bullet squarely against a man who
had been standing just abaft the galley window. He
collapsed with a grunt. My shoulder had knocked the
wind completely out of him.

"Ugh! —" he gasped —"ugh! You son of perdition —
ugh! Why in thunder don't you look where you 're running — ugh! — I 'll break your rascally young neck—ugh
— when I get my wind."

It was Kipping, and for the second time he had lost
his mildness.

As he clutched at me fiercely, I dodged and fled. Later,
when I was hauling at his side, he seemed to have forgotten the accident; but I knew well enough that he
had not. He was not the kind that forgets accidents.
His silence troubled me. How much, I wondered, had
he heard of what was going on in the galley?

CHAPTER IV

A PIECE OF PIE

At two bells there sounded the sonorous call, "Sail ho!"

"Where away?" cried Mr. Falk.

"One point off the larboard bow."

In all the days since we had lost sight of land, we had seen but one other sail, which had appeared only to disappear again beyond the horizon. It seemed probable, however, that we should speak this second vessel, a brig whose course crossed our own. Captain Whidden came on deck and assumed command, and the men below, getting wind of the excitement, trooped up and lined the bulwarks forward. Our interest, which was already considerable, became even keener when the stranger hove out a signal of distress. We took in all studding-sails and topgallantsails fore and aft, and lay by for her about an hour after we first had sighted her.

Over the water, when we were within hailing distance, came the cry: "Ship ahoy!"

Captain Whidden held the speaking trumpet. "Hullo!"

"What ship is that, pray?"

"The ship Island Princess, from Salem, bound to Canton. Where are you from?"

"The brig Adventure, bound from the Straits to Boston. Our foretopmast was carried away four hours ago. Beware of —"

Losing the next words, the Captain called, "I did n't hear that last."

"Beware,"— came again the warning cry, booming

deeply over the sea while one and all we strained to hear it — "beware of any Arab ship. Arabs have captured the English ship Alert and have murdered her captain and fifteen men."

Squaring her head-yards, the brig dropped her mainsail, braced her crossjack-yard sharp aback, put her helm a-weather and got sternway, while her after sails and helm kept her to the wind. So she fell off from us and the two vessels passed, perhaps never to meet again.

Both forward and aft, we aboard the Island Princess were sober men. Kipping and the second mate were talking quietly together, I saw (I saw, too, that Captain Whidden and some of the others were watching them sharply) Mr. Thomas and Roger Hamlin were leaning side by side upon the rail, and forward the men were gathering in groups. It was indeed an ominous message that the brig had given us. But supper broke the tension, and afterwards a more cheerful atmosphere prevailed.

As I was sweeping down the deck next day, Roger, to my great surprise,— for by now I was accustomed to his amused silence,— came and spoke to me with something of the old, humorous freedom that was so characteristic of him.

"Well, Bennie," said he, "we 're quite a man now, are we not?"

"We are," I replied shortly. Although I would not for a great deal have given him the satisfaction of knowing it, I had been much vexed, secretly, by his rigidly ignoring me.

"Bennie," he said in a low voice, "is there trouble brewing in the forecastle?"

I was startled. "Why, no. I 've seen no sign of trouble."

"No one has talked to you, then?"

"Not in such a way as you imply."

"Hm! Keep your eyes and ears open, anyway, and if you hear anything that sounds like trouble, let me know — quietly, mind you, even secretly."

"What do you mean?"

"We are carrying a valuable cargo, and we have very particular orders. All must be thus and so,— exactly thus and so,— and it means more to the owners, Bennie, than I think you realize. Now you go on with your work. But remember — eyes and ears open."

That night, as I watched the restless sea and the silent stars, my imagination was stirred as never before. I felt the mystery and wonder of great distances and far places. We were so utterly alone! Except for the passing hail of some stranger, we had cut ourselves off for months from all communication with the larger world. Whatever happened aboard ship, in whatever straits we found ourselves, we must depend solely upon our own resources; and already it appeared that some of our shipmates were scheming and intriguing against one another. Thus I meditated, until the boyish and more natural, perhaps more wholesome, thought of the cook's promise came to me.

Pie! My remembrance of pie was almost as intangible as a pleasant dream might be some two days later. With care to escape observation, I made my way to the galley and knocked cautiously.

"Who's dah?" asked softly the old cook, who had barricaded himself for the night according to his custom, and was smoking a villainously rank pipe.

"It's Ben Lathrop," I whispered.

"What you want heah?" the cook demanded.

"The pie you promised me," I answered.

"Humph! Ain't you fo'got dat pie yet? You got de

most miraculous memorizer eveh Ah heared of. You wait."

I heard him fumbling inside the galley; then he opened the door and stepped out on deck as if he had just decided to take a breath of fresh air. Upon seeing me, he pretended to start with great surprise, and exclaimed rather more loudly than before: —

"What you doin' heah, boy, at dis yeh hour o' night?"

But all this was only crafty by-play. Having made sure, so he thought, that no one was in sight, he grabbed me by the collar and yanked me into the galley, at the same time shutting the door so that I almost stifled in the rank smoke with which he had filled the place.

Scowling fiercely, he reached into a little cupboard and drew out half an apple pie that to my eager eyes seemed as big as a half moon on a clear night.

"Dah," he said. "Eat it up. Mistah Falk, he tell stew'd he want pie and he gotta have pie, and stew'd he come and he say, 'Frank,' says he, 'dat Mistah Falk, his langwidge is like he is in liquo'. He *gotta* have pie.' 'All right,' Ah say, 'if he gotta have pie, he gotta wait twill Ah make pie. Cap'n, he et hearty o' pie lately.' Stew'd he say, 'Cap'n ain't had but one piece and Mistah Thomas, he ain't had but one piece, and Mistah Hamlin, he ain't had any. Dah's gotta be pie. You done et dat pie yo'se'f,' says he. 'Oh, no,' says Ah. 'Ah never et no pie. You fo'get 'bout dat pie you give Cap'n foh breakfas'.' Den stew'd he done crawl out. He don' know Ah make two pies yestidday. Dat's how come Ah have pie foh de boy. Boys dey need pie to make 'em grow. It's won'erful foh de indignation, pie is."

I was appalled by the hue and cry that my half-circle of pastry had occasioned, and more than a little fearful of the consequences if the truth ever should transpire;

but the pie in hand was compensation for many such intangible difficulties in the future, and I was making great inroads on a wedge of it, when I thought I heard a sound outside the window, which the cook had masked with a piece of paper.

I stopped to listen and saw that Frank had heard it too. It was a scratchy sound as if some one were trying to unship the glass.

"Massy sake!" my host gasped, taking his vile pipe out of his mouth.

Although it was quite impossible for pallor to make any visible impression on his surpassing blackness, he obviously was much disturbed.

"Gobble dat pie, boy," he gasped, "gobble up ev'y crumb an' splinter."

Now, as the scratchy noise sounded at the door, the cook laid his pipe on a shelf and glanced up at a big carving-knife that hung from a rack above his head.

"Who 's dah?" he demanded cautiously.

"Lemme in," said a mild, low voice, "I want some o' that pie."

"Massy sake!" the cook gasped in disgust, "ef it ain't dat no 'count Kipping."

"Lemme in," persisted the mild, plaintive voice. "Lemme in."

"Aw, go 'long! Dah ain't no pie in heah," the cook retorted. "You 's dreamin', dat 's what you is. You needs a good dose of medicine, dat 's what you needs."

"I 'm dreaming, am I?" the mild voice repeated. "Oh, yes, I 'm dreaming I am, ain't I? I did n't sneak around the galley yesterday morning and hear you tell that cocky little fool to come and get a piece of pie to-night. Oh, no! I did n't see him come prowling around when he thought no one was looking. Oh, no! I did n't see you come out of the galley like you did n't know there was anybody on deck, and walk right under the rigging where I was waiting for just such tricks. Oh, no! I was dreaming, I was. Oh, yes."

"Dat Kipping," the cook whispered, "he 's hand and foot with Mistah Falk." •

"Lemme in, you woolly-headed son of perdition, or I swear I 'll take the kinky scalp right off your round old head."

"He 's gettin' violenter," the cook whispered, eyeing me questioningly.

Saying nothing, I swallowed the last bit of pie. I had made the most of my opportunity.

Kipping now shook the door and swore angrily. Finally he kicked it with the full weight of his heel.

It rattled on its hinges and a long crack appeared in the lower panel.

"He 's sho' coming in," the African said slowly and reflectively. "He 's sho' coming in and when he don't get no pie, he 's gwine tell Mistah Falk, and you and me 's gwine have trouble." Putting his scowling face close to my ear, the cook whispered, "Ah 's gwine scare him good."

Amazed by the dramatic turn that events were taking, I drew back into a corner.

From the rack above his head the cook took down the carving-knife. Dropping on hands and knees and creeping across the floor, he held the weapon between his even white teeth, sat up on his haunches, and noiselessly drew the bolt that locked the door. Then with a deft motion of an extraordinarily long arm he put out the lantern behind him and threw the galley into darkness.

CHAPTER V

KIPPING

I THOUGHT that Kipping must have abandoned his quest. In the darkness of the galley the silence seemed hours long. The coals in the stove glowed redly, and the almost imperceptible light of the starry sky came in here and there around the door. Otherwise not a thing was visible in the absolute blackness that shrouded my strange host, who seemed for the moment to have reverted to the savage craft of his Slave Coast ancestors. Surely Kipping must have gone away, I thought. He was so mild a man, one could expect nothing else. Then somewhere I heard the faint sigh of indrawn breath.

"You blasted nigger, open that door," said the mild, sad voice. "If you don't, I 'm going to kick it in on top of you and cut your heart out right where you stand."

The silence, heavy and pregnant, was broken by the shuffling of feet. Evidently Kipping drew off to kick the door a second time. His boot struck it a terrific blow, but the door, instead of breaking, flew open and crashed against the pans behind it.

Then the cook, who so carefully had prepared the simple trap, swinging the carving-knife like a cutlass, sprang with a fierce, guttural grunt full in Kipping's face. Concealed in the dark galley, I saw it all silhouetted against the starlit deck. With the quickness of a weasel, Kipping evaded the black's clutching left hand and threw himself down and forward. Had the cook really intended to kill Kipping, the weapon scarcely could have failed to cut flesh in its terrific swing, but he gave it an upward turn that carried it safely above Kipping's head. When Kipping, however, dived under Frank's feet, Frank, who had expected him to turn and run, tripped and fell, dropping the carving-knife, and instantly black man and white wriggled toward the weapon.

It would have been funny if it had n't been so dramatic. The two men sprawled on their bellies like snakes, neither of them daring to take time to stand, each, in the snap of a finger, striving with every tendon and muscle to reach something that lay just beyond his finger-tips. I found myself actually laughing — they looked so like two fish just out of water.

But the fight suddenly had become bitter earnest, Kipping unquestionably feared for his life, and the cook knew well that the weapon for which they fought would be turned against him if his antagonist once got possession of it.

As Kipping closed his fingers on the handle, the cook grabbed the blade. Then the mate appeared out of the dark.

"Here, what's this?" he demanded, looming on the scene of the struggle.

I saw starlight flash on the knife as it flew over the bulwark, then I heard it splash. Kipping got away by a quick twist and vanished. The cook remained alone to face the mate, for you can be very sure that I had every discreet intention not to reveal my presence in the dark galley.

"Yass, sah," said the cook, "yass, sah. Please to 'scuse me, sah, but Ah did n't go foh no promeditation of disturbance. It is quite unintelligible, sah, but one of de men, sah, he come round, sah, and says Ah gotta give him a pie, sah, and of co'se Ah can't do nothin' like dat, sah. Pies is foh de officers and gen'lems, sah, and of co'se Ah don't give pie to de men, sah, not even in dey vittles, sah, even if dey was pie, which dey wa'n't, sah, foh dis ve'y day Mistah Falk he wants pie and stew'd he come, and me and he, sah, we sho' ransack dis galley, sah, and try like we can, not even two of us togetheh, sah, can sca' up a piece of pie foh Mistah Falk, sah, and he —"

Unwilling to listen longer, the mate turned with a grunt of disgust and walked away.

After he had gone, the cook stood for a time by the galley, looking pensively at the stars. Long-armed, broad-shouldered, bullet-headed, he seemed a typical savage. Yet in spite of his thick lips and protruding chin, his face had a certain thoughtful quality, and not even that deeply graven scowl could hide the dog-like faithfulness of his dark eyes.

After all, I wondered, was he not like a faithful dog: loyal to the last breath, equally ready to succor his friend or to fight for him?

"Boy," he said, when he came in, "Ah done fool 'em. Dey ain' gwine believe no gammon dat yeh Kipping tells 'em — leastwise, no one ain't onless it 's Mistah Falk. Now you go 'long with you and don't you come neah me foh a week without you act like Ah ain't got no use foh you. And boy," he whispered, "you jest look out and keep clear of dat Kipping. Foh all he talk' like he got a mouth full of butter, he 's an uncommon fighter, he is, yass sah, an uncommon fighter."

He paused for a moment, then added in such a way that I remembered it long afterward, "Ah sho' would like to know whar Ah done see dat Kipping befo'."

I reached the forecastle unobserved, and as I started to climb into my bunk, I felt very well satisfied with myself indeed. Not even Kipping had seen me come. But a

disagreeable surprise awaited me; my hand encountered
a man lying wrapped in my blankets.

It was Kipping!

He rolled out with a sly smile, looked at me in silence
a long time, and then pretended to shake with silent
laughter.

"Well," I whispered, "what's the matter with you?"

"There was n't any pie," he sighed — so mildly. "How
sad that there was n't any pie."

He then climbed into his own bunk and almost immediately, I judged, went to sleep.

If he desired to make me exceedingly uncomfortable,
he had accomplished his purpose. For days I puzzled
over his queer behavior. I wondered how much he knew,
how much he had told Mr. Falk; and I recalled, sometimes, the cook's remark, "Ah sho' would like to know
whar Ah done see dat Kipping befo'."

Of one thing I was sure: both Kipping and Mr. Falk
heartily disliked me. Kipping took every occasion to
annoy me in petty ways, and sometimes I discovered Mr.
Falk watching me sharply and ill-naturedly. But he always looked away quickly when he knew that I saw him.

We still lacked several days of having been at sea a
month when we sighted Madeira, bearing west southwest
about ten leagues distant. Taking a fresh departure the
next day from latitude 32° 22' North, and longitude
16° 36' West of London, we laid our course south southwest, and swung far enough away from the outshoulder-
ing curve of the Rio de Oro coast to pass clear of the
Canary Islands.

"Do you know," said Bill Hayden one day, some five
weeks later, when we were aloft side by side, "they don't
like you any better than they do me."

It was true; both Kipping and Mr. Falk showed it constantly.

"And there's others that don't like us, too," Bill added. "I told 'em, though, that if they got funny with me or you, I'd show 'em what was what."

"Who are they?" I asked, suddenly remembering Roger Hamlin's warning.

"Davie Paine is one."

"But I thought he did n't like Kipping or Mr. Falk!"

"He did n't for a while; but there was something happened that turned his mind about them."

I worked away with the tar-bucket and reflected on this unexpected change in the attitude of the deep-voiced seaman who, on our first day aboard ship, had seen Kipping wink at the second mate. It was all so trivial that I was ready to laugh at myself for thinking of it twice, and yet stupid old Bill Hayden had noticed it. A new suspicion startled me. "Bill, did any one say anything to you about any plan or scheme that Kipping is concerned in?" I asked.

"Why, yes. Did n't they speak to you about it?"

"About what?"

"Why, about a voyage that all the men was to have a venture in. I thought they talked to every one. I did n't want anything to do with it if Kipping was to have a finger in the pie. I told 'em 'No!' and they swore at me something awful, and said that if ever I blabbed I'd never see my little wee girl at Newburyport again. So I never said nothing." He looked at me with a frightened expression. "It's funny they never said nothing to you. Don't you tell 'em I talked. If they thought I'd split, they'd knock me in the head, that's what they'd do."

"Who's in it besides Kipping and Davie Paine?"

"The two men from Boston and Chips and the steward. Them 's all I know, but there may be others. The men have been talking about it quiet like for a good while now."

As Mr. Falk came forward on some errand or other, we stopped talking and worked harder than ever at tarring down the rigging.

Presently Bill repeated without turning his head, "Don't you tell 'em I said anything, will you, Bennie? Don't you tell 'em."

And I replied, "No."

We then had passed the Canaries and the Cape Verdes, and had crossed the Line; from the most western curve of Africa we had weathered the narrows of the Atlantic almost to Pernambuco, and thence, driven by fair winds, we had swept east again in a long arc, past Ascension Island and Tristan da Cunha, and on south of the Cape of Good Hope.

The routine of a sailor's life is full of hard work and petty detail. Week follows week, each like every other. The men complain about their duties and their food and the officers grow irritable. There are few stories worth telling in the drudgery of life at sea, but now and then in a long, long time fate and coincidence conspire to unite in a single voyage, such as that which I am chronicling, enough plots and crimes and untoward incidents to season a dozen ordinary lifetimes spent before the mast.

I could not, of course, even begin as yet to comprehend the magnitude that the tiny whirlpool of discontented and lawless schemers would attain. But boy though I was, in those first months of the voyage I had learned enough about the different members of the crew to realize that serious consequences might grow from such a clique.

Kipping, whom I had thought at first a mild, harmless man, had proved himself a vengeful bully, cowardly in a sense, yet apparently courageous enough so far as physical combat was concerned. Also, he had disclosed an unexpected subtlety, a cat-like craft in eavesdropping and underhanded contrivances. The steward I believed a mercenary soul, tricky so far as his own comfort and gain were concerned, who, according to common report, had ingratiated himself with the second mate by sympathizing with him on every occasion because he had not been given the chief mate's berth. The two men from Boston I cared even less for; they were slipshod workmen and ill-tempered, and their bearing convinced me that, from the point of view of our officers and of the owners of the ship, they were a most undesirable addition to such a coterie as Kipping seemed to be forming. Davie Paine and the carpenter prided themselves on being always affable, and each, although slow to make up his mind, would throw himself heart and body into whatever course of action he finally decided on. But significant above all else was Kipping's familiarity with Mr. Falk.

The question now was, how to communicate my suspicions secretly to Roger Hamlin. After thinking the matter over in all its details, I wrote a few letters on a piece of white paper, and found opportunity to take counsel with my friend the cook, when I, as the youngest in the crew, was left in the galley to bring the kids forward to the men in the forecastle.

"Doctor," I said, "if I wanted to get a note to Mr. Hamlin without anybody's knowing,— particularly the steward or Mr. Falk,—how should I go about it?"

The perpetually frowning black heaped salt beef on the kids. "Dah 's enough grub foh a hun'erd o'nary men.

Dey's enough meat dah to feed a whole regiment of Sigambeezel cavalry — yass, sah, ho'ses and all. And yet Ah 'll bet you foh dollahs right out of mah pay, doze pesky cable-scrapers fo'ward 'll eat all dat meat and cuss me in good shape 'cause it ain't mo', and den, mah golly, dey 'll sot up all night, Ah 'll bet you, yass, sah, a-kicking dey heads off 'cause dey ain't fed f'om de cabin table. Boy, if you was to set beefsteak and bake' 'taters and ham and eggs down befo' dem fool men ev'y mo'ning foh breakfas', dey 'd come heah hollerin' and cussin' and tellin' me dey wah n't gwine have dey innards spiled on all dat yeh truck jest 'cause dem aft can't eat it."

Turning his ferocious scowl full upon me, the savage-looking darky handed me the kids. "Dah! you take doze straight along fo'ward." Then, dropping his voice to a whisper, he said, "Gimme yo' note."

Knowing now that the cook approached every important matter by an extraordinarily indirect route, I had expected some such conclusion, and I held the note ready.

"Go 'long," he said, when I had slipped it into his huge black hand. "Ah 'll do it right."

So I departed with all confidence that my message would go secretly and safely to its destination. Even if it should fall into other hands than those for which it was intended, I felt that I had not committed myself dangerously. I had written only one word: "News."

II

IN WHICH WE ENCOUNTER
AN ARAB SHIP

CHAPTER VI

THE COUNCIL IN THE CABIN

SOMETIMES in the night I dream of the forecastle of the Island Princess, and see the crew sitting on chests and bunks, as vividly as if only yesterday I had come through the hatchway and down the steps with a kid of "salt horse" for the mess, and had found them waiting, each with his pan and spoon and the great tin dipper of tea that he himself had brought from the galley. There was Chips, the carpenter, who had descended for the moment from the dignity of the steerage; calmly he helped himself to twice his share, ignoring the oaths of the others, and washed down his first mouthful with a great gulp of tea. Once upon a time Chips came down just too late to get any meat, and tried to kill the cook; but as the cook remarked to me afterwards, "Foh a drea'ful impulsive pusson, he wah n't ve'y handy with his fists." There was Bill Hayden, who always got last chance at the meat, and took whatever the doubtful generosity of his shipmates had left him — poor Bill, as happy in the thought of his little wee girl at Newburyport as if all the wealth of the khans of Tartary were waiting for him at the end of the voyage. There was the deep-voiced Davie, almost out of sight in the darkest corner, who chose his food carefully, pretending the while to be considerate of the others, and growled amiably about his hard lot. Also there was Kipping, mild and evasive, yet amply able to look out for his own interests, as I, who so often brought down the kids, well knew.

When, that evening, Bill Hayden had scraped up the last poor slivers of meat, he sat down beside me on my chest.

"If I did n't have my little wee girl at Newburyport," he said, "I might be as gloomy as Neddie Benson. Do you suppose if I went to see a fortune-teller I 'd be as gloomy as Neddie is? I never used to be gloomy, even before I married, and I married late. I was older than Neddie is now when I married. Neddie ought to get a wife and stop going to see fortune-tellers, and then he would n't be so gloomy."

Bill would run on indefinitely in his stupid, kindly way, for I was almost the only person aboard ship who listened to him at all, and, to tell the truth, even I seldom more than half listened. But already he had given me valuable information that day, and now something in the tone of his rambling words caught my attention.

"Has Neddie Benson been talking about the fortune-teller again?" I asked.

"He 's had a lot to say about her. He says the lady said to him — "

"But what started him off?"

"He says things is bound to come to a bad end."

"What things?"

As I have said before, I had a normal boy's curiosity about all that was going on around us. Perhaps, I have come to think, I had more than the ordinary boy's sense for important information. Roger Hamlin's warning had put me on my guard, and I intended to learn all I could and to keep my mouth shut where certain people were concerned.

"It 's queer they don't say nothing to you about what 's going on," Bill remarked.

For my own part I understood very well why they

should say nothing of any underhanded trickery to one
who ashore was so intimately acquainted with Captain
Whidden and Roger Hamlin. But I kept my thoughts to
myself and persisted in my questions.

"What is going on?"

"Oh, I don't just make out what." Bill's stupidity
was exasperating at times. "It's something about Mr.
Falk. Kipping, he — "

"Yes?" said that eternally mild voice. "Mr. Falk?
And Kipping? What else please?"

Both Bill and I were startled to find Kipping at our
elbows. But before either of us could answer, some one
called down the hatch:—

"Lathrop is wanted aft."

Relieved at escaping from an embarrassing situation,
I jumped up so promptly that my knife fell with a clatter,
and hastened on deck, calling "Ay, ay," to the man who
had summoned me. I knew very well why I was wanted
aft.

Mr. Falk, who was on duty on the quarter-deck, completely ignored me as I passed him and went down the
companionway.

"At least," I thought, "he can't come below now."

The steward, when I appeared, raised his eyebrows and
almost dropped his tray; then he paused in the door,
inconspicuously, as if to linger. But Captain Whidden
glanced round and dismissed him by a sharp nod, and I
found myself alone in the cabin with the captain, Mr.
Thomas, and Roger Hamlin.

"I understand there's news forward, Lathrop," said
Captain Whidden.

Roger looked at me with that humorous, exasperating
twinkle of his eyes,— I thought of my sister and of how
she had looked when she learned that he was to sail for

Canton,— and Mr. Thomas folded his arms and leaned back in his chair.

"Yes, sir," I replied, "although it seems pretty unimportant to be worth much as news."

"Tell us about it."

To all that I had gathered from Bill Hayden I added what I had learned by my own observations, and it seemed to interest them, although for my own part I doubted whether it was of much account.

"Has any one approached you directly about these things?" Captain Whidden asked when I was through.

"No, sir."

"Have you heard any one say just what this little group is trying to accomplish, or just when it is going to act?"

"No, sir."

"Do you, Lathrop, know anything about the cargo of the Island Princess? Or anything about the terms under which it is carried?"

"Only in a general way, sir, that it is made up of ginseng and woolen goods shipped to Canton."

Captain Whidden looked at me very sharply indeed. "You are positive that that is all you know?"

"Yes, sir — except, in a general way, that the cargo is uncommonly important."

The three men exchanged glances, and Roger Hamlin nodded as if to corroborate my reply.

"Lathrop," Captain Whidden began again, "I want you to say nothing about this interview after you leave the cabin. It is more important that you hold your peace than you may ever realize — than, I trust, you ever *will* realize. I am going to ask you to give me your word of honor to that effect."

It seemed to me then that I saw Captain Whidden in a new light. We of the younger generation had inclined to belittle him because he continued to follow the sea at an age when more successful men had established their counting-houses or had retired from active business altogether. But twice his mercantile adventures had proved unfortunate, and now, though nearly sixty years old and worth a very comfortable fortune, he refused to leave again for a less familiar occupation the profession by which he had amassed his competence. I noticed that his hair was gray on his temples, and that his weathered face revealed a certain stern sadness. I felt as if suddenly, in spite of my minor importance on board his ship, I had come closer to the straightforward gentleman, the true Joseph Whidden, than in all the years that I had known him, almost intimately, it had seemed at the time, in my father's house.

"I promise, sir," I said.

He took up a pencil and with the point tapped a piece of paper.

"Tell me who of all the men forward absolutely are not influenced by this man Kipping."

"The cook," I returned, "and Bill Hayden, and, I think, Neddie Benson. Probably there are a number of others, but only of those three am I absolutely sure."

"That's what I want — the men you are absolutely sure of. Hm! The cook, useful but not particularly quick-witted. Hayden, a harmless, negative body. Benson, a gloomy soul if ever there was one. It might be better but —" He looked at Mr. Thomas and smiled. "That is all, Lathrop; you may go now. Just one moment more, though: be cautious, keep your eyes and ears open, and if anything else comes up, communicate with Mr. Hamlin or, — " he hesitated, but finally said it, — "or directly with me."

As I went up on deck, I again passed Mr. Falk and

again he pretended not to see me. But although he seemed to be intent on the rolling seas to windward, I was very confident that, when I had left the quarter-deck, he turned and looked after me as earnestly as if he hoped to read in my step and carriage everything that had occurred in the cabin.

CHAPTER VII

THE SAIL WITH
A LOZENGE–SHAPED PATCH

IT was not long before we got another warning even more ominous than the one from the captain of the Adventure. On Friday, July 28, in latitude 19° 50′ South, longitude 101° 53′ East,— the log of the voyage, kept beyond this point in Mr. Thomas's own hand, gives me the dates and figures to the very day for it still is preserved in the vaults of Hamlin, Lathrop & Company,— we sighted a bark to the south, and at the captain's orders wore ship to speak her. When she also came about, we served out pikes and muskets as a precaution against treachery, and Mr. Falk saw that our guns were shotted. But she proved to be in good faith, and in answer to our hail she declared herself the Adrienne of Liverpool, eight days from the Straits, homeward bound. Her master, it appeared, wished to compare notes on longitude, and a long, dull discussion followed; but in parting Captain Whidden asked if there was news of pirates or marauders.

"Yes," was the reply. "Much news and bad news." And the master of the Adrienne thereupon launched into a tale of piracy and treachery such as I never had heard before. Leaning over the taffrail, his elbows out-thrust and his big hands folded, he roared the story at us in a great booming voice that at times seemed to drown the words in its own volume. Now, as the waves and the wind snatched it away, it grew momentarily fainter and clearer; now it came bellowing back again, loud, hoarse, and indistinct.

It was all about an Arab ship off Benkulen; Ladrone-sers and the havoc they had wrought among the American ships in the China Sea; a warning not to sail from Macao for Whampoa without a fleet of four or five sail; and again, about the depredations of the Malays. The grizzled old captain seemed to delight in repeating horrible yarns of the seas whence he came, whither we were going. He roared them after us until we had left him far astern; and at the last we heard him laughing long and hoarsely.

"What dat yeh man think we all am? He think we all gwine believe dat yeh? Hgh!" the cook growled.

But Neddie Benson dolefully shook his head.

Parting, the Adrienne and the Island Princess continued, each on her course, the one back round the Cape of Good Hope and north again to Liverpool, the other on into strange oceans beset with a thousand dangers.

We sailed now a sea of opalescent greens and purples that shimmered and changed with the changing lights. Strange shadows played across it, even when the sky was cloudless, and it rolled past the ship in great, regular swells, ruffled by favoring breezes and bright beneath the clear sun.

At daylight on August 3 we saw land about nine miles away, bearing from east by south to north, a long line of rugged hills, which appeared to be piled one above another, and which our last lunar observations indicated were in longitude 107° 15' East; and we made out a single sail lying off the coast to the north.

The sail caught and held our attention — not that, so far as we then could see, that particular sail was at all remarkable: any sail, at that time and in that place, would have interested us unusually. Mindful of the warnings we had received, we paused in our work to watch it. Kipping, with a sly glance aft, left the winch with which

he was occupied and leaned on the rail. Here and there
the crew conversed cautiously, and on the quarter-deck
a lively discussion, I could see, was in progress.

We were so intent on that distant spot of canvas which
pricked the horizon, that a fierce squall, sweeping down
upon us, almost took us aback.

The cry, "All hands on deck!" brought the sleeping
watch from the bunks below, and the carpenter, steward,
and sailmaker from the steerage. The foresail ripped
from its bolt ropes with a deafening crack, and tore to
ribbons in the gale. As the ship lay into the wind, I
could hear the captain's voice louder than the very storm,
"Meet her! — Meet her! — Ease her off!" But the reply
of the man at the wheel was lost in the rush of wind and
rain.

I had been well drilled long since in furling the royals,
for on them the green hands were oftenest practised;
and now, from his post on the forecastle, Mr. Thomas
spied me as I slipped and fell half across the deck. I
alone at that moment was not hard at work, and, in obedience to the captain's orders, during a lull that gave us
a momentary respite, he sent me aloft.

It was quite a different thing from furling a royal in a
light breeze. When I had got to the topgallant masthead, the yard was well down by the lifts and steadied
by the braces, but the clews were not hauled chock up
to the blocks. Leaning out precariously, I won Mr.
Thomas's attention with greatest difficulty, and shrieked
to have it done. This he did. Then, casting the yard-
arm gaskets off from the tye and laying them across
between the tye and the mast, I stretched out on the
weather yard-arm and, getting hold of the weather leech,
brought it in to the slings taut along the yard. Mind
you, all this time I, only a boy, was working in a gale of

wind and driven rain, and was clinging to a yard that was sweeping from side to side in lurching, unsteady flight far above the deck and the angry sea. Hauling the sail through the clew, and letting it fall in the bunt, I drew the weather clew a little abaft the yard, and held it with my knee while I brought in the lee leech in the same manner. Then, making up my bunt and putting into it the slack of the clews, the leech and footrope and the body of the sail, I hauled it well up on the yard, smoothed the skin, brought it down abaft, and made fast the bunt-gasket round the mast. Passing the weather and lee yard-arm gaskets round the yard in turn, and hauling them taut and making them fast, I left all snug and trim.

From aft came faintly the clear command, "Full and by!" And promptly, for by this time the force of the squall was already spent, the answer of the man at the wheel, "Full and by, sir."

In this first moment of leisure I instinctively turned, as did virtually every man aboard ship, to look for the sail that had been reported to the north of us. But although we looked long and anxiously, we saw no sail, no trace of any floating craft. It had disappeared during the squall, utterly and completely. Only the wild dark sea and the wild succession of mountain piled on mountain met our searching eyes.

A sail there had been, beyond all question, where now there was none. Driven by the storm, it had vanished completely from our sight.

As well as we could judge by our lunar observations, the land was between Paga River and Stony Point, and when we had sailed along some forty miles, the shore, as it should be according to our reckoning, was less mountainous.

It was my first glimpse of the Sunda Islands, of which I had heard so much, and I well remember that I stood by the forward rigging watching the distant land from where it seemed on my right to rise from the sea, to where it seemed on my left to go down beyond the horizon into the sea again, and that I murmured to myself in a small, awed voice: —

"This is Java!"

The very name had magic in it. Already from those islands our Salem mariners had accumulated great wealth. Not yet are the old days forgotten, when Elias Hasket Derby's ships brought back fortunes from Batavia, and when Captain Carnes, by one voyage in Jonathan Peele's schooner Rajah to the northern coast of Sumatra for wild pepper, made a profit of seven hundred per cent of both the total cost of the schooner itself and the whole expense of the entire expedition. I who lived in the exhilarating atmosphere of those adventurous times was thrilled to the heart by my first sight of lands to which hundreds of Salem ships had sailed.

It really was Java, and night was falling on its shores. Far to the northeast some tiny object pricked above the skyline, and a point of light gleamed clearly, low against the blue heavens in which the stars had just begun to shine.

"A sail!" I cried.

Before the words had left my lips a deep voice aloft sonorously proclaimed: —

"Sa-a-ail ho!"

"Where away?" Mr. Thomas cried.

"Two points off the larboard bow, sir."

The little knot of officers on the quarter-deck already were intent on the tiny spot of almost invisible canvas, and we forward were crowding one another for a better sight of it. Then in the gathering darkness it faded and was gone. Could it have been the same that we had seen before?

There was much talk of the mysterious ship that night, and many strange theories were offered to account for it. Davie Paine, in his deep, rolling voice, sent shivers down our backs by his story of a ghost-ship manned by dead men with bony fingers and hollow eyes, which had sailed the seas in the days of his great-uncle, a stout old mariner who seemed from Davie's account to have been a hard drinker. Kipping was reminded of yarns about Malay pirates, which he told so quietly, so mildly, that they seemed by contrast thrice as terrible. Neddie Benson lugubriously recalled the prophecy of the charming fortune-teller and argued the worst of our mysterious stranger. "The lady said," he repeated, "that there 'd be a dark man and a light man and no end o' trouble. She was a nice lady, too." But Neddie and his doleful fortune-teller as usual banished our gloom, and the forecastle reëchoed with hoarse laughter, which grew louder and louder when Neddie once again narrated the lady's charms, and at last cried angrily that she was as plump as a nice young chicken.

"If you was to ask me," Bill Hayden murmured, "I 'd say it was just a sail." But no one asked Bill Hayden, and with a few words about his "little wee girl at Newburyport," he buried himself in his old blankets and was soon asleep.

During the mid-watch that same night, the cook prowled the deck forward like a dog sneaking along the wharves. Silently, the whites of his eyes gleaming out of the darkness, he moved hither and thither, careful always to avoid the second mate's observation. As I watched him, I became more and more curious, for I

could make nothing of his veering course. He went now
to starboard, now to larboard, now to the forecastle, now
to the steerage, always silently, always deliberately.
After a while he came over and stood beside me.

"It ain't right," he whispered. "Ah tell you, boy, it
ain't right."

"What 's not right?" I asked.

"De goin's on aboa'd dis ship."

"What goings on?"

"Boy, Ah 's been a long time to sea and Ah 's cooked
foh some bad crews in my time, yass, sah, but Ah 's gwine
tell you, boy, 'cause Ah done took a fancy to you, dis am
de most iniquitous crew Ah eveh done cook salt hoss foh.
Yass, sah."

"What do you mean?"

The negro ignored my question.

"Ah 's gwine tell you, boy, dis yeh crew am bad 'nough,
but when dah come a ha'nt boat a-sailin' oveh yondeh
jest at dahk, boy, Ah wish Ah was back home whar Ah
could somehow come to shoot a rabbit what got a lef'
hind-foot. Yass, sah."

For a long time he silently paced up and down by the
bulwark; but finally I saw him momentarily against the
light of his dim lantern as he entered his own quarters.

Morning came with fine breezes and pleasant weather.
At half-past four we saw Winerow Point bearing northwest by west. At seven o'clock we took in all studding-
sails and staysails, and the fore and mizzen topgallantsails. So another day passed and another night. An
hour after midnight we took in the main topgallantsail,
and lay by with our head to the south until six bells, when
we wore ship, proceeding north again, and saw Java
Head at nine o'clock to the minute.

We now faced Sunda Strait, the channel that separates

Java from Sumatra and unites the Indian Ocean with the Java Sea. From the bow of our ship there stretched out on one hand and on the other, far beyond the horizon, Borneo, Celebes, Banka, and Billiton; the Little Sunda Islands — Bali and Lombok, Simbawa, Flores and Timor; the China Sea, the Philippines, and farther and greater than them all, the mainland of Asia.

While we were still intent on Java Head there came once more the cry, "Sail ho!"

This time the sail was not to be mistaken. Captain Whidden trained on it the glass, which he shortly handed to Mr. Thomas. "See her go!" the men cried. It was true. She was running away from us easily. Now she was hull down. Now we could see only her topgallant-sails. Now she again had disappeared. But this time we had found, besides her general appearance and the cut of her sails, which no seaman could mistake, a mark by which any landsman must recognize her: on her fore-topsail there was a white lozenge-shaped patch.

At eleven o'clock in the morning, with Prince's Island bearing from north to west by south, we entered the Straits of Sunda. At noon we were due east of Prince's Island beach and had sighted the third Point of Java and the Isle of Cracato.

Fine breezes and a clear sky favored us, and the islands, green and blue according to their distance, were beautiful to see. Occasionally we had glimpses of little native craft, or descried villages sleeping amid the drowsy green of the cocoanut trees. It was a peaceful, beautiful world that met our eyes as the Island Princess stood through the Straits and up the east coast of Sumatra; the air was warm and pleasant, and the leaves of the tufted palms, lacily interwoven, were small in the distance like the fronds of ferns in our own land. But Captain Whidden and Mr. Thomas remained on deck and constantly searched the horizon with the glass; and the men worked uneasily, glancing up apprehensively every minute or two, and starting at slight sounds. There was reason to be apprehensive, we all knew.

On the evening of Friday, August 11, beyond possibility of doubt we sighted a ship; and that it was the same which we already had seen at least once, the lozenge-shaped patch on the foresail proved to the satisfaction of officers and men.

CHAPTER VIII

ATTACKED

In the morning we were mystified to see that the sail once again had disappeared. But to distract us from idle speculations, need of fresh water now added to our uneasiness, and we anchored on a mud bottom while the captain and Mr. Thomas went ashore and searched in vain for a watering-place.

During the day we saw a number of natives fishing in their boats a short distance away; but when our own boat approached them, they pulled for the shore with all speed and fled into the woods like wild men. Thus the day passed,— so quietly and uneventfully that it lulled us into confidence that we were safe from harm,— and a new day dawned.

That morning, as we lay at anchor, the strange ship, with the sun shining brightly on her sails, boldly reappeared from beyond a distant point, and hove to about three miles to the north-northeast. As she lay in plain sight and almost within earshot, she seemed no more out of the ordinary than any vessel that we might have passed off the coast of New England. But on her great foresail, which hung loose now with the wind shaken out of it, there was a lozenge-shaped patch of clean new canvas.

Soon word passed from mouth to mouth that the captain and Mr. Falk would go in the gig to learn the stranger's name and port.

To a certain extent we were relieved to find that our phantom ship was built of solid wood and iron; yet we were decidedly apprehensive as we watched the men pull away in the bright sun. The boat became smaller and smaller, and the dipping oars flashed like gold.

With his head out-thrust and his chin sunk below the level of his shoulders, the cook stood by the galley, in doubt and foreboding, and watched the boat pull away.

His voice, when he spoke, gave me a start.

"Look dah, boy! Look dah! Dey's sumpin' funny, yass, sah. 'Tain't safe foh to truck with ha'nts, no sah! You can't make, dis yeh nigger think a winkin' fire-bug of a fly-by-night ship ain't a ha'nt."

"Ha'nts," said Kipping mildly, "ha'nts is bad things for niggers, but they don't hurt white men."

"Lemme tell you, you Kipping, it ain't gwine pay you to be disrespectable to de cook." Frank stuck his angry face in front of the mild man's. "Ef you think — ha!" — He stopped suddenly, his eyes fixed on something far beyond Kipping, over whose shoulder he now was looking. "Look dah! Look dah! What Ah say? Hey? What Ah say? Look dah! Look dah!"

Startled by the cook's fierce yell, we turned as if a gun had been fired; but we saw only that the boat was coming about.

"Look dah! Look dah! See 'em row! Don' tell me dat ain't no ha'nt!" Jumping up and down, waving his arms wildly, contorting his irregular features till he resembled a gorilla, he continued to yell in frenzy.

Although there seemed to be no cause for any such outburst, the rest of us now were alarmed by the behavior of the men in the boat. Having come about, they were racing back to the Island Princess as fast as ever they could, and the captain and Mr. Falk, if we could judge by their gestures, were urging them to even greater efforts.

"Look dah! Look dah! Do n't you tell me dey ain't seen a ha'nt, you Kipping!"

As they approached, I heard Roger Hamlin say sharply to the mate, "Mr. Thomas, that ship yonder is drifting down on us rapidly. See! They're sheeting home the topsail."

I could see that Mr. Thomas, who evidently thought Roger's fear groundless, was laughing, but I could not hear his reply. In any case he gave no order to prepare for action until the boat came within earshot and the captain abruptly hailed him and ordered him to trip anchor and prepare to make sail.

As the boat came aboard, we heard news that thrilled us. "She's an Arab ship," spread the word. "They were waiting for our boat, with no sign of hostility until Mr. Falk saw the sunlight strike on a gun-barrel that was intended to be hidden behind the bulwark. As the boat veered away, the man with the gun started to fire, but another prevented him, probably because the distance was so great."

Instantly there was wild activity on the Island Princess. While we loosed the sails and sheeted them home and, with anchor aweigh, braced the yards and began to move ahead, the idlers were tricing up the boarding nettings and double-charging our cannon, of which we carried three — a long gun amidships and a pair of stern chasers. Men to work the ship were ordered to the ropes. The rest were served pikes and loaded muskets.

We accomplished the various preparations in an incredibly short time, and, gathering way, stood ready to receive the stranger should she force us to fight.

For the time being we were doubtful of her intentions, and seeing us armed and ready, she stood off as if still unwilling to press us more closely. But some one aboard her, if I guess aright, resented so tame an end to a long pursuit and insisted on at least an exchange of volleys.

Now she came down on us, running easily with the wind on her quarter, and gave us a round from her muskets.

"Hold your fire," Captain Whidden ordered. "They 're feeling their way."

Emboldened by our silence, she wore ship and came nearer. It seemed now that she would attempt to board us, for we spied men waiting with grapnels, and she came steadily on while our own men fretted at their guns, not daring to fire without the captain's orders, till we could see the triumphant sneer on the dark face of her commander.

Now her muskets spoke again. I heard a bullet sing over my head and saw one of our own seamen in the waist fall and lie quite still. Should we never answer her in kind? In three minutes, it seemed, we should have to meet her men hand to hand.

Now our helmsman luffed, and we came closer into the wind, which gave our guns a chance.

"Now, then," Captain Whidden cried, "let them have the long gun and hold the rest."

With a crash our cannon swept the deck of the Arab, splintering the cabin and accomplishing ten times as much damage as all her muskets had done to us. But she in turn, exasperated by the havoc we had wrought, fired simultaneously her two largest guns at point-blank range.

I ducked behind the bulwark and looked back along the deck. One ball had hit the scuttle-butt and had splashed the water fifteen feet in every direction. Another had splintered the crossjack-yard. Suddenly, in the brief silence that followed the two thunderous reports, a single pistol-shot rang out sharply and I saw Captain Whidden spin round and fall.

Our own guns, as we came about, sent an answer that cut the Arab's lower sail to ribbons, disabled many men

Suddenly, in the brief silence that followed the two thunderous reports, a
pistol shot rang out sharply, and I saw Captain Whidden
spin round and fall.

and, I am confident, killed several. But there was no time to load again. Although by now we showed our stern to the enemy, and had a fair chance to outstrip her in a long race, her greater momentum was bringing her down upon us rapidly. From aft came the order, — it was Mr. Thomas who gave it, — "All hands to the pikes and repel boarders!"

There was, however, no more fighting. Our assailants took measure of the stout nets and the strong battery of pikes, and, abandoning the whole unlucky adventure, bore away on a new course.

One man forward was killed and four were badly hurt. Mr. Thomas sat with his back against the cabin, very white of face, with streams of red running from his nostrils and his mouth; and Captain Whidden lay dead on the deck. An hour later word passed through the ship that Mr. Thomas, too, had died.

CHAPTER IX

BAD SIGNS

It was strange that, while some of us in the forecastle were much cast down by the tragic events of the day, others should seem to be put in really good humor by it all. Neddie Benson soberly shook his head from time to time; old Bill Hayden lay in his bunk without even a word about his "little wee girl in Newburyport," and occasionally complained of not feeling well; and various others of the crew faced the future with frank hopelessness.

For my own part, it seemed to me as unreal as a nightmare that Captain Joseph Whidden actually had been shot dead by a band of Arab pirates. I was bewildered — indeed, stunned — by the incredible suddenness of the calamity. It was so complete, so appallingly final! To me, a boy still in his 'teens, that first intimate association with violent death would have been in itself terrible, and I keenly felt the loss of our chief mate. But Captain Whidden to me was far more than master of the ship. He had been my father's friend since long before I was born; and from the days when I first discriminated between the guests at my father's house, I had counted him as also a friend of mine. Never had I dreamed that so sad an hour would darken my first voyage.

Kipping, on the other hand, and Davie Paine and the carpenter seemed actually well pleased with what had happened. They lolled around with an air of exasperating superiority when they saw any of the rest of us looking at them; and now and then they exchanged glances that I was at a loss to understand until all at once a new thought dawned on me: since the captain and the first mate were dead, the command of the ship devolved upon Mr. Falk, the second mate.

No wonder that Kipping and Davie and the carpenter and all the rest of that lawless clique were well pleased. No wonder that old Bill Hayden and some of the others, for whom Kipping and his friends had not a particle of use, were downcast by the prospect.

I was amazed at my own stupidity in not realizing it before, and above all else I now longed to talk with some-one whom I could trust — Roger Hamlin by prefer-ence; as second choice, my friend the cook. But for the time being I was disappointed in this. Almost immedi-ately Mr. Falk summoned all hands aft.

"Men," he said, putting on a grave face that seemed to me assumed for the occasion, "men, we 've come through a dangerous time, and we are lucky to have come alive out of the bad scrape that we were in. Some of us have n't come through so well. It 's a sad thing for a ship to lose an officer, and it is twice as sad to lose two fine officers like Captain Whidden and Mr. Thomas. I 'll now read the service for the burial of the dead, and after that I 'll have something more to say to you."

One of the men spoke in an undertone, and Mr. Falk cried, "What 's that?"

"If you please, sir," the man said, fidgeting nervously, "could n't we go ashore and bury them decently?"

Others had thought of the same thing, and they showed it by their faces; but Mr. Falk scowled and replied, "Nonsense! We 'd be murdered in cold blood."

So we stood there, bareheaded, silent, sad at heart, and heard the droning voice of the second mate,— even then he could not hide his unrighteous satisfaction, — who read from a worn prayer-book, that had belonged to Captain

Whidden himself, the words committing the bodies of three men to the deep, their souls to God.

When the brief, perfunctory service was over, Mr. Falk put away the prayer-book,— I verily believe he put away with it all fear of the Lord,— folded his arms and faced us arrogantly.

"By the death of Captain Whidden and Mr. Thomas," he said, "I have become the rightful master of this ship. Now I 've got a few things to say to you, and I 'm going to have them understood. If you heed them and work smartly, you 'll get along as well as you deserve. If you don't heed them, you 'd better be dead and done with it. If you don't heed them — " he sneered disagreeably — "if you don't heed them I 'll lash the skin off the back of every bloody mother's son of ye. This voyage from now on is to be carried out for the best interests of all concerned." He stopped and smiled and repeated significantly, "*Of* ALL *concerned.*" After another pause, in which some of the men exchanged knowing glances, he went on, "I have no doubt that the most of us will get along as well as need be. So far, well and good. But if there 's those that try to cross my bows," — he swore roundly,— "heaven help 'em! They 'll need it. That 's all. Wait! One thing more: we 've got to have officers, and as I know you 'll not be bold to pick from among yourselves, I 'll save you the trouble. Kipping from this time on will be chief mate. You 'll take his things aft, and you 'll obey him from now on and put the handle to his name. Paine will be second mate. That 's all. Go forward."

Kipping and Davie Paine! I was thunderstruck. But some of the men exchanged glances and smiles as before, and I saw by his expression that Roger, although ill pleased, was by no means so amazed as I should have expected him to be.

For the last time as seaman, Kipping, mild and quiet, came to the forecastle. But as he packed his bag and prepared to leave us, he smiled constantly with a detestable quirk of his mouth, and before going he stopped beside downcast old Bill Hayden. "Straighten up, be a man," he said softly; "I 'll see that you 're treated right." He fairly drawled the words, so mildly did he speak; but when he had finished, his manner instantly changed. Thrusting out his chin and narrowing his eyes, he deliberately drew back his foot and gave old Bill one savage kick.

I was right glad that chance had placed me in the second mate's watch.

As for Davie Paine, he was so overcome by the stroke of fortune that had resulted in his promotion, that he could not even collect his belongings. We helped him pile them into his chest, which he fastened with trembling fingers, and gave him a hand on deck. But even his deep voice had failed him for the time being, and when he took leave of us, he whispered piteously, "'Fore the Lord, I dunno how it happened. I ain't never learned to figger and I can 't no more than write my name."

What was to become of us? Our captain was a weak officer. Our present chief mate no man of us trusted. Our second mate was inexperienced, incompetent, illiterate. More than ever I longed to talk with Roger Hamlin, but there was no opportunity that night.

Our watch on deck was a farce, for old Davie was so unfamiliar with his new duties and so confused by his sudden eminence that, according to the men at the wheel, he did n't know north from south or aloft from alow. Evading his confused glances, I sought the galley, and without any of the usual complicated formalities was admitted to where the cook was smoking his rank pipe.

*We helped him pile his belongings into his chest
and gave him a hand on deck.*

Rolling his eyes until the whites gleamed, he told me the following astounding story.

"Boy," he said, "dis am de most unmitigated day ol' Frank ever see. Cap'n, he am a good man and now he's a dead un. Mistah Thomas he am a good man and now *he's* a dead un. What Ah tell you about dem ha'nts? Ef Ah could have kotched a rabbit with a lef' hind-leg, Ah guess we'd be better off. Hey? Mistah Falk, he am cap'n — Lo'd have mercy on us! Dat Kipping, he am chief mate — Lo'd have mercy on us mis'able sinners! Davie Paine, he am second mate — Lo'd perserve ou' souls! Ah guess you don't know what Ah heah Mistah Falk say to stew'd! He says, 'Stew'd, we got ev'ything — ev'ything. And we ain't broke a single law!' Now tell me what he mean by dat? What's stew'd got, Ah want to know? But dat ain't all — no, sah, dat ain't all."

He leaned forward, the whites of his eyes rolling, his fixed frown more ominous than ever. "Boy, Ah see 'em when dey's dead, Ah did. Ah see 'em all. Mistah Thomas, he have a big hole in de middle of his front, and dat po' old sailo' man he have a big hole in de middle of his front. Yass, sah, Ah see 'em! But cap'n, he have a little roun' hole in the back of his head.— Yass, sah — *he was shot f'om behine!*"

The sea that night was as calm and as untroubled as if the day had passed in Sabbath quiet. It seemed impossible that we had endured so much, that Captain Whidden and Mr. Thomas were dead, that the space of only twenty-four hours had wrought such a change in the fortunes of all on board.

I could not believe that one of our own men had shot our captain. Surely the bullet must have hit him when he was turning to give an order or to oversee some particular duty. And yet I could not forget the cook's words. They hummed in my ears. They sounded in the strumming of the rigging, in the "talking" of the ship: —

"A little roun' hole in the back of his head — yass, sah — he was shot f'om behine."

Without the captain and Mr. Thomas the Island Princess was like a strange vessel. Both Kipping and Davie Paine had been promoted from the starboard watch, leaving us shorthanded; so a queer, self-confident fellow named Blodgett was transferred from the chief mate's watch to ours. But even so there were fewer hands and more work, and the spirit of the crew seemed to have changed. Whereas earlier in the voyage most of the men had gone smartly about their duties, always glad to lend a hand or join in a chantey, and with an eye for the profit and welfare of the owners as well as of themselves, now there came over the ship, silently, imperceptibly, yet so swiftly and completely that, although no man saw it come, in twenty-four hours it was with us and upon us in all its deadening and discouraging weight, a spirit of lassitude and procrastination. You would have expected some of the men to find it hard to give old Davie Paine quite all the respect to which his new berth entitled him, and for my own part I liked Kipping less even than I had liked Mr. Falk. But although my own prejudice should have enabled me to understand any minor lapses from the strict discipline of life aboard ship, much occurred in the next twenty-four hours that puzzled me.

For one thing, those men whom I had thought most likely to accord Kipping and Mr. Falk due respect were most careless in their work and in the small formalities observed between officers and crew. The carpenter and the steward, for example, spent a long time in the galley at an hour when they should have been busy with their own duties. I was near when they came out, and heard the cook's parting words: "Yass, sah, yass, sah, it ain't neveh no discombobilation to help out gen'lems, sah. Yass, sah, no, sah."

And when, a little later, I myself knocked at the door, I got a reception that surprised me beyond measure.

"Who dah," the cook cried in his usual brusque voice. "Who dah knockin' at mah door?"

Coming out, he brushed past me, and stood staring fiercely from side to side. I knew, of course, his curiously indirect methods, and I expected him by some quick motion or muttered command to summon me, as always before, into his hot little cubby-hole. Never was boy more taken aback! "Who dah knockin' at mah door?" he said again, standing within two feet of my elbow, looking past me not two inches from my nose. "Humph! Somebody knockin' at mah door better look at what dey doin' or dey gwine git into a peck of trouble."

He turned his back on me and reëntered the galley.

Then I looked aft, and saw Kipping and the steward grinning broadly. Before, I had been disconcerted. Now I was enraged. How had they turned old black Frank against me, I wondered? Kipping and the steward, whom the negro disliked above all people on board! So the steward and the carpenter and Kipping were working hand in glove! And Mr. Falk probably was in the same boat with them. Where was Roger Hamlin, and what was he doing as supercargo to protect the goods below decks? Then I laughed shortly, though a little angrily, at my own childish impatience.

Certainly any suspicions of danger to the cargo were entirely without foundations. Mr. Falk — Captain Falk, I must call him now — might have a disagreeable personality, but there was nothing to indicate that he was not in most respects a competent officer, or that the ship and cargo would suffer at his hands. The cook had been companionable in his own peculiar way and a very convenient friend indeed; but, after all, I could get along very well on my own resources.

The difference that a change of officers makes in the life and spirit of a ship's crew is surprising to one unfamiliar with the sea. Captain Whidden had been a gentleman and a first-class sailor; by ordering our life strictly, though not harshly or severely, he had maintained that efficient, smoothly working organization which is best and pleasantest for all concerned. But Captain Falk was a master whose sails were cut on another pattern. He lacked Captain Whidden's straightforward, searching gaze. From the corners of his mouth lines drooped unpleasantly around his chin. His voice was not forceful and commanding. I was confident that under ordinary conditions he never would have been given a ship; I doubted even if he would have got a chief mate's berth. But fortune had played into his hands, and he now was our lawful master, resistance to whom could be construed as mutiny and punished in any court in the land.

Never, while Captain Whidden commanded the ship, would the steward and the carpenter have deserted their work and have hidden themselves away in the cook's galley. Never, I was positive, would such a pair of officers as Kipping and old Davie Paine have been promoted from the forecastle. To be sure, the transgressions of the carpenter and the steward were only petty as yet, and if no worse came of our new situation, I should be very foolish to take it all so seriously. But it was not easy to regard our situation lightly. There were too many straws to show the direction of the wind.

CHAPTER X

THE TREASURE–SEEKER

It was a starlit night while we still lingered off the coast of Sumatra for water and fresh vegetables. The land was low and black against the steely green of the sky, and a young moon like a silver thread shone in the west. Blodgett, the new man in our watch, was the centre of a little group on the forecastle.

He was small and wrinkled and very wise. The more I saw and heard of him, the more I marveled that he had not attracted my attention before; but up to this point in the voyage it was only by night that he had appeared different from other men, and I thought of him only as a prowler in the dark.

In some ways he was like a cat. By day he would sit in corners in the sun when opportunity offered, or lurk around the galley, shirking so brazenly, that the men were amused rather than angry. Even at work he was as slow and drowsy as an old cat, half opening his sleepy eyes when the officers called him to account, and receiving an occasional kick or cuff with the same mild surprise that a favorite cat might show. But once darkness had fallen, Blodgett was a different man. He became nervously wakeful. His eyes distended and his face lighted with strange animation. He walked hither and yon. He fairly arched his neck. And sometimes, when some ordinary incident struck his peculiar humor, he would throw back his head, open his great mouth, and utter a screech of wild laughter for all the world like the yowl of a tom-cat.

On that particular night he walked the forecastle, always keeping close to the bulwarks, till the rest of us

assembled by the rigging and watched him with a kind
of fascination. After a time he saw us gathered there
and came over to where we were. His eyes were large
and his wrinkled features twitched with eagerness. He
seemed very old; he had traveled to the farthest lands.

"Men," he cried in his thin, windy voice, "yonder 's
the moon."

The moon indeed was there. There was no reason to
gainsay him. He stood with it over his left shoulder and
extended his arms before him, one pointing somewhat to
the right, the other to the left. "The right hand is the
right way," he cried, "but the left we 'll never leave."

We stared at the man and wondered if he were mad.

"No," he said, smiling at our puzzled glances, "we 'll
never leave the left."

"Belay that talk," said one of the men sharply. "Ye 'll
have to steer a clearer course than that if you ,want us
to follow you."

Blodgett smiled. "The course is clear," he replied.
"Yonder" — he waved his right hand — "is Singapore
and the Chinese Sea and Whampoa. It 's the right
course. Our orders is for that course. Our cargo is for
that course. It 's the course that will make money for
the owners. It 's the right — you understand? — my
right hand and the right course according to orders. But
yonder" — this time he waved his left hand — "is the
course that won't be left. And yet it 's the left you know
— my left hand."

He explained his feeble little joke with an air of pride.

"Why won't it be left?" the gruff seaman demanded.

"Because," said Blodgett, "we ain't going to leave it.
There 's gold there and no end of treasure. Do you suppose Captain Falk is going to leave it all for some one
else to get? He 's going to sail through Malacca Strait and

across the Bay of Bengal to Calcutta. That 's what he 's going to do. I 've been in India myself and seen the heaps of gold lying on the ground by the money-changer's door and no body watching it but a sleepy Gentoo."

"But what 's this treasure you 're talking about," some one asked.

"Sure," said Blodgett in a husky whisper, "it 's a treasure such as never was heard of before. There 's barrels and barrels of gold and diamonds and emeralds and rubies and no end of such gear. There 's idols with crowns of precious stones, and eyes in their carved heads that would pay a king's ransom. There 's money enough in gold mohurs and rupees to buy the Bank of England."

It was a cock-and-bull story that the little old man told us; but, absurd though it was, he had an air of impressive sincerity; and although every one of us would have laughed the yarn out of meeting had it been told of Captain Whidden, affairs had changed in the last days aboard ship. Certainly we did not trust Captain Falk. I thought of the cook's dark words, "A little roun' hole in the back of his head — he was shot f'om behine!" As we followed the direction of Blodgett's two hands,— the right to the northeast and the Chinese shore, the left to the northwest and the dim lowlands of Sumatra that lay along the road to Burma,— anything seemed possible. Moon-madness was upon us, and we were carried away by the mystery of the night.

Such madness is not uncommon. Of tales in the forecastle during a long voyage there is no end. Extraordinary significance is attributed to trivial happenings in the daily life of the crew, and the wonders of the sea and the land are overshadowed completely by simple incidents that superstitious shipmates are sure to exaggerate and to dwell upon.

After a time, though, as Blodgett walked back and forth along-the bulwark, like a cat that will not go into the open, my sanity came back to me.

"That's all nonsense," I said — perhaps too sharply; "Mr. Falk is an honest seaman. His whole future would be ruined if he attempted any such thing as that."

"Ay, hear the boy," Blodgett muttered sarcastically. "What does the boy think a man rich enough to buy all the ships in the king's navy will care for such a future as Captain Falk has in front of him? Hgh! A boy that don't know enough to call his captain by his proper title!"

Blodgett fairly bristled in his indignation, and I said no more, although I knew well enough — or thought I did — that such a scheme was quite too wild to be plausible. Captain Falk might play a double game, but not such a silly double game as that.

"No," said Bill Hayden solemnly, as if voicing my own thought, "the captain ain't going to spoil his good name like that." Poor, stupid old Bill!

Blodgett snorted angrily, but the others laughed at Bill — silly old butt of the forecastle, daft about his little girl! — and after speculating at length concerning the treasure that Blodgett had described so vaguely, fell at last into a hot argument about how far a skipper could disobey the orders of his owners without committing piracy.

Thus began the rumor that revealed the scatterwitted convictions so characteristic of the strange, cat-like Blodgett, which later were to lead almost to death certain simple members of the crew; which served, by a freak of chance, to involve poor Bill Hayden in an affair that came to a tragic end; and which, by a whim of fortune almost as remote, though happier, placed me in closer touch with Roger Hamlin than I had been since the Island Princess sailed from Salem harbor.

An hour later I saw the cook standing silently by his galley. He gave me neither look nor word, although he must have known that I was watching him, but only puffed at his rank old pipe and stared at the stars and the hills. I wondered if the jungle growth reminded him of his own African tropics; if behind his grim, seamed face an unsuspected sense of poetry lurked, a sort of half-beast, half-human imagination.

Never glancing at me, never indicating by so much as a quiver of his black features that he had perceived my presence, he sighed deeply, walked to the rail and knocked the dead ashes from his pipe into the water. He then turned and went into the galley and barricaded himself against intruders, there to stay until, some time in the night, he should seek his berth in the steerage for the few hours of deep sleep that were all his great body required. But as he passed me I heard him murmuring to himself, "Dat Bill Hayden, he betteh look out, yass, sah. He say Mistah Captain Falk don't want to go to spoil his good name. Dat Hayden he betteh look out."

With a bang of his plank door the old darky shut himself away from all of us in the darkness of his little kingdom of pots and pans.

III

WHICH APPROACHES A CRISIS

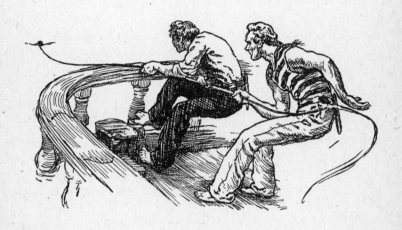

CHAPTER XI

A HUNDRED THOUSAND DOLLARS IN GOLD

UNQUESTIONABLY the negro had known that I was there. Never otherwise could he have ignored me so completely. I was certain too, that his cryptic remarks about Bill Hayden were intended for my ears, for he never acted without a reason, obscure, perhaps, and far-fetched, but always, according to his own queer notions, sufficient.

Sometimes it seemed as if he despised me; sometimes, as if he were concealing a warm, friendly regard for me.

An hour later, hearing the murmur of low voices, I discovered a little group of men by the mainmast; and moved by the curiosity that more than once had led me where I had no business to go, I silently approached.

"Ah," said one of the men, "so you 're keeping a weather eye out for my good name, are you?" It was Captain Falk.

I was startled. It seemed as if the old African were standing at my shoulder, saying, "What did Ah told you, hey?" The cook had used almost those very words. Where, I wondered, had he got them? It was almost uncanny.

"No, sir," came the reply, — it was poor Bill Hayden's voice,— "no, sir, I did n't say that. I said —"

"Well, what *did* you say? Speak up!"

"Why, sir, it — well, it was n't that, I know. I would n't never ha' said that. I — well, sir, it sounded something like that, I got to admit — I — I ain't so good at remembering, sir, as I might be."

The shadowy figures moved closer together.

"You 'll admit, then, that it *sounded* like that?" There was the thud of a quick blow. "I 'll show you. I don't care what you *said*, as long as that was what you *meant*. Take that! I 'll show you."

"Oh! — I — that 's just it, sir, don't hit me! — It may have sounded like that, but — Oh! — it never *meant* anything like that. I can't remember just how the words was put together — I ain't so good at remembering but — Oh! —"

The scene made me feel sick, it was so brutal; yet there was nothing that the rest of us could do to stop it. Captain Falk was in command of the ship.

I heard a mild laugh that filled me with rage. "That 's the way to make 'em take back their talk, captain. Give him a good one," said the mild voice. "He ain't the only one that 'll be better for a sound beating."

There was a scuffle of footsteps, then I heard Bill cry out, "Oh — oh! — oh!"

Suddenly a man broke from the group and fled along the deck.

"Come back here, you scoundrel!" the captain cried with vile oaths; "come back here, or I swear I 'll seize you up and lash you to a bloody pulp."

The fugitive now stood in the bow, trembling, and faced those who were approaching him. "Don't," he cried piteously, "I did n't go to do nothing."

"Oh, no, not you!" said the mild voice, followed by a mild laugh. "He did n't do nothing, captain."

"Not he!" Captain Falk muttered. "I 'll show him who 's captain here."

There was no escape for the unfortunate man. They closed in on him and roughly dragged him from his retreat straight aft to the quarter-deck, and there I heard their brief discussion.

"Had n't you better call up the men, captain?" asked the mild voice. "It 'll do 'em good, I 'll warrant you." "No," the captain replied, hotly. "This is a personal affair. Strip him and seize him up."

I heard nothing more for a few minutes, but I could see them moving about, and presently I distinguished Bill's bare back and arms as they spread-eagled him to the rigging. Then the rope whistled in the air and Bill moaned.

Unable to endure the sight, I was turning away, when some one coming from the cabin broke in upon the scene. "Well," said Roger Hamlin, "what 's all this about?"

Roger's calm voice and composed manner were so characteristic of him that for the moment I could almost imagine myself at home in Salem and merely passing him on the street.

"I 'll have you know, sir," said Captain Falk, "that I 'm master here."

"Evidently, sir."

"Then what do you mean, sir, by challenging me like that?"

"From what I have heard, I judge that the punishment is out of proportion to the offense, even if the steward's yarn was true."

"I 'll have you know, that I 'm the only man aboard this ship that has any judgment," Falk snarled.

"Judgment?" Roger exclaimed; and the twist he gave the word was so funny that some one actually snickered.

"Yes, judgment!" Falk roared; and he turned on Roger with all the anger of his mean nature choking his voice. "I 'll — I 'll beat you, you young upstart, you! I 'll beat you in that man's place," he cried, with a string of oaths.

"No," said Roger very coolly, "I think you won't."

"By heaven, I will!"

The two men faced each other like two cocks in the pit at the instant before the battle. There was a deathly silence on deck.

Such a scene, as I saw it there, if put on the stage in a theatre, would be a drama in itself without word or action. The sky was bright with stars; the land lay low and dark against the horizon; the sea whispered round the ship and sparkled with golden phosphorescence. Over our heads the masts towered to slender black shafts, which at that lofty height seemed far too frail to support the great network of rigging and spars and close-furled canvas. Dwarfed by the tall masts, by the distances of the sea, and by the vastness of the heavens, the small black figures stood silent on the quarter-deck. But one of those men was bound half-naked to the rigging, and two faced each other in attitudes that by outline alone, for we could discern the features of neither, revealed antagonism and defiance.

"No," said Roger once more, very coolly, "I think you won't."

As the captain lifted his rope to hit Bill again, Roger stepped forward.

The captain looked sharply at him; then with a shrug he said, "Oh, well, the fellow's had enough. Cut him down, cut him down."

So they unlashed Bill, and he came forward with his clothes in his arms and one long, raw welt across his back.

"Now, what did I say?" he whimpered. "What did I say to make 'em do like that?"

What had he said, indeed? Certainly nothing culpable. Some one had twisted his innocent remarks in such a way as to irritate the captain and had carried tales to the cabin. With decent officers such a thing never would have happened. Affairs had run a sad course since Captain Falk had read the burial service over Captain Whidden and Mr. Thomas, both of whom had been strict, fair, honorable gentlemen. There was a sober time in the forecastle that night, and none of us had much to say.

Next day we sent a boat ashore again, and got information that led us to sail along five miles farther, where there was a settlement from which we got a good supply of water and vegetables. This took another day, and on the morning of the day following we made sail once more and laid our course west of Lingga Island, which convinced us for a time that we really were about to bear away through Malacca Strait and on to Burma, at the very least.

I almost believed it myself, India seemed so near; and Blodgett, sleepy by day, wakeful by night, prowled about with an air of triumph. But in the forenoon watch Roger Hamlin came forward openly and told me certain things that were more momentous than any treasure-hunting trip to India that Blodgett ever dreamed of.

Captain Falk and Mr. Kipping — I suppose they must be given their titles now — watched him, and I could see that they did n't like it. They exchanged glances] and stared after him suspiciously, even resentfully; but there was nothing that they could do or say. So he came on slowly and confidently, looking keenly from one man to another as he passed.

, By this time the two parties on board were sharply divided, and from the attitude of the men as they met Roger's glance their partisanship was pretty plainly revealed. The two from Boston, who were, I was confident, on friendly and even familiar terms with Captain Falk and Mr. Kipping, gave him a half-concealed sneer. There was no doubt where their sympathies would lie, should Roger cross courses with our new master. The carpenter, working on a plank laid on deck, heard him coming, glanced up, and seeing who it was, continued at his labor without moving so much as a hair's breadth to let him by; the steward looked him in the eye brazenly and impersonally; and others of the crew, among them the strange Blodgett, treated him with a certain subtle rudeness, even contempt. Yet here and there a man was glad to see him coming and gave him a cordial nod, or a cheerful "Ay, ay, sir," in answer to whatever observation he let fall.

The cook alone, as I watched the scene with close interest, I could not understand. To a certain extent he seemed surly, to a certain extent, subservient. Perhaps he intended that we — and others — should be mystified.

One thing I now realized for the first time: although the crew was divided into two cliques, the understanding was much more complete on the side of Captain Falk. Among those who enjoyed the favor of our new officers there was, I felt sure, some secret agreement, perhaps even some definite organization. There seemed to be a unity of thought and manner that only a common purpose could explain, whereas the rest drifted as the wind blew.

"Ben," Roger said, coming to me where I sat on the forecastle, "I want to talk to you. Step over by the mast."

I followed him, though surprised.

"Here we can see on all sides," he said. "There are no hiding-places within earshot. Ben" — He hesitated as if to find the right words.

All were watching us now, the captain and the mate from the quarter-deck, the others from wherever they happened to be.

"I am loath to draw your sister's younger brother into danger," Roger began. His adjective was tactfully chosen. "I am almost equally reluctant to implicate you in what seems likely to confront us, because you are an old friend of mine and a good deal younger than I am. But when the time comes to go home, Ben, I 'm sure we want to be able to look your sister and all the others squarely in the eyes, with our hands clean and our consciences clear — if we go home. How about it, Ben?"

I was too bewildered to answer, and in Roger's eyes something of his old twinkle appeared.

"Ultimately," he continued, grave once more and speaking still in enigmas, "we shall be vindicated in any case. But I fear that, before then, I, for one, shall have to clasp hands with mutiny, perhaps with piracy. How would you like that, Ben, with a thundering old fight against odds, a fight that likely enough will leave us to sleep forever on one of these green islands hereabouts?"

Still I did not understand.

Roger regarded me thoughtfully. "Tell me all that you know about our cargo."

"Why," said I, finding my tongue at last, "it 's ginseng and woollen goods for Canton. That 's all I know."

"Then you don't know that at this moment there is one hundred thousand dollars in gold in the hold of the Island Princess?"

"What?" I gasped.

"One hundred thousand dollars in gold."

I could not believe my ears. Certainly, so far as I was concerned, the secret had been well kept.

Then a new thought came to me. "Does Captain Falk know?" I asked.

"Yes," said Roger, "Captain Falk knows."

CHAPTER XII

A STRANGE TALE

ROGER HAMLIN'S words were to linger a long time in my ears, and so far as I then could see, there was little to say in reply. A hundred thousand dollars in gold had bought, soul and body, many a better man than Captain Falk. At that very moment Falk was watching us from the quarter-deck with an expression on his face that was partly an amused smile, partly a sneer. Weak and conceited though he was, he was master of that ship and crew in more ways than one.

But Roger had not finished. "Do you remember, Ben," he continued in a low voice, but otherwise unmindful of those about us, "that some half a dozen years ago, when Thomas Webster was sore put to it for enough money to square his debts and make a clean start, the brig Vesper, on which he had sent a venture, returned him a profit so unbelievably great that he was able to pay his creditors and buy from the Shattucks the old Eastern Empress, which he fitted out for the voyage to Sumatra that saved his fortunes?"

I remembered it vaguely — I had been only a small boy when it happened — and I listened with keenest interest. The Websters owned the Island Princess.

"Not a dozen people know all the story of that voyage. It's been a kind of family secret with the Websters. Perhaps they're ashamed to be so deeply indebted to a Chinese merchant. Well, it's a story I shouldn't tell under other conditions, but in the light of all that's come to pass, it's best you should hear the whole tale, Ben;

and in some ways it's a fine tale, too. The Websters, as you probably know, had had bad luck, what with three wrecks and pirates in the West Indies. They were pretty much by the head in those days, and it was a dark outlook before them, when young Webster signed the Vesper's articles as first officer and went aboard, with all that the old man could scrape together for a venture, and with the future of his family hanging in the balance. At Whampoa young Webster went up to the Hong along with the others, and drove what bargains he could, and cleared a tidy little sum. But it was nowhere near enough to save the family. If only they could get the money to tide them over, they'd weather the gale. If not, they'd go on a lee shore. Certain men — you'd know their names, but such things are better forgotten — were waiting to attach the ships the Websters had on the ways, and if the ships were attached there would be nothing left for the Websters but stools in somebody's counting-house.

"As I've heard the story, young Webster was waiting by the river for his boat, with a face as long as you'd hope to see, when a Chinese who'd been watching him from a little distance came up and addressed him in such pidgin English as he could muster and asked after his father. Of course young Webster was taken by surprise, but he returned a civil answer, and the two fell to talking together. It seemed that, once upon a time, when the Chinese was involved, head and heels, with some rascally down-east Yankee, old man Webster had come to the rescue and had got him out of the scrape with his yellow hide whole and his money-bags untapped.

"The Chinaman seemed to suspect from the boy's long face that all was not as it should be, and he squeezed more

or less of the truth out of the young fellow, had him up
to the Hong again, gave him various gifts, and sent him
back to America with five teak-wood chests. Just five
ordinary teak-wood chests — but in those teak-wood
chests, Ben, was the money that put the Websters on their
feet again. The hundred thousand dollars below is for
that Chinese merchant."

It was a strange tale, but stranger tales than that
were told in the old town from which we had sailed.

"And Captain Falk — ?" I began questioningly.

"Captain Falk was never thought of as a possible
master of this ship."

"Will he try to steal the money?"

Roger raised his brows. "Steal it? Steal is a disagreeable word. He thinks he has a grievance because
he was not given the chief mate's berth to begin with.
He says, at all events, that he will not hand over any
such sum to a yellow heathen. He thinks he can return
it to the owners two-fold. Although he seldom reads
his Bible, I believe he referred to the man who was given
ten talents."

"But the owners' orders!" I exclaimed.

"The owners' orders in that respect were secret. They
were issued to Captain Whidden and to me, and Captain
Falk refuses to accept my version of them."

"And you?"

Roger smiled and looked me hard in the eye. "I am
going to see that they are carried out," he said. "The
Websters would be grievously disappointed if this com-
mission were not discharged. Also —" his eyes twinkled
in the old way — "I am not convinced that Captain
Falk is in all respects an honest — no, let us not speak
too harshly — let us say, a *reliable* man."

"So there 'll be a fight," I mused.

"We 'll see," Roger replied. "In any case, you know the story. Are you with me?"

After fifty years I can confess without shame that I was frightened when Roger asked me that question, for Roger and I were only two, and Falk, by hook or by crook, had won most of the others to his side. There was Bill Hayden, to be sure, on whom we could count; but he was a weak soul at best, and of the cook's loyalty to Roger and whatever cause he might espouse I now held grave doubts. Yet I managed to reply, "Yes, Roger, I am with you."

I thought of my sister when I said it, and of the white flutter of her handkerchief, which had waved so bravely from the old wharf when Roger and I sailed out of Salem harbor. After all, I was glad even then that I had answered as I did.

"I 'll have more to say later," said Roger; "but if I stay here much longer now, Falk and Kipping will be breaking in upon us." And, turning, he coolly walked aft.

Falk and Kipping were still watching us with sneers, and not a few of the crew gave us hostile glances as we separated. But I looked after Roger with an affection and a confidence that I was too young fully to appreciate. I only realized that he was upright and fearless, and that I was ready to follow him anywhere.

More and more I was afraid of the influence that Captain Falk had established in the forecastle. More and more it seemed as if he actually had entered into some lawless conspiracy with the men. Certainly they grumbled less than before, and accepted greater discomforts with better grace; and although I found myself excluded from their councils without any apparent reason, I overheard occasional snatches of talk from which I gathered that they derived great satisfaction from their scheme, whatever it was. Even the cook would have none of me in the galley of an evening; and Roger in the cabin, where no doubt he was fighting his own battles, was far away from the green hand in the forecastle. I was left to my own devices and to Bill Hayden.

To a great extent, I suppose, it counted against me that I was the son of a gentleman. But if I was left alone forward, so Roger, I learned now and then, was left alone aft.

Continually I puzzled over the complacency of the men. They would nod and smile and glance at me pityingly, even when I was getting my meat from the same kids and my tea from the same pot; and chance phrases, which I caught now and then, added to my uneasiness.

Once old Blodgett, prowling like a cat in the night, was telling how he was going to "take his money and buy a little place over Ipswich way. There's nice little places over Ipswich way where a man can settle snug as you please and buy him a wife and end his days in comfort. We'll go home by way of India, too, I'll warrant you, and take each of us our handful of round red rubies. Right's right, but right'll be left — mind what I tell you."

Another time — on the same day, as I now recall it — I overheard the carpenter saying that he was going to build a brick house in Boston up on Temple Place. "And there'll be fan-lights over the door," he said, "their panels as thin as rose-leaves, and leaded glass in a fine pattern." The carpenter was a craftsman who aspired to be an artist.

But where did old Blodgett or the carpenter hope to get the money to indulge the tastes of a prosperous merchant? I suspected well enough the answer to that question, and I was not far wrong.

The cook remained inscrutable. I could not fathom the expressions of his black frowning face. Although

Captain Falk of course had no direct communication with him openly, I learned through Bill Hayden that indirectly he treated him with tolerant and friendly patronage. It even did not surprise me greatly to be told that sometimes he secretly visited the galley after dark and actually hobnobbed with black Frank in his own quarters. It was almost incredible, to be sure; but so was much else in which Captain Falk was implicated, and I could see revealed now in the game that he was playing his desire to win and hold the men until they had served his ends, whatever those ends might be.

"Yass, sah," black Frank would growl absently as he passed me without a glance, "dis am de most appetizin' crew eveh Ah cooked foh. Dey's got no mo' bottom to dey innards dan a sponge has. Ah's a-cookin' mah head off to feed dat bunch of wuthless man-critters, a-a-a-a-h!" And he would stump to the galley with a brimming pail of water in each hand.

I came sadly to conclude that old Frank had found other friends more to his taste than the boy in the forecastle, and that Captain Falk, by trickery and favoritism, really was securing his grip on the crew. In all his petty manœuvres and childish efforts to please the men and flatter them and make them think him a good officer to have over them, he had made up to this point only one or two false steps.

Working our way north by west to the Straits of Singapore, and thence on into the China Sea, where we expected to take advantage of the last weeks of the southwest monsoon, we left far astern the low, feverous shores of Sumatra. There were other games than a raid on India to be played for money, and the men thought less and less now of the rubies of Burma and the gold mohurs and rupees of Calcutta.

CHAPTER XIII

TROUBLE FORWARD

In the starboard watch, one fine day when there was neither land nor sail in sight, Davie Paine was overseeing the work on the rigging and badly botching it. The old fellow was a fair seaman himself, but for all his deep voice and big body, his best friend must have acknowledged that as an officer he was hopelessly incompetent. "Now unlay the strands so," he would say. "No, that ain't right. No, so! No, that ain't right either. Supposing you form the eye so. No, that ain't right either."

After a time we were smiling so broadly at his confused orders that we caught the captain's eye.

He came forward quickly — say what you would against Captain Falk as an officer, no one could deny that he knew his business — and instantly he took in the whole unfortunate situation. "Well, *Mister* Paine," he cried, sarcastically stressing the title, "are n't you man enough to unlay a bit of rope and make a Flemish eye?"

Old Davie flushed in hopeless embarrassment, and even the men who had been chuckling most openly were sorry for him. That the captain had reason to be dissatisfied with the second mate's work, we were ready enough to admit; but he should have called him aside and rebuked him privately. We all, I think, regarded such open interference as unnecessary and unkind.

"Why — y-yes, sir," Davie stammered.

"To make you a Flemish eye," Captain Falk continued in cold sarcasm, "you unlay the end of the rope and open up the yarns. Then you half-knot some half the inside

yarns over that bit of wood you have there, and scrape
the rest of them down over the others, and marl, parcel,
and serve them together. That's the way you go to
make a Flemish eye. Now then, *Mister* Paine, see that
you get a smart job done here and keep your eyes open,
you old lubber. I thought you shipped for able seaman.
A fine picture of an able seaman you are, you doddering
old fool!"

It is impossible to reproduce the meanness with which
he gave his little lecture, or the patronizing air with which
he walked away. Old Davie was quite taken aback by
it and for a time he could not control his voice enough to
speak. It was pitiful to see him drop all the pretensions
of his office and, as if desiring only some friendly word,
try to get back on the old familiar footing of the forecastle.

"I know I ain't no great shakes of a scholar," he managed to mutter at last, "and I ain't no great shakes of a
second mate. But he made me second mate, he did, and
he had n't ought to shame me in front of all the men, now
had he? It was him that gave me the berth. If he don't
like me in it, now why don't he take it away from me?
I did n't want to be second mate when he made me do it,
and I can't read figures good nor nothing. Now why don't
he send me forrard if he don't like the way I do things?"

The old man ran on in a pathetic monologue, for none
of us felt exactly at liberty to put in our own oars, and he
could find relief only in his incoherent talk. It had been
a needless and unkind thing and the men almost unanimously disapproved of it. Why indeed should Captain
Falk not send Davie back to the forecastle rather than
make his life miserable aft? The captain was responsible
only to himself for the appointment, and its tenure depended only on his own whims; but that, apparently, he
had no intention of doing.

"'Tain't right," old Blodgett murmured, careful not to let Captain Falk see him talking. "He didn't ought to use a man like that."

"No, he didn't," Neddie Benson said in his squeaky voice, turning his face so that neither Davie nor Captain Falk should see the motion of his lips. "I didn't ought to ship for this voyage, either. The fortune teller — she was a lady, she was, a nice lady — she says, 'Neddie, there'll be a dark man and a light man and a store of trouble.' She kind of liked me, I think. But I up and come. I'm always reckless."

A ripple of low, mild laughter, which only Kipping could have uttered, drifted forward, and the men exchanged glances and looked furtively at old Davie.

The murmur of disapproval went from mouth to mouth, until for a time I dared hope that Captain Falk had quite destroyed the popularity that he had tried so hard to win. But, though Davie was grieved by the injustice and though the men were angry, they seemed soon to forget it in the excitement of that mysterious plot from which Roger and I were virtually the only ones excluded.

Nevertheless, like certain other very trivial happenings aboard the Island Princess, Captain Falk's unwarrantable insult to Davie Paine — it seems incongruous to call him "mister" — was to play its part later in events that as yet were only gathering way.

We had not seen much of Kipping for a time, and perhaps it was because he had kept so much to himself that to a certain extent we forgot his sly, tricky ways. His laugh, mild and insinuating, was enough to call them to mind, but we were to have a yet more disagreeable reminder.

All day Bill Hayden had complained of not feeling

well, and now he leaned against the deck-house, looking white and sick. Old Davie would never have troubled him, I am sure, but Kipping was built by quite another mould.

Unaware of what was brewing, I turned away, sorry for poor Bill, who seemed to be in much pain, and in response to a command from Kipping, I went aloft with an "Ay, ay sir," to loose the fore-royal. Having accomplished my errand, I was on my way down again, when I heard a sharp sound as of slapping.

Startled, I looked at the deck-house. I was aware at the same time that the men below me were looking in the same direction.

The sound of slapping was repeated; then I heard a mild, gentle voice saying, "Oh, he's sick, is he? Poor fellow! Ain't it hard to be sick away from home?" Slap — slap. "Well, I declare, what do you suppose we'd better do about it? Shan't we send for the doctor? Poor fellow!" Slap — slap. "Ah! ah! ah!" Kipping's voice hardened. "You blinking, bloody old fool. You would turn on me, would you? You would give me one, would you? You would sojer round the deck and say you're sick, would you? I'll show you — take that — I'll show you!"

Now, as I sprang on deck and ran out where I could see what was going forward, I heard Bill's feeble reply. "Don't hit me, sir. I didn't go to do nothing. I'm sick. I've got a pain in my innards. I *can't* work — so help me, I *can't* work."

"Aha!" Again Kipping laughed mildly. "Aha! *Can't* work, eh? I'll teach you a lesson."

Bill staggered against the deck-house and clumsily fell, pressing his hands against his side and moaning.

"Hgh!" Kipping grunted. "Hgh!"

At that moment the day flashed upon my memory when I had sat on one side of that very corner while Kipping attempted to bully Bill on the other side of it — the day when Bill had turned on his tormentor. I now understood some of Kipping's veiled references, and a great contempt for the man who would use the power and security of his office to revenge himself on a fellow sea-man who merely had stood up bravely for his rights swept over me. But what could I or the others do? Kipping now was mate, and to strike him would be open mutiny. Although thus far, in spite of the dislike with which he and Captain Falk regarded me, my good be-havior and my family connections had protected me from abuse, I gladly would have forfeited such security to help Bill; but mutiny was quite another affair.

We all stood silent, while Kipping berated Bill with many oaths, though poor Bill was so white and miser-able that it was almost more than we could endure. I, for one, thought of his little girl in Newburyport, and I remember that I hoped she might never know of what her loving, stupid old father was suffering.

Enraged to fury by nothing more or less than Bill's yielding to his attacks, Kipping turned suddenly and reached for the carpenter's mallet, which lay where Chips had been working nearby. With a round oath, he yelled, "I 'll make you grovel and ask me to stop."

Kipping had moved quickly, but old Bill moved more quickly still. Springing to his feet like a flash, with a look of anguish on his face such as I hope I never shall see again, he warded off a blow of the mallet with his hand and, running to the side, scrambled clean over the bulwark into the sea.

We stood there like men in a waxwork for a good min-ute at the very least; and if you think a minute is not a long time, try it with your eyes shut. Kipping's angry snarl was frozen on his mean features,— it would have been ludicrous if the scene had not been so tragic,— and his outstretched hand still held the mallet at the end of the blow. The carpenter's mouth was open in amazement. Neddie Benson, the first to move or break the silence, had spread his hands as if he were about to clutch at a butterfly or a beetle; dropping them to his side, he gasped huskily, "She said there'd be a light man and a dark man — I — oh, Lord!"

It was the cook, as black as midnight and as inscrutable as a figurehead, who brought us to our senses. Silently observing all that had happened, he had stood by the galley, without lifting his hand or changing the expression of a single feature; but now, taking his pipe from his mouth, he roared, "Man ovehboa'd!" Then, snatching up the carpenter's bench with one hand and gathering his great body for the effort, he gave a heave of his shoulders and tossed the bench far out on the water.

As if waking from a dream, Mr. Kipping turned aft, smiling scornfully, and said with a deliberation that seemed to me criminal, "Put down the helm!"

So carelessly did he speak, that the man at the wheel did not hear him, and he was obliged to repeat the order a little more loudly. "Did n't you hear me? I say, put down the helm."

"Put down the helm, sir," came the reply; and the ship began to head up in the wind.

At this moment Captain Falk, having heard the cook's shout, appeared on deck, breathing hard, and took command. However little I liked Captain Falk, I must confess in justice to him that he did all any man could have done under the circumstances. While two or three hands cleared away a quarter-boat, we hauled up the mainsail, braced the after yards and raised the head sheets, so that the ship, with her main yards aback, drifted down in the general direction in which we thought Bill must be.

Not a man of us expected ever to see Bill again. He had flung himself overboard so suddenly, and so much time had elapsed, that there seemed to be no chance of his keeping himself afloat. . I saw that the smile actually still hovered on Kipping's mean, mild mouth. But all at once the cook, near whom I was standing, grasped my arm and muttered almost inaudibly, "If dey was to look behine, dey 'd get ahead, yass, sah."

Taking his hint, I looked astern and cried out loudly. Something was bobbing at the end of the log line. It was Bill clinging desperately.

When we got him on board, he was nearer dead than alive, and even the stiff drink that the captain poured between his blue lips did not really revive him. He moaned continually and now and then he cried out in pain. Occasionally, too, he tried to tell us about his little girl at Newburyport, and rambled on about how he had married late in life and had a good wife and a comfortable home, and before long, God willing, he would be back with them once more and would never sail the seas again. It was all so natural and homely that I did n't realize at the time that Bill was delirious; but when I helped the men carry him below, I was startled to find his face so hot, and presently it came over me that he did not recognize me.

Poor old stupid Bill! He meant so well, and he wished so well for all of us! It was hard that he should be the one who could not keep out of harm's way.

But there were other things to think of, more important even than the fate of Bill Hayden, and one of them was an extraordinary interview with the cook.

I heard laughter in the galley that night, and lingered near as long as I dared, with a boy's jealous desire to learn who was enjoying the cook's hospitality. By his voice I soon knew that it was the steward, and remembering how black Frank once was ready to deceive him for the sake of giving me a piece of pie, I was more disconsolate than ever. After a while I saw him leave, but I thought little of that. I still had two more hours to stand watch, so I paced along in the darkness, listening to the sound of the waves and watching the bright stars.

When presently I again passed the galley I thought I heard a suspicious sound there. Later I saw something move by the door. But neither time did I go nearer. I had no desire for further rebuffs from the old negro.

When I passed a third time, at a distance of only a foot or two, I was badly startled. - A long black arm reached out from the apparently closed door; a black hand grasped me, lifted me bodily from the floor, and silently drew me into the galley, which was as dark as Egypt. I heard the cook close the door behind me and bolt it and cover the deadlight with a tin pan. What he was up to, I had not the remotest idea; but when he had barricaded and sealed every crack and cranny, he lighted a candle and set it on a saucer and glared at me ferociously.

"Mind you, boy," he said in a very low voice, "don't you think Ah 'm any friend of yo's. No, sah. Don't you think Ah 'm doing nothin' foh you. No, sah. 'Cause Ah ain't. No, sah. Ah 'm gwine make a fo'tune dis yeh trip, Ah am. Yass, sah. Dis yeh nigger 's gwine go home putty darn well off. Yass, sah. So don't you think dis yeh nigger 's gwine do nothin' foh you. No, sah."

For a moment I was completely bewildered; then, as I recalled the darky's crafty and indirect ways, my confidence returned and I had the keenest curiosity to see what would be forthcoming.

"Boys, dey's a pest," he grumbled. "Dey did n't had ought to have boys aboa'd ship. No, sah. Cap'n Falk, he say so, too."

The negro was looking at me so intently that I searched his words for some hidden meaning; but I could find none.

"No, sah, boys am de mos' discombobulationest eveh was nohow. Yass, sah. Dey's been su'thin' happen aft. Yass, sah. Ah ain't gwine tell no boy, nohow. No, sah. 'Taint dis nigger would go tell a boy dat Mistah Hamlin he have a riot with Mistah Cap'n Falk, no sah. Ah ain't gwine tell no boy dat Mistah Hamlin, he say dat Mistah Cap'n Falk he ain't holdin' to de right co'se, no, sah; nor dat Mistah Cap'n Falk he bristle up like a guinea gander and he say, while he's swearin' most amazin', dat he know what co'se he's sailin', no, sah. Ah ain't gwine tell no boy dat Mistah Hamlin, he say he am supercargo, an' dat he reckon he got orders f'om de owners; and Mistah Cap'n Falk, he say he am cap'n and he cuss su'thin' awful 'bout dem orders; and Mistah Roger Hamlin he say Mistah Cap'n Falk his clock am a hour wrong and no wonder Mistah Kipping am writing in de log-book dat de ship am whar she ain't; and Mistah Kipping he swear dre'ful pious and he say by golly he am writer of dat log-book and he reckon he know what's what ain't. No, sah, Ah ain't gwine tell a boy dem things 'cause Ah tell stew'd Ah ain't, an' stew'd, him an' me is great friends, what's gwine make a fo'tune *when Mistah Cap'n Falk git dat money!*"

He said those last words in a whisper, and stared at me intently; in that same whisper, he repeated them, "*When Mistah Cap'n Falk git dat money!*"

Then, in a strangely meditative way, as if an unfamiliar process of thought suddenly occupied all his attention, he muttered absently, letting his eyes fall, "Seem like Ah done see dat Kipping befo'; Ah jes' can't put mah finger on him." It was the second time that he had made such a remark in my hearing.

The candle guttered in the saucer that served for a candlestick, and its crazy, wavering light shone unsteadily on the black face of the cook, who continued to stare at me grimly and apparently in anger. A pan rattled as the ship rolled. Water splashed from a bucket. I watched the drops falling from the shelf. One — two — three — four — five — six — seven! Each with its *pht*, its little splash. They continued to drip interminably. I lost all count of them. And still the black face, motionless except for the wildly rolling eyes, stared at me across the galley stove.

CHAPTER XIV

BILL HAYDEN COMES TO THE
END OF HIS VOYAGE

I was ejected from the galley as abruptly and strangely as I had been drawn into it. The candle went out at a breath from the great round lips; the big hand again closed on my shoulder and lifted me bodily from my chair. The door opened and shut, and there was I, dazed by my strange experience and bewildered by the story I had heard, outside on the identical spot from which I had been snatched ten minutes before.

In my ears the negro's parting message still sounded, "Dis nigger would n't tell a boy one word, no sah, not dis nigger. If he was to tell a boy jest one leetle word, dat boy, he might lay hisself out ready foh a fight. Yass, sah."

For a long time I puzzled over the whole extraordinary experience. It was so like a dream, that only the numbness of my arm where the negro's great fist had gripped it convinced me that the happenings of the night were real. But as I pondered, I found more and more significance in the cook's incoherent remarks, and became more and more convinced that their incoherence was entirely artful. Obviously, first of all, he was trying to pacify his conscience, which troubled him for breaking the promise of secrecy that he probably had given the steward, from whom he must have learned the things at which he had hinted. Also he had established for himself an alibi of a kind, if ever he should be accused of tattling about affairs in the cabin.

That Captain Falk had promised to divide the money

among the crew, I long had suspected; consequently
that part of the cook's revelations did not surprise me.
But the picture he gave of affairs in the cabin, discon-
nected though it was, caused me grave concern. After
all, what could Roger do to preserve the owners' property
or to carry out their orders? Captain Falk had all the
men on his side, except me and perhaps poor old Bill
Hayden. Indeed, I feared for Roger's own safety if he
had detected that rascally pair in falsifying the log; he
then would be a dangerous man when we all went back
to Salem together. I stopped as if struck: what assurance had I that we should go back to Salem together —
or singly, for that matter? There was no assurance
whatever, that all, or any one of us, would ever go back
to Salem. If they wished to make way with Roger, and
with me too, for that matter, the green tropical seas
would keep the secret until the end of time.

I am not ashamed that I frankly was white with fear
of what the future might bring. You can forgive in a
boy weaknesses of which a man grown might have been
guilty. But as I watched the phosphorescent sea and
the stars from which I tried to read our course, I gradually
overcame the terror that had seized me. I think that
remembering my father and mother, and my sister, for
whom I suspected that Roger cared more than I, perhaps,
could fully realize, helped to compose me; and I am sure
that the thought of the Roger I had known so long,—
cool, bold, resourceful, with that twinkle in his steady
eyes — did much to renew my courage. When eight
bells struck and some one called down the hatch, "Lar-
bowlines ahoy," and the dim figures of the new watch
appeared on deck, and we of the old watch went below,
I was fairly ready to face whatever the next hours might
bring.

"Roger and I against them all," I thought, feeling very much a martyr, "unless," I mentally added, "Bill Hayden joins us." At that I actually laughed, so that Blodgett, prowling restlessly in the darkness, asked me crossly what was the matter. I should have been amazed and incredulous if anyone had told me that poor Bill Hayden was to play the deciding part in our affairs.

He lay now in his bunk, tossing restlessly and muttering once in a while to himself. When I went over and asked if there was anything that I could do for him, he raised himself on his elbow and stared at me more stupidly than ever. It seemed to come to him slowly who I was. After a while he made out my face by the light of the dim, swinging lantern, and thanked me, and said if I would be so good as to give him a drink of water — He never completed the sentence; but I brought him a drink carefully, and when he had finished it, he thanked me again and leaned wearily back.

His face seemed dark by the lantern-light, and I judged that it was still flushed. Muttering something about a "pain in his innards," he apparently went to sleep, and I climbed into my own bunk. The lantern swung more and more irregularly, and Bill tossed with ever-increasing uneasiness. When at last I dozed off, my own sleep was fitful, and shortly I woke with a start.

Others, too, had waked, and I heard questions flung back and forth: —

"Who was that yelled?"

"Did you hear that? Tell me, did you hear it?"

Some one spoke of ghosts,— none of us laughed,— and Neddie Benson whimpered something about the lady who told fortunes. "She said the light man and the dark man would make no end o' trouble," he cried; "and he —"

"Keep still," another voice exclaimed angrily. "It

was Bill Hayden," the voice continued. "He hollered."

Getting out of my bunk, I crossed the forecastle. "Bill," I said, "are you all right?"

He started up wildly. "Don't hit me!" he cried. "That was n't what I said — it —I don't remember *just* what I said, because I ain't good at remembering, but it was n't that — don't — oh! oh! — I *know* it was n't that."

Two of the men joined me, moving cautiously for the ship was pitching now in short, heavy seas.

"What 's that he 's saying?" one of them asked.

Before I could answer, Bill seemed suddenly to get control of himself. "Oh," he moaned. "I 've got such a pain in my innards! I 've got a rolling, howling old pain in my innards."

There was little that we could do, so we smoothed his blankets and went back to our own. The Island Princess was pitching more fiercely than ever now, and while I watched the lantern swing and toss before I went to sleep, I heard old Blodgett saying something about squalls and cross seas. There was not much rest for us that night. No sooner had I hauled the blankets to my chin and closed my eyes, than a shout came faintly down to us, "All — hands — on deck!"

Some one called, "Ay, ay," and we rolled out again wearily — all except Bill Hayden whose fitful tossing seemed to have settled at last into deep sleep.

Coming on deck, we found the ship scudding under close-reefed maintopsail and reefed foresail, with the wind on her larboard quarter. A heavy sea having blown up, all signs indicated that a bad night was before us; and just as we emerged from the hatch, she came about suddenly, which brought the wind on the starboard quarter and laid all aback.

In the darkness and rain and wind, we sprang to the

ropes. Mr. Kipping was forward at his post on the fore-castle and Captain Falk was on the quarter-deck. As the man at the wheel put the helm hard-a-starboard, we raised the fore tack and sheet, filled the foresail and shivered the mainsail, thus bringing the wind aft again, where we met her with the helm and trimmed the yards for her course. For the moment we were safe, but already it was blowing a gale, and shortly we lay to, close-reefed, under what sails we were carrying.

In a lull I heard Blodgett, who was pulling at the ropes by my side, say to a man just beyond him, "Ay, it's a good thing for *us* that Captain Falk got command. We'd never make our bloody fortunes under the old officers."

As the wind came again and drowned whatever else may have been said, I thought to myself that they never would have. Plainly, Captain Falk and Kipping had won over the simple-minded crew, which was ready to follow them with never a thought of the chance that that precious pair might run off with the spoils themselves and leave the others in the lurch.

But now Kipping's indescribably disagreeable voice, which we all by this time knew so well, asked, "Has anybody seen that sojering old lubber, Hayden?"

"Ay, ay, sir," Blodgett replied. "He's below sick."

"Sick?" said the mild voice. "Sick is he? Supposing, Blodgett, you go below and bring him on deck. He ain't sick, he's sojering."

"But, sir, — " Blodgett began.

"But what?" roared Kipping. His mildness changed to fierceness. "*You go!*" He snapped out the words, and Blodgett went.

Poor stupid old Bill!

When he appeared, Blodgett had him by the arm to help him.

"You sojering, bloody fool," Kipping cried; "do you think I 'm so blind I can't see through such tricks as yours?"

A murmur of remonstrance came from the men, but Kipping paid no attention to it.

"You think, do you, that I ain't on to your slick tricks? Take that."

Bill never flinched.

"So!" Kipping muttered. "So! Bring him aft."

Though heavy seas had blown up, the squalls had subsided, and some of the men, for the moment unoccupied, trailed at a cautious distance after the luckless Bill. We could not hear what those on the quarter-deck said; but Blodgett, who stood beside me and stared into the darkness with eyes that I was convinced could see by night, cried suddenly, "He 's fallen!"

Then Captain Falk called, "Come here, two or three of you, and take this man below."

Old Bill was moaning when we got there. "Sure," he groaned, "I 've got a rolling — howling — old Barney's bull of a pain in my innards." But when we laid him in his bunk, he began to laugh queerly, and he seemed to pretend that he was talking to his little wee girl; for we heard him saying that her old father had come to her and that he was never going to leave her again.

To me — only a boy, you must remember — it was a horrible experience, even though I did not completely understand all that was happening; and to the others old Bill's rambling talk seemed to bring an unnamed terror.

All night he restlessly tossed, though he soon ceased his wild talking and slept lightly and fitfully. The men watching him were wakeful, too, and as I lay trying to sleep and trying not to see the swaying lantern and the fantastic shadows, I heard at intervals snatches of their low conversation.

"They had n't ought to 'a' called him out. It war n't human. A sick man has got *some* rights," one of the men from Boston repeated interminably. He seemed unable to hold more than one idea at a time.

Then Blodgett would say, "Ay, it don't seem right. But we 've all got to stand by the skipper. That 's how we 'll serve our ends best. It don't do to get too much excited."

I imagined that Blodgett's voice did not sound as if he were fully convinced of the doctrine he was preaching.

"Ay," the other would return, "but they had n't ought to 'a' called him out. It war n't human. A sick man has got *some* rights, and he was allers quiet."

They talked on endlessly, while I tried in vain to sleep and while poor Bill tossed away, getting no good from the troubled slumber that the Lord sent him.

No sooner, it seemed to me, did I actually close my eyes than I woke and heard him moaning, "Water — a — drink — of — water."

The others by then had left him, so I got up and fetched water, and he muttered something more about the "pain in his innards." Then my watch was called and I went on deck with the rest.

For the most part it was a day of coarse weather. Now intermittent squalls from the southwest swept upon us with lightning and thunder, driving before them rain in solid sheets; now the ship danced in choppy waves, with barely enough wind to give her steerage-way and with a warm, gentle drizzle that wet us to the skin and penetrated into the forecastle, where blankets and clothing soon became soggy and uncomfortable. But the greater part of the time we lurched along in a gale of

wind, with an occasional dash of rain, which we accepted
as a compromise between those two worse alternatives,
the cloudbursts that accompanied the squalls, and the
enervating warm drizzle.

That Bill Hayden did not stand watch with the others,
no one, apparently, noticed.   The men were glad enough
to forget him, I think, and the officers let his absence pass,
except Davie Paine, who found opportunity to inquire
of me secretly about him and sadly shook his gray head
at the tidings I gave.

Below we could not forget him.   I heard the larboard
watch talking of it when they relieved us; and no sooner
had we gone below in turn than Blodgett cried, "Look
at old Bill!   His face is all of a sweat."

He was up on his elbow when we came down, staring
as if he had expected some one; and when he saw who it
was, he kept his eyes on the hatch as if waiting for still
another to come.   Presently he fell back in his bunk.
"Oh, I've got such a pain in my innards," he moaned.

By and by he began to talk again, but he seemed to
have forgotten his pain completely, for he talked about
doughnuts and duff, and Sundays ashore when he was a
little shaver, and going to church, and about the tiny wee
girl on the bank of the Merrimac who would be looking
for her dad to come home, and lots of things that no one
would have thought he knew.   He seemed so natural
now and so cheerful that I was much relieved about him,
and I whispered to Blodgett that I thought Bill was better.
But Blodgett shook his head so gravely that I was frightened in spite of my hopes, and we lay there, some of us
awake, some asleep, while Bill rambled cheerily on and the
lantern swung with the motion of the ship.

To-day I remember those watches below at that time
in the voyage as a succession of short unrestful snatches

of sleep broken by vivid pictures of the most trivial things — the swinging lantern, the distorted shadows, the muttered comments of the men, Bill leaning on his elbow at the edge of his bunk and staring toward the hatch as if some one long expected were just about to come. I do not pretend to understand the reason, but in my experience it is the trifling unimportant things that after a time of stress or tragedy are most clearly remembered.

When next I woke I heard the bell — *clang-clang, clang-clang, clang-clang, clang* — faint and far off. Then I saw that Blodgett was sitting on the edge of his bunk, counting the strokes on his fingers. When he had finished he gravely shook his head and nodded toward Bill who was breathing harder now. "He 's far gone," Blodgett whispered. "He ain't going to share in no split-up at Manila. He ain't going to put back again to India when we 've got rid of the cargo. His time 's come."

I did n't believe a word that Blodgett said then, but I sat beside him as still as the grave while the forecastle lantern nodded and swung as casually as if old Bill were not, for all we knew, dying. By and by we heard the bell again, and some one called from the hatch, "Eight bells! Roll out!"

The very monotony of our life — the watches below and on deck, each like every other, marked off by the faint clanging of the ship's bell — made Bill's sickness seem less dreadful. There is little to thrill a lad or even, after a time, to interest him, in the interminable routine of a long voyage.

When we came on deck Davie Paine looked us over and said, "Where 's Bill?"

Blodgett shook his head. Even this simple motion had a sleepy quality that made me think of a cat.

"I 'm afraid, sir," he replied, "that Bill has stood his last watch."

"So!" said old Davie, reflectively, in his deep voice, "so! — I was afraid of that." Ignorant though Davie was, and hopelessly incompetent as an officer, he had a certain kindly tolerance, increased, perhaps, by his own recent difficulties, that made him more approachable than any other man in the cabin. After a time he added, "I cal'ate I got to tell the captain." Davie's manner implied that he was taking us into his confidence.

"Yes," Neddie Benson muttered under his breath, "tell the captain! If it was n't for Mr. Kipping and the captain, Bill would be as able a man this minute as any one of us here. It did n't do to abuse him. He ain't got the spirit to stand up under it."

Davie shuffled away without hearing what was said, and soon, instead of Captain Falk, Mr. Kipping appeared, bristling with anger.

"What 's all this?" he snapped, with none of the mildness that he usually affected. "Who says Bill Hayden has stood his last watch? Is mutiny brewing? I 'll have you know I 'm mate here, legal and lawful, and what 's more I 'll show you I 'm mate in a way that none of you won't forget if he thinks he can try any more of his sojering on me. I 'll fix him. You go forward, Blodgett, and drag him out by the scalp-lock."

Blodgett walked off, keeping close to the bulwark, and five minutes later he was back again.

Mr. Kipping grew very red. "Well, my man," he said in a way that made my skin creep, "are you a party to this little mutiny?"

"N-no, sir," Blodgett stammered. "I — he —it ain't no use, he *can't* come."

The mate looked sternly at Blodgett, and I thought he

was going to hit him; but instead, after a moment of hesitation, he started forward alone.

We scarcely believed our eyes.

By and by he came back again, but to us he said nothing. He went into the cabin, and when next we saw him Captain Falk was by his side.

"I don't like the looks of it," Kipping was saying. "I don't at all."

As the captain passed me he called, "Lathrop, go to the galley and get a bucket of hot water."

Running to the deck-house, I thrust my head into the galley and made known my want with so little ceremony that the cook was exasperated. Or so at least his manner intimated.

"You boy," he roared in a voice that easily carried to where the others stood and grinned at my discomfiture, "you boy, what foh you come promulgatin' in on me with 'gimme dis' and 'gimme dat' like Ah wah n't ol' enough to be yo' pa? Ain't you got no manners nohow? You vex me, yass, sah, you vex me. If we gotta have a boy on boa'd ship, why don' dey keep him out of de galley?"

Then with a change of voice that startled me, he demanded in an undertone that must have been inaudible a dozen feet away, "Have things broke? Is de fight on? Has de row started?"

Bewildered, I replied, "Why, no—it's only Bill Hayden."

Instantly he resumed his loud and abusive tone. "Well, if dey gwine send a boy heah foh wateh, wateh he's gotta have. Heah, you wuthless boy, git! Git out of heah!"

Filling a bucket with boiling water, he thrust it into my hand and shoved me half across the deck so roughly that I narrowly escaped scalding myself, then returned to his work, muttering imprecations on the whole race of boys. He was too much of a strategist for me.

When I took the bucket to the forecastle, I found the captain and Mr. Kipping looking at poor old Bill.

"Dip a cloth in the water," the captain said carelessly, "and pull his clothes off and lay the cloth on where it hurts."

I obeyed as well as I could, letting the cloth cool a bit first; and although Bill cried out sharply when it touched his skin, the heat eased him of pain, and by and by he opened his eyes for all the world as if he had been asleep and looked at Captain Falk and said in a scared voice, "In heaven's name, what 's happened?"

The captain and Mr. Kipping laughed coldly. It seemed to me that they did n't care whether he lived or died. Certainly the men of the larboard watch, who were lying in their bunks at the time, did n't like the way the two behaved. I caught the word "heartless" twice repeated.

"Well," said Captain Falk at last, "either he 'll live or he 'll not. How about it, Mr. Kipping?"

The mate laughed as if he had heard a good joke. "That 's one of the truest things ever was said aboard a ship," he replied, in his slow, insincere way. "Yes, sir, it hits the nail on the head going up and coming down."

"Well, then, let 's leave him to make up his mind."

So the two went aft together as if they had done a good day's work. But there was a buzz of disapproval in the forecastle when they had gone, and one of the men from Boston, of whom I hitherto had had a very poor opinion, actually got out of his blankets and came over to help me minister to poor Bill's needs.

"It ain't right," he said dipping the cloth in the hot water; "they never so much as gave him a dose of medicine. A man may be only a sailor, but he 's worth a dose of medicine. There never come no good of denying poor Jack his pill when he 's sick."

"Ay, heartless!" one of the others exclaimed. "*I could tell things if I would.*"

That remark, I ask you to remember. The man who made it, the other of the two from Boston, had black hair and a black beard, and a nose that protruded in a big hook where he had broken it years before. It was easy to recognize his profile a long way off because of the peculiar shape of the nose. The remark itself is of little importance, of course; but a story is made up of things that seem to be of little importance, yet really are more significant by far than matters that for the moment are startling.

It was touching to see the solicitude of the men and the clumsy kindness of their efforts to help poor Bill when the captain and the mate had left him. They crowded up to his bunk and smoothed out his blankets and spoke to him more gently than I should have believed possible. So angry were they at the brutality of the two officers, that the coldest and hardest of them all gave the sick man a muttered word of sympathy or an awkward helping hand.

We worked over him, easing him as best we could, while the bell struck the half hours and the hours; and for a while he seemed more comfortable. In a moment of sanity he looked up at me with a sad smile and said, "I wish, lad, I surely wish I could do something for *you.*" But long before the watch was over he once more began to talk about the tiny wee girl at Newburyport — "Cute she is as they make 'em," he reiterated weakly, "a-waiting for her dad to come home." And by and by he spoke of his wife,— "a good wife," he called her,— and then he made a little noise in his throat and lay for a long time without moving.

"He's dead," the man from Boston said at last;

and there was no sound in the forecastle except the rattle of the swinging lantern and the *chug-chug* of waves.

I was younger than the others and more sensitive, so I went on deck and leaned on the bulwark, looking at the ocean and seeing nothing.

IV

IN WHICH THE TIDE OF OUR FORTUNES EBBS

CHAPTER XV

MR. FALK TRIES TO COVER HIS TRACKS

How long I leaned on the bulwark I do not know; I had no sense of passing time. But after a while some one told me that the captain wished to see me in the cabin, and I went aft with other tragic memories in mind. I had not entered the cabin since Captain Whidden died — "*shot f'om behine.*" The negro's phrase now flashed upon my memory and rang over and over again in my ears.

The cabin itself was much as it had been that other day: I suppose no article of its furnishings had been changed. But when I saw Captain Falk in the place of Captain Whidden and Kipping in the place of Mr. Thomas, I felt sick at heart. All that encouraged me was the sight of Roger Hamlin, and I suspected that he attended uninvited, for he came into the cabin from his stateroom at the same moment when I came down the companionway, and there was no twinkle now in his steady eyes.

Captain Falk glanced at him sharply. "Well, sir?" he exclaimed testily.

"I have decided to join you, sir," Roger said, and calmly seated himself.

For a moment Falk hesitated, then, obviously unwilling, he assented with a grimace.

"Lathrop," he said, turning to me, "you were present when Hayden died, and also you had helped care for him previously. Mr. Kipping has written a statement of the circumstances in the log and you are to sign it. Here's the place for your name. Here's a pen and ink. Be careful not to blot or smudge it."

He pushed the big, canvas-covered book over to me and placed his finger on a vacant line. All that preceded it was covered with paper.

"Of course," said Roger, coldly, "Lathrop will read the statement before signing it." He was looking the captain squarely in the eye.

Falk scowled as he replied, "I consider that quite unnecessary."

"A great many of the ordinary decencies of life seem to be considered unnecessary aboard this ship."

"If you are making any insinuations at me, Mr. Hamlin, I'll show you who's captain here."

"You need n't. You 've done it sufficiently already. Anyhow, if Lathrop were foolish enough to sign the statement without reading it, I should know that he had n't read it and I assure you that it would n't pass muster in any court of law."

As Captain Falk was about to retort even more angrily, Kipping touched his arm and whispered to him.

"Oh, well," he said with ill grace, "as you wish, Mr. Kipping. There's nothing underhanded about this. Of course the account is absolutely true and the whole world could read it; only I don't intend a silly young fop shall think he can bully me on my own ship. Show Lathrop the statement."

Kipping withdrew the paper and I began to read what was written in the log, but Roger now interrupted again.

"Read it aloud," he said.

"What in heaven's name do you think you are, you young fool? If you think you can bully Nathan Falk like that, I 'll lash you to skin and pulp."

"Oh, well," said Roger comically, in imitation of the

captain's own air of concession, "since you feel so warmly on the subject, I 'm quite willing to yield the point. It 's enough that Lathrop should read it before he signs." Then, turning to me suddenly, he cried, "Ben, what 's the course according to the log?"

The angry red of Captain Falk's face deepened, but before he could speak, I had seen and repeated it:—

"Northeast by north."

Roger smiled. "Go on," he said. "Read the statement."

The statement was straightforward enough for the most part — more straightforward, it seemed to me, than either of the two men who probably had collaborated in writing it; but one sentence caught my attention and I hesitated.

"Well," said Roger who was watching me closely, "is anything wrong?"

"Why, perhaps not exactly wrong," I replied, "though I do think most of the men forward would deny it."

"See here," cried Captain Falk, cutting off Kipping, who tried to speak at the same moment, "I tell you, Mr. Hamlin, if you thrust your oar in here again I 'll thrash you within an inch of your life! I 'll keelhaul you, so help me! I 'll —" He wrinkled up his nose and twisted his lips into a sneer before he added, almost in a whisper, "I 'll do worse than that."

"No," said Roger calmly, "I don't think you will. What 's the sentence, Benny?"

Without waiting for another word from anyone I read aloud as follows:—

"'And the captain and the chief mate tended Hayden carefully and did what they might to make his last hours comfortable.'"

"Well," said Falk, "did n't we?"

"No, by heaven, you did n't," Roger cried suddenly,

taking the floor from me. "I know how you beat Hayden. I know how you two drove him to throw himself overboard. You 're a precious pair! And what 's more, all the men forward know it. While we 're about it, Captain Falk, here 's something else I know. According to the log, which you consistently have refused to let me see, the course is northeast by north. According to the men at the wheel,— I will not be still! I will not close my mouth! If you assault me, sir, I will break your shallow head,— according to the men at the wheel, of whom I have inquired, according to the ship's compass when I 've taken a chance to look at it, according to the tell-tale that you yourself can see at this very minute and — " Roger laid on the table a little box of hard wood bound with brass — "according to this compass of my own, which I know is a good one, our course is now and has been for two days east-northeast. Captain Falk, do you think you can make us believe that Manila is Canton?"

"It may be that I do, and it may be that I do not," Falk retorted hotly. "As for you, Mr. Hamlin, I 'll attend to your case later. Now sign that statement, Lathrop."

Falk was standing. His hands, a moment before lifted for a blow, rested on the table; but the knuckles were streaked with red along the creases, and the nails of his fingers, which were bent under, he had pressed hard against the dull mahogany. When he had finished speaking, he sat down heavily.

"Sign it, Ben," said Roger; "but first draw your pen through that particular sentence."

Quick as thought I did what Roger told me, leaving a single broad line through the words "and did what they might to make his last hours comfortable"; then I wrote my name and laid the pen on the table.

Leaning over to see what I had done, Falk leaped up

"Sign that statement, Lathrop," said Captain Falk.

white with passion. "Good God!" he yelled, "that's worse than nothing."

"Yes," said Roger coolly, "I think it is."

"What —" Falk stopped suddenly. Kipping had touched his sleeve. "Well?"

Kipping whispered to him.

"No," Falk snarled, glancing at me, "I'm going to take that young pup's hide off his back and salt it."

Again Kipping whispered to him.

This time he seemed half persuaded. He was a weak man, even in his passions. "All right," he said, after reflecting briefly. "As you say, it don't make so much odds. Myself, I'm for slitting the young pup's ears — but later on, later on. And though I'd like to straighten out the record as far as it goes — Well, as you say."

For all of Captain Falk's bluster and pretension, I was becoming more and more aware that the subtle Kipping could twist him around his little finger, and that for some end of his own Kipping did not wish affairs to come yet to a head.

He leaned back in his chair, twirling his thumbs behind his interlocked fingers, and smiled at us mildly. His whole bearing was odious. He fairly exhaled hypocrisy. I remembered a dozen episodes of his career aboard the Island Princess — the wink he had given Captain Falk, then second mate; his coming to the cook's galley for part of my pie; his bullying poor old Bill Hayden; his cold selfishness in taking the best meat from the kids, and many other offensive incidents. Was it possible that Captain Falk was not at the bottom of all our troubles? that Captain Falk had been from the first only somebody's tool?

We left the cabin in single file, the captain first, Kipping second, then Roger, then I.

CHAPTER XVI

A PRAYER FOR THE DEAD

In the last few hours we had sighted an island, which lay now off the starboard bow; and as I had had no opportunity hitherto to observe it closely, I regarded it with much interest when I came on deck. Inland there were several cone-shaped mountains thickly wooded about the base; to the south the shore was low and apparently marshy; to the north a bold and rugged promontory extended. Along the shore and for some distance beyond it there were open spaces that might have been great tracts of cleared land; and a report prevailed among the men that a fishing boat had been sighted far off, which seemed to put back incontinently to the shore. Otherwise there was no sign of human habitation, but we knew the character of the natives of such islands thereabouts too well to approach land with any sense of security.

Captain Falk and Kipping were deep in consultation, and the rest were intent upon the sad duty that awaited us. On the deck there lay now a shape sewed in canvas. The men, glancing occasionally at the captain, stood a little way off, bare-headed and ill at ease, and conversed in whispers. For the moment I had forgotten that we were to do honor for the last time — and, I fear me, for the first — to poor Bill Hayden. Poor, stupid Bill! He had meant so well by us all, and life had dealt so hardly with him! Even in death he was neglected.

As time passed, the island became gradually clearer, so that now we could see its mountains more distinctly and pick out each separate peak. Although the wind

was light and unsteady, we were making fair progress;
but Captain Falk and Mr. Kipping remained intent on
their conference.

I could see that Roger Hamlin, who was leaning on the
taffrail, was imperturbable; but Davie Paine grew nervous
and walked back and forth, looking now and then at the
still shape in canvas, and the men began to murmur among
themselves.

"Well," said the captain at last, "what does all this
mean, Mr. Paine? What in thunder do you mean by letting the men stand around like this?"

He knew well enough what it meant, though, for all
his bluster. If he had not, he would have been ranting
up the deck the instant he laid eyes on that scene of
idleness such as no competent officer could countenance.

Old Davie, who was as confused as the captain had intended that he should be, stammered a while and finally
managed to say, "If you please, sir, Bill Hayden's dead."

"Yes," said the captain, "it looks like he's dead."

We all heard him and more than one of us breathed
hard with anger.

" Well, why don't you heave him over and be done
with it?" he asked shortly, and turned away.

The men exchanged glances.

"If you please, sir,—" it was Davie, and a different
Davie from the one we had known before,— "if you please,
sir, ain't you goin' to read the service and say the words?"

I turned and stared at Davie in amazement. His voice
was sharper now than ever I had heard it and there was
a challenge in his eyes as well.

"What?" Falk snapped out angrily.

"Ain't you goin' to read the Bible and say the words,
sir?"

I am convinced that up to this point Captain Falk had

intended, after badgering Davie enough to suit his own unkind humor, to read the service with all the solemnity that the occasion demanded. He was too eager for every prerogative of his office to think of doing otherwise. But his was the way of a weak man; at Davie's challenge he instantly made up his mind not to do what was desired, and having set himself on record thus, his mulish obstinacy held him to his decision in spite of whatever better judgment he may have had.

"Not I!" he cried. "Toss him over to suit yourself."

When an angry murmur rose on every side, he faced about again. "Well," he said, "what do you want, anyway? I 'm captain here, and if you wish I 'll *show* you I 'm captain here. I 'll read the service or I 'll not read it, just as I please. If any man here 's got anything to say about it, I 'll do some saying myself. If any man here wants to read the service over that lump of clay, let him read it." Then, turning with an air of indifference, he leaned on the rail with a sneer, and smiled at Kipping.

What would have happened next I do not know, so angry were the men at this wretched exhibition on the part of the captain, if Roger had not stepped forward.

"Very well, sir," he said facing the captain, "since you put it that way, *I 'll* read the service." And without ceremony he took from the captain's hand the prayer-book that Falk had brought on deck.

Disconcerted by this unexpected act and angered by the murmur of approval from the men, Falk started to speak, then thought better of it and sidled over beside Kipping, to whom he whispered something at which they both laughed heartily. Then they stood smiling scornfully while Roger went down beside poor Bill's body.

Roger opened the prayer-book, turned the pages deliberately, and began to read the service slowly and with

feeling. He was younger and more slender than many
of the men, but straight and tall and handsome, and I
remember how proud of him I felt for taking affairs in
his own hands and making the best of a bad situation.

"We therefore commit his body to the deep," he read,
"looking for the general Resurrection in the last day,
and the life of the world to come, through our Lord Jesus
Christ; at whose second coming in glorious majesty to
judge the world, the sea shall give up her dead; and the
corruptible bodies of those who sleep in Him shall be
changed and made like unto his glorious body; according
to the mighty working whereby He is able to subdue all
things unto Himself."

Then Blodgett, Davie Paine, the cook, and the man
from Boston lifted the plank and inclined it over the
bulwark, and so passed all that was mortal of poor Bill
Hayden.

Suddenly, in the absolute silence that ensued when
Roger closed the prayer-book, I became aware that he
was signaling me to come nearer, and I stepped over
beside him. At the same instant the reason for it burst
upon me. Now, if ever, was the time to turn against
Captain Falk.

"Men," said Roger in a low voice, "are you going to
stand by without lifting a hand and see a shipmate's
dead body insulted?"

The crew came together in a close group about their
supercargo. With stern faces and with the heavy breathing of men who contemplate some rash or daring deed,
they were, I could see, intent on what Roger had to say.

He looked from one to another of them as if to appraise
their spirit and determination. "I represent the owners,"
he continued tersely. "The owners' orders are not being
obeyed. Mind what I tell you — *the owners' orders are*

not being obeyed. You know why as well as I do, and
you remember this: though it may seem on the face of
it that I advocate mutiny or even piracy, if we take the
ship from the present captain and carry out the voyage
and obey the owners' orders, I can promise you that
there 'll be a fine rich reward waiting at Salem for every
man here. What 's more, it 'll be an honest reward, with
credit from the owners and all law-abiding men. But
enough of that! It 's a matter of ordinary decency — of
common honesty! The man who will conspire against
the owners of this ship is a contemptible cur, a fit ship-
mate with the brute who horsed poor Bill to death."

I never had lacked faith in Roger, but never before had
I appreciated to the full his reckless courage and his un-
yielding sense of personal honor.

He paused and again glanced from face to face. "What
say, men? Are you with me?" he cried, raising his voice.

Meanwhile Captain Falk, aware that something was
going on forward, shouted angrily, "Here, here! What 's
all this! Come, lay to your work, you sons of perdition,
or I 'll show you what 's what. You, Blodgett, go forward and heave that lead as you were told."

In his hand Blodgett held the seven-pound dipsey lead,
but he stood his ground.

"Well?" Falk came down on us like a whirlwind.
"Well? You, Hamlin, what in Tophet are you backing
and hauling about?"

"I? Backing and hauling?" Roger spoke as calmly
as you please. "I am merely advocating that the men
take charge of the ship in the name of the lawful owners
and according to their orders."

As Captain Falk sprang forward to strike him down,
there came a thin, windy cry, "No you don't; no, you
don't!"

To my amazement I saw that it was old Blodgett.
"It don't do to insult the dead," he cried in a voice
like the yowl of a tom-cat. "You can kill us all you like.
It's captain's rights. But, by the holy, you ain't got no
rights whatsoever to refuse a poor sailor a decent burial."

With a vile oath, Captain Falk contemplated this new
factor in the situation. Suddenly he yelled, "Kipping!
It's mutiny! Help!" And with a clutch at his hip he
drew his pistol.

"'Heave the lead' is it?" Blodgett muttered. "Ay,
I'll heave the lead." He whipped up his arm and hurled
the missile straight at Captain Falk's head.

The captain dodged, but the lead struck his shoulder
and felled him.

Seeing Kipping coming silently with a pistol in each
hand, I ducked and tried to pull Roger over beside Blodgett; but Roger, instantly aware of Kipping's move, spun
on his heel as the first bullet flew harmlessly past us, and
lithely stepped aside. With a single swing of his right
arm he cut Kipping across the face with a rope's end and
stopped him dead.

As the welt reddened on his face, Kipping staggered,
leveled his other pistol point-blank and pulled the trigger.

For the moment I could not draw breath, but the
pistol missed fire.

"Flashed in the pan!" Roger cried, and tugged at his
own pistol, which had caught inside his shirt where he
had carried it out of sight. "That's not all — that's
flashed in the pan!"

"Now then, you fools," Kipping shrieked. "Go for
'em! Go for 'em! The bell's struck! Now's the time!"

So far it all had happened so suddenly and so extraordinarily swiftly, with one event fairly leaping at the
heels of another, that the men were completely dazed.

Captain Falk sat on the deck with his hand pressed against his injured shoulder and with his pistol lying beside him where he had dropped it when he fell. Kipping, the red bruise showing across his face, confronted us with one pistol smoking, the other raised; Blodgett, having thrown the lead, was drawing his knife from the sheath; Roger was pulling desperately at his own pistol; and for my part I was in a state of such complete confusion that to this day I don't know what I did or said. In the moments that followed we were to learn once and for all the allegiance of every man aboard the Island Princess.

One of the men from Boston, evidently picking me out as the least formidable of the trio, shot a quick glance back at Kipping as if to be sure of his approval, and springing at me, knocked me flat on my back. I felt sure he was going to kill me when he reached for my throat. But I heard behind me a thunderous roar, "Heah Ah is! Heah Ah is!" And out of the corner of my eye I saw the cook, the meat-cleaver in his hand, leaping to my rescue, with Roger, one hand still inside his shirt, scarcely a foot behind him.

The man from Boston scrambled off me and fled.

"Ah's with you-all foh one," the cook cried, swinging his cleaver. "Ah ain't gwine see no po' sailor man done to death and me not say 'What foh!'"

"You fool! You black fool!" Chips shrieked, shaking his fist, "Stand by and share up! Stand by and share up!"

Neddie Benson jumped over beside the cook. "Me too!" he called shrilly. "Bad luck or good luck, old Bill he done his best and was fair murdered."

Poor Bill! His martyrdom stood us in good stead in our hour of need.

On the other side of the deck there was a lively struggle

from which came fierce yells as each man sought to persuade his friends to his own way of thinking:

"Stand by, lads, stand by —"

"—— the bloody money! —"

"Hanged for mutiny —"

"I know where my bed 's made soft —"

The greater part of the men, it seemed, were lining up behind Kipping and Captain Falk, when a scornful shout rose and I was aware that some one else had come over to our side. It was old Davie Paine. "He did n't ought to shame me in front of all the men," Davie muttered. "No, sir, it wa' n't right. And what 's more, there 's lots o' things aboard this ship that ain't as they should be. I may be poor and ignorant and no shakes of a scholar, but I ain't goin' to put up with 'em."

So we six faced the other twelve with as good grace as we could muster,— Roger, the cook, Blodgett, Neddie Benson, Davie, and I,— and there was a long silence. But Roger had got out his pistol now, and the lull in the storm was ominous.

CHAPTER XVII

MAROONED

THAT it was important to control the after part of the ship, I was well aware, and though we were outnumbered two to one, I hoped that by good fortune we might win it.

I was not long in doubt of Roger's sharing my hope. He analyzed our opponents' position at a single glance, and ignoring their advantage in numbers, seized upon the only chance of taking them by surprise. Swinging his arm and crying, "Come, men! All for the cabin!" he flung himself headlong at Falk. I followed close at his heels — I was afraid to be left behind. I heard the cook grunt hoarsely as he apprehended the situation and sprang after us. Then the others met us with knives and pistols.

Our attack was futile and soon over, but while it lasted there was a merry little fight. As a man slashed at Roger with a case-knife, laying open a long gash in his cheek, Roger fired a shot from his pistol, and the fellow pitched forward and lay still except for his limbs, which twitched sickeningly. For my own part, seeing another who had run aft for a weapon swing at me with a cutlass, I threw myself under his guard and got my arms round both his knees. As something crashed above me, I threw the fellow back and discovered that the cook had met the cutlass in full swing with the cleaver and had shattered it completely. Barely in time to escape a murderous blow that the carpenter aimed at me with his hammer, I scrambled to my feet and leaped back beside Roger, who held his cheek with his hand.

I believe it was the cook's cleaver that saved our lives for the time being. Falk and Kipping had fired the charges in their pistols, and no one was willing to venture within reach of the black's long arm and brutal weapon. So, having spent our own last charge of powder, we backed away into the bow with our faces to the enemy, and the only sounds to be heard were flapping sails and rattling blocks, the groans of the poor fellow Roger had shot, and the click of a powder-flask as Falk reloaded and passed his ammunition to Kipping.

"So," said Falk at last, "we have a fine little mutiny brewing, have we?" He looked first at us, then at those who remained true to him and his schemes. "Well, Mr. Kipping, with the help of Chips here, we can make out to work the ship at a pinch. Yes, I think we can dispense with these young cocks altogether. Yes, —" he raised his voice and swore roundly — "yes, we can follow our own gait and fare a damned sight better without them. We 'll let them have a boat and row back to Salem. A voyage of a few thousand miles at the oars will be a rare good thing to tone down a pair of young fighting cocks." Then he added, smiling, "If they meet with no Ladronesers or Malays to clip their spurs."

Captain Falk looked at Kipping and his men, and they all laughed.

"Ay, so it will," cried Kipping. "And old Davie Paine 'll never have a mister to his name again. You old lubber, you, your bones will be rotting at the bottom of the sea when we 're dividing up the gold."

Again the men laughed loudly.

Davie flushed and stammered, but Blodgett spoke out bitterly.

"So they will, before you or Captain Falk divide with any of the rest. Ah! Red in the face, are ye? That shot told. Davie 'd rather take his chances with a gentleman than be second mate under either one o' you two. He may not know when he 's well off, but he knows well when he ain't."

For all Blodgett spoke so boldly, I could see that Davie in his own heart was still afraid of Kipping. But Kipping merely smiled in his mean way and slowly looked us over.

"If we was to walk them over a plank," he suggested, deferentially, to the captain, "there would be an end to all bother with them."

"No," said Falk, "give them a boat. It 's all the same in the long run, and I ain't got the stomach to watch six of them drown one after another."

Kipping raised his eyebrows at such weakness; then a new thought seemed to dawn on him. His accursed smile grew broader and he began to laugh softly. For the moment I could not imagine what he was laughing at, but his next words answered my unspoken question. "Ha ha ha! Right you are, captain! Just think of 'em, a-sailing home in a ship's boat! Oh, won't they have a pretty time?"

The predicament of six fellow men set adrift in an open boat pleased the man's vile humor. We knew that he believed he was sending us to certain death, and that he delighted in it.

"This fine talk is all very well," said Roger, "and I 've no doubt you think yourselves very witty, but let that be as it may. As matters stand now, you 've got the upper hand — though I wish you joy of working the ship. However, if you give us the long-boat and a fair allowance of water and bread, we 'll ask nothing more."

"Ah," said Falk, with a leer at Kipping who was smiling quietly, "the long-boat and a fair allowance of water and bread! Ay, next they 'll be wanting us to set 'em up in

their own ship." He changed suddenly from a leer to
a snarl. "You 'll take what I give you and nothing more
nor less. Now then, men, we 'll just herd these hearties
overboard and bid them a gay farewell."

He stood there, pointing the way with a grand gesture,
and the late afternoon sun sparkled on the buttons of his
coat and shone brightly on the fine white shirt he wore,
which in better days had belonged to Captain Whidden.
"Murderer and thief!" I thought. For although about
Captain Whidden's death I knew nothing more than the
cook's never-to-be-forgotten words, "a little roun' hole in
the back of his head — he was shot f'om behine," I laid
Bill Hayden's death at Captain Falk's door, and I knew
well by now that our worthy skipper would not scruple
at stealing more than shirts.

When Falk pointed to the quarter-boat, the men,
laughing harshly, closed in on us and drove us along by
threatening us with pistols and pikes, which the bustling
steward by now had distributed. And all the while Kipping stood just behind the captain, smiling as if no unkind
thought had ever ruffled his placid nature. I could not
help but be aware of his meanness, and I suppose it was
because I was only a boy and not given to looking under
the surface that I did not yet completely recognize in
him the real leader of all that had gone astray aboard the
Island Princess.

We let ourselves be driven toward the boat. Since we
were outnumbered now eleven to six,— not counting
the wounded man of course,— and since, compared with
the others, we were virtually unarmed, we ought, I suppose, to have been thankful that we were not murdered
in cold blood, as doubtless we should have been if our
dangerous plight had not so delighted Kipping's cruel
humor, and if both Falk and Kipping had not felt certain

that they would never see or hear of us again. But we found little comfort in realizing that, as matters stood, although in our own minds we were convinced absolutely that Captain Falk and Mr. Kipping had conspired with the crew to rob the owners, by the cold light of fact we could be proved in the wrong in any court of admiralty.

So far as Roger and I were concerned, our belief was based after all chiefly on supposition; and so craftily had the whole scheme been phrased and manœuvred that, if you got down to categorical testimony, even Blodgett and Davie Paine would have been hard put to it to prove anything culpable against the other party. Actually we were guilty of mutiny, if nothing more.

The cook still carried his great cleaver and Blodgett unobtrusively had drawn and opened a big dirk knife; but Neddie Benson, Davie, and I had no weapons of any kind, and Roger's pistol was empty.

We worked the boat outboard in silence and made no further resistance, though I knew from Roger's expression as he watched Falk and Kipping and their men, that, if he had seen a fair chance to turn the scales in our favor, he would have seized it at any cost.

Meanwhile the sails were flapping so loudly that it was hard to hear Roger's voice when he again said, "Surely you 'll give us food and water."

"Why — no," said Falk. "I don't think you 'll need it. You won't want to row right home without stopping to say how-d'y'-do to the natives."

Again a roar of laughter came from the men on deck.

As the boat lay under the side of the ship, they crowded to the rail and stared down at us with all sorts of rough gibes at our expense. Particularly they aimed their taunts at Davie Paine and Blodgett, who a short time before had been hand-in-glove with them; and I was no little relieved to see that their words seemed only to confirm the two in their determination, come what might, never to join forces again with Falk and Kipping. But Kipping singled out the cook and berated him with a stream of disgusting oaths.

"You crawling black nigger, you," he yelled. "Now what 'll *you* give *me* for a piece of pie?"

Holding the cleaver close at his side, the negro looked up at the fox who was abusing him, and burst into wild vituperation. Although Kipping only laughed in reply, there was a savage and intense vindictiveness in the negro's impassioned jargon that chilled my blood. I remember thinking then that I should dread being in Kipping's shoes if ever those two met again.

As we cast off, we six in that little boat soon to be left alone in the wastes of the China Sea, we looked up at the cold, laughing faces on which the low sun shone with an orange yellow light, and saw in them neither pity nor mercy. The hands resting on the bulwark, the hands of our own shipmates, were turned against us.

The ship was coming back to her course now, and some of us were looking at the distant island with the cone-shaped peaks, toward which by common consent we had turned our bow, when the cook, who still stared back at Kipping, seemed to get a new view of his features. Springing up suddenly, he yelled in a great voice that must have carried far across the sea:—

"You Kipping, Ah got you — Ah got you — Ah knows who you is — Ah knows who you is — you crimp's runner, you! You blood-money sucker, you! Ah seen you in Boston! Ah seen you befo' now! A-a-a-ah! — a-a-a-ah!" And he shook his great black fist at the mate.

The smile on Kipping's face was swept away by a look of consternation. With a quick motion he raised his loaded pistol, which he had primed anew, and fired on us; then, snatching another from one of the crew, he fired again, and stood with the smoking weapons, one in each hand, and a snarl fixed on his face.

Captain Falk was staring at the negro in wrath and amazement, and there was a stir on the deck that aroused my strong curiosity. But the cook was groaning so loudly that we could hear no word of what was said, so we bent to the oars with all our strength and rowed out of range toward the distant island.

Kipping's second ball had grazed the negro's head and had left a deep furrow from which blood was running freely. But for the thickness of his skull I believe it would have killed him.

Once again the sails of the Island Princess, as we watched her, filled with wind and she bore away across the sapphire blue of the sea with all her canvas spread, as beautiful a sight as I have ever seen. The changing lights in the sky painted the water with opalescent colors and tinted the sails gold and crimson and purple, and by and by, when the sun had set and the stars had come out and the ocean had darkened, we still could make her out, smaller and ghostlike in the distance, sailing away before light winds with the money and goods all under her hatches.

Laboring at the oars, we rowed on and on and on. Stars, by which we now held our course, grew bright overhead, and after a time we again saw dimly the shores of the island. We dared not stay at sea in a small open boat without food or water, and the island was our only refuge.

Presently we heard breakers and saw once more the bluff headlands that we had seen from the deck of the Island Princess. Remembering that there had been low shores farther south, we rowed on and on, interminably, and at last, faint and weary, felt the keel of the boat grate on a muddy beach.

At all events we had come safely to land.

CHAPTER XVIII

ADVENTURES ASHORE

As we rested on our oars by the strange island, and smelled the warm odor of the marsh and the fragrance of unseen flowers, and listened to the *wheekle* of a night-hawk that circled above us, we talked of one thing and another, chiefly of the men aboard the Island Princess and how glad we were to be done with them forever.

"Ay," said Davie Paine sadly, "never again 'll I have the handle before my name. But what of that? It 's a deal sight jollier in the fo'castle than in the cabin and I ain't the scholar to be an officer." He sighed heavily.

"It war n't so jolly this voyage," Neddie Benson muttered, "what with Bill Hayden passing on, like he done."

We were silent for a time. For my own part, I was thinking about old Bill's "little wee girl at Newbury-port" waiting for her stupid old dad to come back to her, and I have an idea that the others were thinking much the same thoughts. But soon Blodgett stirred restlessly, and the cook, the cleaver on his knees, cleared his throat and after a premonitory grunt or two began to speak.

"Boy, he think Ah ain't got no use foh boys," he chuckled. "Hee-ha ha! Ah fool 'em. Stew'd, he say, 'Frank, am you with us o' without us?' He say, 'Am you gwine like one ol' lobscozzle idjut git cook 's pay all yo' life?'

"'Well,' Ah says, 'what pay you think Ah 'm gwine foh to git? Cap'n's pay, maybe? O' gin'ral's pay? Yass, sah. Ef Ah 'm cook Ah 'm gwine git cook's pay.'

"Den he laff hearty and slap his knee and he say, 'Ef you come in with us, you won't git cook's pay, no, sah. You is gwine git pay like no admiral don't git if you come in with us. Dah's money 'board dis yeh ol' ship.'

"'Yass, sah,' says I, suspicionin' su'thin' was like what it did n't had ought to be. 'But dat's owner's money.'

"Den stew'd, he say, 'Listen! You come in with me and Cap'n Falk and Mistah Kipping, and we 's gwine split dat yeh money all up 'twix' one another. Yass, sah! But you all gotta have nothin' to do with dat yeh Mistah Hamlin and dat yeh cocky li'le Ben Lathrop.'

"'Oh no,' Ah says inside, so stew'd he don't heah me. 'Guess you all don't know me and dat yeh Ben Lathrop is friends.'

"Den Ah stop sudden. 'Mah golly,' Ah think, 'dey's a conspiration a-foot, yass, sah, and if dis yeh ol' nigger don't look out dey gwine hu't de boy.' If Ah gits into dat yeh conspiration, den Ah guess Ah 'll snoop roun' and learn what Ah did n't had ought to, and when time come, den mah golly, Ah 'll took good keer of dat boy. So Ah done like Ah'm sayin' now, and Ah says to stew'd, 'Yass, sah, yass, sah,' and Ah don't let boy come neah de galley and Ah don't give him no pie nor cake, but when time come Ah take good keer of him, and Ah 's tellin' you, Ah knows a lot 'bout what dem crawlin' critters yonder on ship think dey gwine foh to do."

With a glance toward me in the darkness that I verily believe expressed as much genuine affection as so villainous a black countenance could show, Frank got out his rank pipe and began packing it full of tobacco.

Here was further evidence of what we so long had suspected. But as I reflected on it, with forgiveness in my

heart for every snub the faithful, crafty old darky had
given me and with amusement at the simple way he had
tricked the steward and Falk and Kipping, I recalled his
parting remarks to our worthy mate.

"What was that you said to Mr. Kipping just as we
gave way this afternoon?" I asked.

"Hey, what dat?" Frank growled.

"When had you seen Kipping before?"

There was a long silence, then Frank spoke quietly
and yet with obvious feeling. "Ah got a bone to pick
with Kipping," he said, "but dat yeh's a matter 'twix'
him and me."

All this time Roger had watched and listened with a
kindly smile.

"Well, men," he now said, "we've had a chance to
rest and get our wind. It's time we set to work. What
do you say, had n't we better haul the boat out?"

Although we tacitly had accepted Roger as commander
of our expedition, he spoke always with a certain deference
to the greater age and experience of Blodgett and Davie
Paine, which won them so completely that they would
have followed him anywhere.

They both looked at the sky and at the darkly rolling
sea on which there now rested a low incoming mist; but
Davie left the burden of reply to old Blodgett, who spoke
nervously in his thin, windy voice.

"Ay, sir, that we had. There's not much wind, nor
is there, I think, likely to be much; but if we was to haul
up into some bushes like those yonder, there won't be
a thousand savages scouring the coast, come daylight,
a-hunting for the men that came in the boat."

That was sound common sense.

We got out and, standing three on a side, hauled the
boat by great effort clean out of water. Then we bent

ropes to each end of three thwarts, and thrust an oar through the bights of each pair of ropes. Thus, with one of us at each end of an oar, holding it in the crooks of his elbows, we made out to lift the boat and drag it along till we got it safely hidden in the bushes with the oars tucked away under it. We then smoothed out our tracks and restored the branches as well as we could, and held a counsel in which every man had an equal voice.

That it would be folly to remain on the beach until daylight, we were all agreed. Immediately beyond the muddy shore there was, so far as we could tell, only a salt marsh overgrown with rank grass and scattered clumps of vegetation, which might conceal us after a fashion if we were willing to lie all day long in mud that probably swarmed with reptile life, but which would afford us no real security and would give us no opportunity to forage for fresh water and food.

Blodgett, wide-eyed and restless, urged that we set out inland and travel as far as possible before daybreak. "You can't tell about a country like this," he said. "Might be we 'd stumble on a temple with a lot of heathen idols full of gold and precious stones to make our everlasting fortunes, or a nigger or two with a bag of rubies tied round his neck with a string."

"Yeah!" the cook grunted, irritated by Blodgett's free use of the word "nigger," "and Ah 's tellin' you he 'll have a Malay kris what 'll slit yo' vitals and chop off yo' head; and nex' time when you gwine come to say howdy, you 'll find yo' ol' skull a-setting in de temple, chockfull of dem rubies and grinnin' like he was glad to see you back again. Ah ain't gwine on no such promulgation, no sah! What Ah wants is a good, cool drink and a piece of pie. Yass, sah."

"Now that's like I feel," said Neddie Benson. "I never thought when the lady was tellin' me about trouble in store, that there war n't goin' to be enough victuals to go round—"

"Ah, you make me tired," Blodgett snapped out. "Food, food, food! And here's a chance to find a nice little temple an' better our fortunes. Of course it ain't like India, but if these here slant-eyed pirates have stole any gold at all, it'll be in the temples."

"What I'd like" — it was Davie Paine's heavy, slow voice — "is just a drink of water and some ship's bread."

"Well," said Roger, "we'll find neither bread nor rubies lying on the beach, and since we're agreed that it's best to get out of sight, let's set off."

He was about to plunge blindly into the marsh, when Blodgett, who had been ranging restlessly while we talked, cried, "Here's a road! As I'm alive here's a road!"

We trooped over to where he stood, and saw, sure enough, an opening in the brush and grass where the ground was beaten hard as if by the passing of many feet.

"Well, let's be on our way," said Blodgett, starting forward.

"No, sah, dat ain't no way foh to go!" the cook exclaimed. He stood there, head thrown forward, chin out-thrust, the cleaver, which he had carried all the time since we left the ship, hanging at his side.

"Why not?" asked Roger.

" 'Cause, sah, whar dey's a road dey's humans and humans heahbouts on dese yeh islands is liable to be drefful free with strangers. Yass, sah, if we go a-walkin' along dat yeh road, fust thing we know we's gwine walk into a whole mob of dem yeh heathens. Den whar'll we be?" In answer to his question, the negro thrust out his left hand and, grasping an imaginary opponent by the throat, raised the cleaver, and swept it through the air with a slicing motion. Looking keenly at us to be sure that we grasped the significance of his pantomime, he remarked, "Ah want mah ol' head to stay put."

"There ain't going to be no village till we come to trees," said Davie Paine slowly. "If there is, we can see it anyhow, and if there is n't, this road 'll take us across the marsh. Once we 're on the other side, we can leave the road and take to the hills."

"There's an idea," Roger cried. "How about it, Bennie?" I nodded.

Blodgett eagerly went first and the cook, apparently fearing that he was on his way to be served as a particularly choice tidbit at somebody else's banquet, came last. The rest of us just jostled along together. But Davie Paine, I noticed, held his head higher than I ever had seen it before; for Roger's appreciation of his sound common sense had pleased him beyond measure and had done wonders to restore his self-confidence.

First there were interwoven bushes and vines beside the road, and then tall reeds and marsh grasses; now there was sand underfoot, now mud. But it was a better path by far than any we could have beaten out for ourselves, and we all — except the cook — were well pleased that we had taken it.

The bushes and tall grasses, which shut us in, prevented our seeing the ocean behind us or the hills ahead, and the miasmic mist that we had noticed some time since billowed around our knees. But the stars were very bright above us, and phosphorescent creatures like fire-flies fluttered here and there, and, all things considered, we made excellent progress.

As it had been Blodgett in his eternal peering and prowling who had found the path, so now it was Blodgett, bending low as he hurried at the head of our irregular line, who twice stopped suddenly and said that he had heard hoarse, distant calls.

Each time, when the rest of us came up to him and listened, they had died away, but Blodgett now had lost his confident air. He bent lower as he walked and he peered ahead in a way that seemed to me more prowling and catlike than ever. As we advanced his uneasiness grew on him, until presently he turned and raised his hand. The five of us crowded close together behind him and listened intently.

For a while, as before, we heard nothing; then suddenly a new, strange noise came to our ears. It was an indistinct sound of trampling, and it certainly was approaching.

The cook grasped my arm. "'Fo' de good Lo'd!" he muttered, "dey's voices!"

Now I, too, and all the others heard occasional grunts and gutturals. We dared not flee back to the beach, for there or in the open marshy land we could not escape observation, and since it had taken us a good half hour to carry our boat to its hiding-place, it would be utter folly to try to launch it and put out to sea.

Not knowing which way to turn, the six of us stood huddled together like frightened sheep, in the starlight, in the centre of that great marsh, with the white mist sweeping up around the bushes, and waited for we knew not what.

As the noise of tramping and the guttural voices grew louder, Blodgett gasped, "Look! In heaven's name, look there!"

Where the path wound over a gentle rise, which was blurred to our eyes by the mist, there appeared a moving black mass above which swayed and rose and fell what seemed to our excited vision the points of a great number of spears.

With one accord we turned and plunged from the path straight into the marsh and ran with all our might and main. The cook, who hitherto had brought up the rear, now forged to the front, springing ahead with long jumps. Occasionally, as he leaped even higher to clear a bush or a stump, I could see his kinky round head against the sky, and catch the flash of starlight on his cleaver, which he still carried. Close behind him ran Neddie Benson, who saw in the adventures of the night a more terrible fulfillment of the plump lady's prophecies than ever he had dreamed of; then came Roger and I, and at my shoulder I heard Davie's heavy breathing and Blodgett's hard gasps.

To snakes or other reptiles that may have inhabited the warm pools through which we splashed, we gave no thought. Somewhere ahead of us there was high land — had we not rowed close enough to the promontory to hear breakers? When Davie and Blodgett fairly panted to us to stop for breath, the cook and Neddie Benson with one voice urged us on to the hills where we could find rocks or trees for a shelter from which to stand off whatever savages might pursue us.

Though we tried to make as little noise as possible, our splashing and crashing as we raced now in single file, now six abreast, now as irregularly as half a dozen sheep, must have been audible to keen ears a mile away. When we came at last to woods and drier ground, we settled down to a steady jog, which was much less noisy, but even then we stumbled and fell and clattered and thrashed as we labored on.

At first we had heard in the night behind us, repeated

over and over again, those hoarse, unintelligible calls and certain raucous blasts, which we imagined came from some crude native trumpet; but as we climbed, the rising mist floated about us, and hearing less of the calling and the blasts, we slowed down to a hard walk and went on up, up, up, through trees and over rocks, with the mist in our faces and obscuring the way until we could not see three feet in front of us, but had to keep together by calling cautiously now and then.

Blodgett, coming first to a ridge of rock, stopped high above us like a shadow cast by the moonlight on the mist.

"Here's the place to make a stand," he cried in his thin voice. "A nat'ral fort to lay behind. Come, lads, over we go!"

Up on the rock we scrambled, all of us ready to jump down on the other side, when Neddie Benson called on us to stop, and with a queer cry let himself fall back the way he had come. Fearing that he was injured, we paused reluctantly.

"Don't go over that rock," he cried.

"Why not?" Roger asked.

"It gives me a sick feeling inside."

"Stuff!" exclaimed Blodgett. "Behind that rock we'll be safe from all the heathen in the Chinese Sea."

"The lady she said there'd be trouble," Neddie wailed insistently, "and I ain't going over that rock. No, sir, not when I feel squeamish like I do now."

With an angry snort Blodgett hesitated on the very summit of the ledge. "Come on, come on," he said.

"Listen dah!" the cook whispered.

I thought of savage yells and trampling feet when, crouching on hands and knees, I listened; but I heard none of them. The sound that came to my ears was the faint, distant rumble of surf breaking on rocks.

Now Roger spoke sharply: "Steady, men, go slow."

"The sea 's somewhere beyond us," I said.

"Come, come," Blodgett repeated tiresomely in his thin windy voice, "over these rocks and we 'll be safe." He was so confident and eager that we were on the very point of following him. I actually leaned out over the edge ready to leap down. Never did a man's strange delusion come nearer to leading his comrades to disaster!

The cook raised his hand. "Look — look dah!"

He was staring past Blodgett's feet, past my hands, down at the rocks whither we were about to drop. The mist was opening slowly. There was nothing for more than six feet below us — for more than twelve feet. Now the mist eddied up to the rock again; now it curled away and opened out until we could look down to the ghostly, phosphorescent whiteness of waves breaking on rough stones almost directly under us. Blodgett, with a queer, frightened expression, crawled back to Neddie Benson.

We were sitting at the brink of a sheer precipice, which fell away more than two hundred feet to a mass of jagged rock on which the sea was booming with a hollow sound like the voice of a great bell.

"Well, here we 'll have to make our stand if they follow us," said Davie.

Although the rest were white with horror at the death we so narrowly had avoided, old Davie did not even breathe more quickly. The man had no more imagination than a porpoise.

Gathering in the lee of the rocky ridge, we took stock of our weapons and recovered our self-possession. The cook again ran his thumb-nail along the edge of the cleaver; Roger examined the lock of his pistol — I saw a queer expression on his face at the time, but he said nothing; Blodgett sharpened his knife on his calloused palm and the rest of us found clubs and stones. We could flee no farther. Here, if we were pursued, we must fight. But although we waited a long time, no one came. The mist gradually passed off; the stars again shone brightly, and the moon presently peeped out from between the cone-shaped mountains on our eastern horizon.

V

IN WHICH THE TIDE TURNS

CHAPTER XIX

IN LAST RESORT

"THEY 'RE not on our heels at all events," said Roger, when we had sat silent and motionless until we were cramped from head to foot. Of our little band, he was by far the least perturbed. "If we should set an anchor watch, we could sleep, turn and turn about. What do you say to that?"

He had a way with him, partly the quiet humor that twinkled in his eyes, partly his courteous manner toward all of us, particularly the older men, that already had endeared him to every member of our company, and a general murmur of assent answered him.

"Blodgett, Neddie, and I 'll stand first watch, then. We 'll make the watches three hours on deck and three below, if you say so. You others had best hunt out an easy place to sleep, but let every man keep his knife or club where he can snatch it up in case of attack."

Remembering his comfortable quarters in the steerage of the Island Princess, the cook groaned; but we found a spot where there was some sun-baked earth, which we covered with such moss as we could lay our hands on, threw ourselves down, and fell asleep forthwith.

We were so stiff when the other three waked us that we scarcely could stand without help; but we gradually worked new life into our sore muscles and took our stations with as much good-will as we could muster. Roger gave us his watch to tell the time by, and we agreed on separate posts from which to guard against surprise — the cook a little way down the hill to the right, Davie

Paine farther to the left, and I on the summit of the rocks whence I could see in all directions.

The wild view from that rock would have been a rare sight for old and experienced voyagers, and to me, a boy in years and in travels, it was fascinating both for its uncommon beauty and for the thousand perils that it might conceal. Who could say what savages were sleeping or prowling about under the dark branches of yonder shadowy woods? What wild creatures lurked in their depths? What pirate proas were steering their course by yonder cone-shaped peaks or by those same bright stars that twinkled overhead?

I studied the outline of the island, with its miles of flat marshland deep in grass and tangled vines, its palms and dense forests, its romantic mountains, and its jagged northern cliffs; I watched the moonbeams sparkling on the water; I watched a single light shining far out at sea. By and by I saw inland, on the side of one of the hills, a light shining in the jungle, and stared at it with a sort of unwilling fascination.

A light in the jungle could mean so many things!

Startled by a sound down in our own camp, I quickly turned and saw old Blodgett scrambling up to where I sat.

"It ain't no use," he said in an undertone. "I can't sleep." He twisted his back and writhed like a cat that wants to scratch itself against a doorpost. "What an island for temples! Ah, Benny, here 's our chance to make our everlasting fortunes."

I touched him and pointed at the distant light shining out of the darkness.

Sitting down beside me, he watched it intently. "I tell ye, Benny," he murmured thoughtfully, "either me and you and the rest of us is going to make our everlasting fortunes out o' these here natives, or we 're going to lay out under these here trees until the trumpet blows for Judgment."

After a time he spoke again. "Ah, but it's a night to be stirring! I'll stake all my pay for this unlucky voyage that there's not a native on the island who hasn't a bag of rubies tied round his neck with a string, or maybe emeralds — there's a stone for you! Emeralds are green as the sea by a sandy shore and bright as a cat's eyes in the dark."

Morning came quickly. Pink and gold tinted the cone-shaped peaks, the sky brightened from the color of steel to a clear cobalt, and all at once the world lay before us in the cool morning air, which the sun was soon to warm to a vapid heat. As we gathered at the summit of the cliff over which Blodgett nearly had let us into eternity, we could see below, flying in and out, birds of the variety, as I afterwards learned, that make edible nests.

It now was apparent that the light I had seen at sea was that of a ship's lantern, for to our amazement the Island Princess lay in the offing. Landward unbroken verdure extended from the slope at our feet to the base of the cone-shaped peaks, and of the armed force that had frightened us so badly the evening before we saw no sign; but when we looked at the marsh we rubbed our eyes and stared anew.

There was the rough hillside that we had climbed in terror; there was the marsh with its still pools, its lush herbage, and the "road" that wound from the muddy beach to the forest on our left. But in the marsh, scattered here and there — ! The truth dawned on us slowly. All at once Blodgett slapped his thin legs and leaned back and laughed until tears started from his faded eyes; Neddie Benson stared at him stupidly, then poured out a flood of silly oaths. The cook burst into a hoarse guffaw, and Roger and Davie Paine chuckled softly. We stopped and looked at each other and then laughed together until we had to sit down on the ground and hold our aching sides.

In the midst of the marsh were feeding a great number of big, long-horned water buffaloes. We now realized that the road we had followed was one of their trails, that the guttural calls and blasts from rude trumpets were their snorts and blats, that the spears we had seen were their horns viewed from lower ground.

The ebbing tide had left our boat far from the water, and since we were faint from our long fast, it was plain that, if we were to survive our experience, we must find help soon.

"If I was asked," Davie remarked thoughtfully, "I'd say the thing to do was to follow along the edge of that there swamp to the forest, where maybe we'll find a bit of a spring and some kind of an animal Mr. Hamlin can shoot with that pistol of his."

Roger drew the pistol from his belt and regarded it with a wry smile. "Unfortunately," he said, "I have no powder."

At all events there was no need to stay longer where we were; so, retracing our steps of the evening before, we skirted the marsh and came to a place where there were many cocoanut trees. We were bitterly disappointed to find that our best efforts to climb them were of no avail. We dared not try to fell them with the cook's cleaver, lest the noise of chopping attract natives; for we were convinced by the light we had seen shining in the jungle that the island was inhabited. So we set off cautiously into the woods, and slowly tramped some distance through an undergrowth that scratched our hands and faces and tore our clothes. On the banks of a small stream we picked some yellow berries, which Blodgett ate with relish, but which the rest of us found unpalatable. We all drank water from the hollows of trees, — we dared not drink from the boggy stream, — and Neddie Benson ate the leaves of some bushes and urged the rest of us to try them. That we refused, we later had reason to be deeply thankful.

Following the stream we crossed a well-marked path, which caused us considerable uneasiness, and came at last to an open glade, at the other end of which we saw a person moving. At that we bent double and retreated as noiselessly as possible. Once out of sight in the woods, we hurried off in single file till we thought we had put a safe distance behind us; but when we stopped to rest we were terrified by a noise in the direction from which we had come, and we hastened to conceal ourselves under the leaves and bushes.

The noise slowly drew nearer, as if men were walking about and beating the undergrowth as they approached. Blodgett stared from his covert with beady eyes; Neddie gripped my wrist; the cook rubbed his thumb along the blade of the cleaver, and Roger fingered the useless pistol. Still the noises approached. At the sight of something that moved I felt my heart leap and stand still, then Blodgett laughed softly; a pair of great birds which flew away as soon as they saw us stirring, had occasioned our fears.

Having really seen a man in the glade by the stream, we were resolved to incur no foolish risks; so we cautiously returned to the hill, whence we could watch the beach and the broad marsh and catch between the mountains a glimpse of a bay to the northeast where we now saw at a great distance some men fishing from canoes. While the rest of us prepared another hiding-place among the bushes, Roger and Blodgett sallied forth once more to reconnoitre in a new direction.

Although we no longer could see the ship, we were much perplexed that she had lingered off the island, and we talked of it at intervals throughout the day. Whatever her purpose, we were convinced that for us it augured ill.

Presently Roger and Blodgett returned in great excitement and reported that the woods were full of Malays. Apparently the natives were unaware of our presence, but we dared not venture again in search of food, so we resumed our regular watches and slept in our turns. As soon as the sun should set we planned to skirt the mountains under the cover of darkness, in desperate hope of finding somewhere food and water with which we could return to our boat and defy death by putting out to sea; but ere the brief twilight of the tropics had settled into night, Neddie Benson was writhing and groaning in mortal agony. We were alarmed, and for a time could think of no explanation; but after a while black Frank looked up from where he crouched by the luckless Neddie and fiercely muttered: —

"What foh he done eat dem leaves? Hey? Tell me dat!"

It was true that Neddie alone had eaten the leaves. A heavy price he was paying for it! We all looked at Blodgett with an anxiety that it would have been kinder, perhaps, to hide, and Blodgett himself seemed uneasy lest he should be poisoned by the berries he had eaten. But no harm came of them, and by the time the stars were shining again Neddie appeared to be over the worst of his sickness and with the help of the rest of us managed to stagger along. So we chose a constellation for our guide and set off through the undergrowth.

Even Blodgett by this time had got over his notion of robbing temples.

"If only we was to run on a yam patch," he said to me as together we stumbled forward, "or maybe some chickens or a little rice or a vegetable garden or a spring of cold water — "

But only a heavy sigh answered him, a grunt from the cook, and a moan from Neddie. Our spirits were too low to be stirred even by Blodgett's visionary tales. It was hard to believe that the moon above the mountains was the same that had shone down upon us long before off the coast of Sumatra.

The woods were so thick that we soon lost sight of our constellation, but we kept on our way, stopping often to rest, and made what progress we could. More than once we heard at a little distance noises that indicated the presence of wild beasts; and the brambles and undergrowth tore our clothes and scratched and cut our skin till blood ran from our hands and faces. But the thing that alarmed us most we heard one time when we had thrown ourselves on the ground to rest. Though it came from a great distance it unmistakably was four distinct gunshots.

Too weak and exhausted to talk, yet determined to carry through our undertaking, we pushed on and on till we could go no farther; then we dropped where we stood, side by side, and slept.

Morning woke us. Through the trees we saw a cone-shaped peak and a great marsh where buffalo were feeding. We unwittingly had circled in the night and had come back to within a quarter of a mile of the very point from which we had set forth.

CHAPTER XX

A STORY IN MELON SEEDS

W E were all gaunt and unkempt after our hardships of the past two days, but Neddie, poor fellow, looked more like a corpse than a living man and moaned with thirst and scarcely could sit up without help. Finding about a pint of water close at hand in the hollow of a tree, we carried him to it and he sucked it up with a straw till it was all gone; but though it relieved his misery, he was manifestly unable to walk, even had we dared stir abroad, so we stayed where we were while the sun rose to the meridian. We could find so little water that we all suffered from thirst, and with Neddie's sickness in mind none of us dared eat more leaves or berries.

The afternoon slowly wore away; the tide came in across the flats; the shadows lengthened hour by hour. But no breath of wind cooled our hot faces. Neddie lay in a heap, moaning fitfully; Blodgett and Davie Paine slept; Roger sat with his back to a tree and watched the incoming tide; the cook stirred about uneasily and muttered to himself.

Coming over to me, he crouched at my side and spoke of Kipping. He was savagely vindictive. "Hgh!" he grunted, "dat yeh crimp! He got dis nigger once, yass, sah. Got me to dat boa'din' house what he was runner foh. Yass, sah. Ah had one hunnerd dollahs in mah pants pocket, yass, sah. Nex' mohnin' Ah woke up th'ee days lateh 'boa'd ship bound foh London. Ah ain' got no hunnerd dollah in mah pants pocket. Dat yeh Kipping he did n't leave me no pants pocket." The old black pulled open his shirt and revealed a jagged scar on his great shoulder. "Look a' dat! Cap'n done dat — dat yeh v'yage. Hgh!"

At dusk Neddie's moaning woke the sleepers, and we held a council in which we debated plans for the future. Daring neither to venture abroad nor to eat the native fruits and leaves, exhausted by exposure, perishing of hunger and thirst, we faced a future that was dark indeed.

"As for me," said Davie calmly, "I can see only one way to end our misery." He glanced at the cook's cleaver as he spoke.

"No, no!" Roger cried sharply. "Let us have no such talk as that, Davie." He hesitated, looking first at us, — his eyes rested longest on Neddie's hollow face, — then at the marsh; then he leaned forward and looked from one to another. "Men," he said, "I see no better way out of our difficulties than to surrender to the natives."

"Oh, no, no, sah! No, sah! Don' do dat, sah! No, no no!" With a yell black Frank threw himself on his knees. "No, sah, no, sah! Dey 's ve'y devils, sah, dey 's wuss 'n red Injuns, sah!"

"Fool!" Roger cried. "Be still!" Seeming to hold the negro in contempt, he turned to the rest of us and awaited our answer.

At the time we were amazed at his harshness, and the poor cook was completely overwhelmed; for little as Roger said, there was something in his manner of saying it that burned like fire. But later, when we looked back on that day and remembered how bitterly we were discouraged, we saw reason to thank God that Roger Hamlin had had the wisdom and the power to crush absolutely the first sign of insubordination.

Staring in a curious way at the cook, who was fairly groveling on the earth, Blodgett spoke up in a strangely listless voice. "I say yes, sir. If we 're to die, we 're to die anyhow, and there 's a bare chance they 'll feed us before they butcher us."

"Ay," said Davie. "Me, too!"

And Neddie made out to nod.

The cook, watching the face of each man in turn, began to blubber; and when I, the youngest and last, cast my vote with the rest, he literally rolled on the ground and bellowed.

"Get up!" Roger snapped out at him.

He did so in a kind of stupid wonder.

"Now then, cook, there 's been enough of this non-sense. Come, let 's sleep. At daylight to-morrow we 'll be on our way."

Apparently the negro at first doubted his ears; but Roger's peremptory tone brought him to his senses, and the frank disapproval of the others ended his perversity.

A certain confidence that our troubles were soon to be ended in one way or another, coupled with exhaustion, enabled me to sleep deeply that night, despite the number-less perils that beset us.

I was aware that the cook continually moaned to him-self and that at some time in the night Roger and Blod-gett were throwing stones at a wild beast that was prowl-ing about. Then the sun shone full on my face and I woke with a start.

Roger and Davie Paine each gave Neddie Benson an arm, Blodgett and I pushed ahead to find the best foot-ing, and the cook, once more palsied with fear, again came last. To this day I have not been able to account for Frank's strange weakness. In all other circumstances he was as brave as a lion.

Staggering along as best we could, we arrived at the stream we had found before — we dared not drink its water, even in our extremity — and followed it to the glade, which this time we boldly entered. At first we saw no one, but when we had advanced a few steps, we came upon three girls fishing from the bank of the stream. As they darted off along the path that led up the glade, we started after them, but we were so weak that, when we had gone only a short distance, we had to sit down on the trunk of a large tree to rest.

About a quarter of an hour later we heard steps, and shortly seven men appeared by the same path.

Indicating by a motion of his hand that he wished the rest of us to remain seated, Roger rose and went fearlessly to meet the seven. When he had approached within a short distance, they stopped and drew their krises, or knives with waved points. Never hesitating, Roger continued to advance until he was within six feet of them, then falling on his knees and extending his empty hands, he begged for mercy.

For a long time they stood with drawn knives, staring at him and at us; then one of them put up his kris, and knelt in front of him and offered him both hands, which, it seemed, was a sign of friendship.

When we indicated by gestures that we were hungry, they immediately gave us each a cocoanut; but meanwhile some twenty or thirty more natives had arrived at the spot where we were, and they now proceeded to take our hats and handkerchiefs, and to cut the buttons from our coats.

Presently they gave us what must have been an order to march. At all events we walked with them at a brisk pace along a well-marked trail, between great ferns and rank canes and grasses, and after a time we came to a village composed of frail, low houses or bungalows, from which other natives came running. Some of them shook their fists at us angrily; some picked up sticks and clubs, or armed themselves with knives and krises, and came trailing along behind. Children began to throw clods and pebbles at us. The mob was growing rapidly, and for some cause, their curiosity to see the white men, the like of whom most of them probably never had seen before, was unaccountably mixed with anger.

If they were going to kill us, why did they not cut our throats and have it done with? Still the people came running, till the whining of their voices almost deafened us; and still they hustled us along, until at last we came to a house larger than any we had passed.

Here they all stopped, and our captors, with as many of the clamoring mob as the place would hold, drove us through the open door into what appeared to be the judgment-hall of the village. Completely at their mercy, we stood by the judgment-seat in the centre of a large circle and waited until, at the end of perhaps half an hour, an even greater uproar arose in the distance.

There was much stirring and talking and new faces continued to appear. From where I stood I could see that the growing throng was armed with spears and knives. More and more natives pressed into the ring that surrounded us and listened intently to a brisk discussion, of which none of us could understand a word.

In one corner was a heap of melons; in another were spears and shields. I was looking at them curiously when something familiar just above them caught my eye and sent a stab of fear through my heart. In that array of savage weapons were *three ship's cutlasses*. I was familiar enough with the life of those Eastern islands to know what that meant.

Everywhere in the dim hall were bared knives, and muttering voices now and then rose to loud shrieks. What with faintness and fatigue and fear, I felt myself growing weak and dizzy. The circle of hostile faces and knives and spears seemed suddenly dim and far-away. In all the hut I could see only the three ship's cutlasses in the corner, and think only of what a grand history theirs must have been.

The distant roar that came slowly nearer seemed so much like a dream that I thought I must be delirious, and rubbed my eyes and ears and tried to compose myself; but the roar continued to grow louder, and now a more intense clamor arose. The crowd parted and in through the open lane came a wild, tall man, naked except for a pair of short breeches, a girdle, and a red handkerchief on his head, who carried a drawn kris. Coming within the circle, he stopped and stared at us. Then everything grew white and I found myself lying on my back on the floor, looking up at them all and wondering if they had killed me already. Small wonder that starvation and exposure had proved too much for me!

Roger was down on his knees beside me,— he told me long afterwards that nothing ever gave him such a start as did my ghastly pallor,— and the others, in the face of our common danger, gathered round me solicitously. All, that is, except the cook; for, although our captors had exhibited a lively curiosity about those of us who were white, they had frightened the poor negro almost out of his wits by feeling of his cheeks and kinky hair and by punching his ribs with their fingers, until now, having been deprived of his beloved cleaver, he cowered like a scared puppy before the gravely interested natives. "O Lo'd," he muttered between chattering teeth, "O Lo'd, why am dis yeh nigger so popolous? O Lo'd,

O Lo'd, dah comes anotheh — dah comes anotheh!"

Of the hostility of our captors there now could be no doubt. The sinister motion of their weapons, the angry glances that they persistently darted at us, the manner and inflection of their speech, all were threatening. But Roger, having made sure that I was not injured, was on his feet and already had faced boldly the angry throng.

Though we could not understand the savages and they could not understand us, Roger's earnestness when he began to speak commanded their attention, and the chief fixed his eyes on him gravely. But some one else repeated twice a phrase that sounded like "Pom-pom, pom-pom!" And the rest burst into angry yells.

Roger indignantly threw his hands down,— palms toward the chief,— as if to indicate that we had come in friendship; but the man laughed scornfully and repeated the phrase, "Pom-pom!"

Again Roger spoke indignantly; again he threw his hands down, palms out. But once more the cry, "Pom-pom, pom-pom," rose fiercely, and the angry throng pressed closer about us. The rest of us had long since despaired of our lives, and for the moment even Roger was baffled.

"Pom-pom, pom-pom!"

What the phrase meant we had not the remotest idea, but that our state now was doubly perilous the renewed hubbub and the closing circle of weapons convinced us.

"Pom-pom, pom-pom!" Again and again in all parts of the hall we heard the mysterious words.

Was there nothing that we could do to prove our good faith? Nothing to show them that at least we did not come as enemies?

Over Davie Paine's face an odd expression now passed. He was staring at the heap of melons.

"Mr. Hamlin," he said in a low voice, "if we was to cut a ship out of one of them melons, and a boat and some men, we could show these 'ere heathen how we did n't aim to bother them, and then maybe they 'd let us go away again."

"Davie, Davie, man," Roger cried, "there 's an idea!"

I was completely bewildered. What could Davie mean, I wondered. Melons and a ship? Were he and Roger mad? From Roger's actions I verily believed they were.

He faced our captors for a moment as if striving to think of some way to impress them; then, with a quick gesture, he deliberately got down on the floor and took the chief's foot and placed it on his head, to signify that we were completely in the fellow's power. Next he rose and faced the man boldly, and began a solemn and impressive speech. His grave air and stern voice held their attention, though they could not understand a word he said; and before their interest had time to fail, he drew from his pocket a penknife, a weapon so small that it had escaped their prying fingers, and walking deliberately to the corner where the melons were heaped up, took one of them and began to cut it.

At first they started forward; but when Roger made no hostile motion, they gathered round him in silence to see what he was doing.

"Here, men, is the ship," he said gravely, "and here the boats." Kneeling and continuing his speech, he cut from the melon-rind a roughly shaped model of a ship, and stuck in it, to represent masts, three slivers of bamboo, which he split from a piece that lay on the floor; then he cut a smaller model, which he laid on the deck of the ship, to represent a boat. On one side of the deck he stuck upright six melon seeds, on the other twelve. Point-

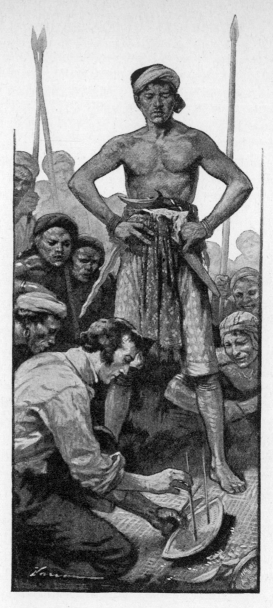

He cut from the melon-rind a roughly shaped model of a ship and stuck in it, to represent masts, three slivers of bamboo.

ing at the six seeds and holding up six fingers, he pointed
at each of us in turn.

Suddenly one of the natives cried out in his own tongue;
then another and another seemed to understand Roger's
meaning as they jabbered among themselves and in turn
pointed at the six seeds and at the six white men whom
they had captured.

Roger then imitated a fight, shaking his fists and slash-
ing as if with a cutlass, and, last of all, he pointed his
finger, and cried, "Bang! Bang!"

At this the natives fairly yelled in excitement and repeated over and over, "Pom — pom — pom — pom!"

"Bang-bang!" — "Pom-pom!" We suddenly understood the phrase that they had used so often.

Now in dead silence, all in the hut, brown men and
white, pressed close around the melon-rind boat on the
floor. So moving the melon seeds that it was obvious
that the six men represented by six seeds were being
driven overboard, Roger next set the boat on the floor
and transferred them to it. Lining up all the rest along
the side of the ship, he cried loudly, "Bang-bang!"

"Cook," he called, beckoning to black Frank, "come
here!"

As the negro reluctantly obeyed, Roger pointed to the
long gash that Kipping's bullet had cut in his kinky scalp.
Crying again, "Bang-bang!" he pointed at one of the
seeds in the boat and then at the cook.

Not one of them who could see the carved boats failed
to understand what Roger meant, and the brown men
looked at Frank and laughed and talked more loudly
and excitedly than ever. Then the chief stood up and
cried to some one in the farthest corner of the room, and
at that there was more laughing and shouting. The
man in the corner seemed much abashed; but those about

him pushed him forward, and he was shoved along through the crowd until he, too, stood beside the table, where a dozen men pointed at his head and cried "Bang-bang!" or "Pom-pom!" as the case might be.

To our amazement we saw that just over his right temple there was torn the path of a bullet, exactly like that on the cook's head.

CHAPTER XXI

NEW ALLIES

Now the chief reached for Roger's knife and deftly whittled out the shape of a native canoe. In it he placed several seeds, then, pushing it against the carved ship, he pointed to the man with the bullet wound on his temple and cried, "Pom-pom!" Next he pointed at two seeds in the boat and said, "Pom-pom," and snapped them out of the canoe with his finger.

"Would you believe it!" Blodgett gasped. "The heathens went out to the ship in one o' them boats, and Falk fired on 'em!"

"And two of 'em was killed!" Davie exclaimed unnecessarily.

Roger now laid half a melon on the floor, its flat side down, and moved the boat slowly over to it.

That the half-melon represented the island was apparent to all. The natives crowded round us, jabbering questions that we could not understand and of course could not answer; they examined the cook's wound and compared it with the wound their friend had suffered; they pointed at the little boats cut out of melon-rind and laughed uproariously.

Now one of them made a suggestion, the others took it up, and the chief split melons and offered a half to each of us.

We ate them like the starving men we were, and did not notice that the chief had assembled his head men for a consultation, until he sent a man running from the hall, who returned shortly with six pieces of betel nut, which

the natives chew instead of tobacco, and gave them to
the chief, who handed one to each of us as a mark of
friendship. Next, to our amazement, one of the natives
produced Roger's useless pistol and handed it back to
him; and as if that were a signal, one after another they
restored our knives and clubs, until, last of all, a funny
little man with a squint handed the cleaver back to the
cook.

With a tremendous sigh of relief, Frank seized the
mighty weapon and laid it on his knee and buried his
big white teeth in half a melon. "Mah golly!" he
muttered, when he had swallowed the huge mouthful and
had wiped his lips and chin with the back of his hand,
"Ah neveh 'spected to see dis yeh felleh again. No,
sah!" And he tapped the cleaver lovingly.

The chief, who had been talking earnestly with his
counselors, now made signs to attract our attention.
Obviously he wished to tell us a story of his own. He
cut out a number of slim canoes from the melon-rind
and laid them on the half-melon that represented the
island; next, he pushed the ship some distance away on
the floor. Blowing on it through pursed lips, he turned
it about and drew it back toward the half-melon that
represented the island. When it was in the lee of the
island, he stopped it and looked up at us and smiled and
pointed out of the door. We were puzzled. Seeing our
blank expressions, he repeated the process. Still we could
not understand.

Persisting in his efforts, he now launched three roughly
carved canoes, in which he placed a number of seeds,
pointing at himself and various others; then in each of
the proas he placed two seeds and pointed at the six of
us, two at a time. Pointing next at the roof of the hut,
he waved his hand from east to west and closed his eyes

as if in sleep, after which he placed his finger on his lips, pushed the carved canoes very slowly across the floor toward the ship, then, with a screech that made our hair stand on end, he rushed them at the seeds that represented Captain Falk and his men, yelling, "Pom-pom-pom-pom!" and snapped the seeds off on the floor.

Leaning back, he bared his teeth and laughed ferociously.

Here was a plot to take the ship! Although we probably had missed the fine points of it, we could not mistake its general character.

"Ay," said Blodgett, as if we had been discussing the matter for hours, "but we 'll be a pack of bloody pirates to be hanged from the yard-arms of the first frigate that overhauls us."

It was true. We should be liable as pirates in any port in Christendom.

"Men," said Roger coolly, " there 's no denying that in the eyes of the law we 'd be pirates as well as mutineers. But if we can take the ship and sail it back to Salem, we 'll be acquitted of any charge of mutiny or piracy, I can promise you. It 'll be easy to ship a new crew at Canton, and we can settle affairs with the Websters' agents there so that at least we 'll have a chance at a fair trial if we are taken on our homeward voyage. Shall we venture it?"

The cook rolled his eyes. "Gimme dat yeh Kipping!" he cried, and with a savage cackle he swung his cleaver.

"Falk for me, curse him!" Davie Paine muttered with a heat that surprised me. I had not realized that emotions as well as thoughts developed so slowly in Davie's big, leisurely frame that he now was just coming to the fullness of his wrath at the indignities he had undergone.

Turning to the native chief, Roger cried, "We 're with you!" And he extended his hand to seal the bargain.

Of course the man could not understand the words.
but in the nods we had exchanged and in the cook's fierce
glee, he had read our consent, and he laughed and talked
with the others, who laughed, too, and pointed at Roger's
pistol and cried, "Pom-pom!" and at the cook's cleaver
and cried, "Whish!"

When by signs Roger indicated that we needed sleep,
the chief issued orders, and half a dozen natives led us
to a hut that seemed to be set apart for our use. But
although we were nearly perishing with fatigue, they
urged by signs that we follow them, and so insistent
were they that we reluctantly obeyed.

Climbing a little hill beyond the village, we came to a
cleared spot surrounded by bushes through which we
looked across between the mountains to where we could
just see the open ocean. There, not three miles away,
the Island Princess rode at anchor.

I remember thinking, as I fell asleep, of the chance
that Falk and Kipping would sail away before it was
dark enough to attack them, and I spoke of it to Roger
and the others, who shared my fear; but when our savage
hosts wakened us, we knew by their eagerness that the
ship still lay at her anchor. Why she remained, we could
not agree. We hazarded a score of conjectures and debated them with lively interest.

Presently the natives brought us rice and sago-bread
and peas.

As I ate and looked out into the darkness where fires
were twinkling, I wondered which was the light I had seen
that night when I watched from the summit of the head-
land.

Though a gentle rain was falling, the whole village was
alive with people. Men armed with spears and krises
squatted in all parts of the hut. Boys came and went

in the narrow circle of light. Women and girls looked on from the door and from the farthest corners. Now and then some one would point at Roger's pistol and cry, "Pom-pom!" or, to the pride and delight of the cook, point at the cleaver and cry, "Whish!" and laugh loudly.

Even black Frank had got over his terror of having natives come up without warning and feel of his arm or his woolly head, though he muttered doubtfully, "Ah ain't sayin' as Ah likes it. Dah's su'thin' so kind of hongry de way dey comes munchin' an' proddin' round dis yeh ol' niggeh."

At midnight we went out into the dark and the rain, and followed single file after our leader along a narrow path that led through dripping ferns and pools of mud and water, over roots and rocks, and under low branches, which time and again swung back and struck our faces.

We were drenched to the skin when we came at last to a sluggish, black little stream, which ran slowly under thick overhanging trees, and in other circumstances we should have been an unhappy and rebellious crew. But now the spell of adventure was upon us. Our savage guides moved silently and surely, and the forest was so mysterious and strange that I found its allurement all but irresistible. The slow, silent stream, on which now and then lights as faint and elusive as wisps of cloud played fitfully, reflected from I knew not where, had a fascination that I am sure the others felt as strongly as I. So we followed in silence and watched all that the dense blackness of the night let us see.

Now the natives launched canoes, which slipped out on the water and lay side by side in the stream. Roger and Neddie Benson got into one; Blodgett and Davie Paine into another; the cook and I into a third. Whatever thoughts or plans we six might have, we could not express them to the natives, and we were too widely separated to put them into practice ourselves. We could only join in the fight with good-will when the time came, and, I assure you, the thought made me very nervous indeed. Also, I now realized that the natives had taken no chance of treachery on our part: *behind each of us sat an armed man.*

The canoes shot ahead so swiftly under the pressure of the paddles that they seemed actually to have come to life. But they moved as noiselessly as shadows. We glided down the stream and out in a long line into a little bay, where we gathered, evidently to arrange the last details of the attack. I heard Roger say in a low voice, "We'll reach the ship about three bells and there could n't be a better hour." Then, with a few low words of command from the native chief, we spread out again into an irregular, swiftly moving fleet, and swept away from the shore.

As I looked back at the island I could see nothing, for the cloudy sky and the drizzly rain completely obscured every object beyond a limited circle of water; but as I looked ahead, my heart leaped and my breath came quickly. We had passed the farthest point of land and there, dimly in the offing, shone a single blurred light, which I knew was on the Island Princess.

CHAPTER XXII

WE ATTACK

In the darkness and rain we soon lost sight even of those nearest us on each side, but we knew by the occasional almost imperceptible whisper of a paddle in the water, or by the faintest murmur of speech, that the others were keeping pace with us.

To this day I do not understand how the paddlers maintained the proper intervals in our line of attack; yet maintain them they did, by some means or other, according to a preconcerted plan, for we advanced without hurry or hesitation.

Approaching the ship more closely, we made out the rigging, which the soft yellow light of the lantern dimly revealed. We saw, too, a single dark figure leaning on the taffrail, which became clear as we drew nearer. I was surprised to perceive that we had come up astern of the ship — quite without reason I had expected to find her lying bow on. Now we rode the gentle swell without sound or motion. The slow paddles held us in the same place with regard to the ship, and minutes passed in which my nervousness rose to such a pitch that I felt as if I must scream or clap my hands simply to shatter that oppressive, tantalizing, almost unendurable silence. But when I started to turn and whisper to the cook, something sharp and cold pricked through the back of my shirt and touched my skin, and from that time on I sat as still as a wooden figurehead.

After a short interval I made out other craft drawing in on our right and left, and I later learned that, while we waited, the canoes were forming about the ship a circle of hostile spears. But it then seemed at every moment as if the man who was leaning on the taffrail must espy us,— it always is hard for the person in the dark, who sees what is near the light, to realize that he himself remains invisible,— and a thousand fears swept over me.

There came now from somewhere on our right a whisper no louder than a mouse's hiss of warning or of threat. I scarcely was aware of it. It might have been a ripple under the prow of the canoe, a slightest turn of a paddle. Yet it conveyed a message that the natives instantly understood. The man just behind me repeated it so softly that his repetition was scarcely audible, even to me who sat so near that I could feel his breath, and at once the canoe seemed silently to stir with life. Inch by inch we floated forward, until I could see clearly the hat and coat-collar of the man who was leaning against the rail. It was Kipping.

From forward came the cautious voices of the watch. The light revealed the masts and rigging of the ship for forty or fifty feet from the deck, but beyond the cross-jack yard all was hazy, and the cabin seemed in the odd shadows twice its real size. I wondered if Falk were asleep, too, or if we should come on him sitting up in the cabin, busy with his books and charts. I wondered who was in the galley, where I saw a light; who was standing watch; who was asleep below. Still we moved noiselessly on under the stern of the ship, until I almost could have put my hands on the carved letters, "Island Princess."

Besides things on deck, the light also revealed our own attacking party. The man in front of me had laid his paddle in the bottom of the canoe and held a spear across his knees. In the boat on our right were five natives armed with spears and krises; in the one on our left, four. Beyond the craft nearest to us I could see others less distinctly — silent shadows on the water, each with her head toward our prey, like a school of giant fish. In the lee of the ship, the pinnace floated at the end of its painter.

Still the watch forward talked on in low, monotonous voices; still Kipping leaned on the rail, his head bent, his arms folded, to all appearances fast asleep.

I had now forgotten my fears. I was keenly impatient for the word to attack.

A shrill wailing cry suddenly burst on the night air. The man in front of me, holding his spear above his head with one hand, made a prodigious leap from the boat, caught the planking with his fingers, got toe-hold on a stern-port, and went up over the rail like a wild beast. With knives between their teeth, men from the proas on my right and left boarded the ship by the chains, by the rail, by the bulwark.

I saw Kipping leap suddenly forward and whirl about like a weasel in his tracks. His yell for all hands sounded high above the clamor of the boarders. Then some one jabbed the butt of a spear into my back and, realizing that mine was not to be a spectator's part in that weird battle, I scrambled up the stern as best I could.

The watch on deck, I instantly saw, had backed against the forecastle where the watch below was joining it. Captain Falk and some one else, of whose identity I could not be sure, rushed armed from the cabin. Then a missile crashed through the lantern, and in the darkness I heard sea-boots banging on the deck as those aft raced forward to join the crew.

I clambered aboard, waving my arms and shouting;

then I stood and listened to the chorus of yells fore and aft, the *slip-slip-slip* of bare feet, the thud of boots as the Americans ran this way and that. I sometimes since have wondered how I escaped death in that wild mêlée in the darkness. Certainly I was preserved by no effort of my own, for not knowing which way to turn, ignored by friend and foe alike, almost stunned by the terrible sounds that rose on every side, I simply clutched the rail and was as unlike the hero that my silly dreams had made me out to be — never had I dreamed of such a night! — as is every half-grown lad who stands side by side with violent death.

Of Kipping I now saw nothing, but as a light momentarily flared up, I caught a glimpse of Captain Falk and his party sidling along back to back, fighting off their assailants while they struggled to launch a boat. Time and time again I heard the spiteful crack of their guns and their oaths and exclamations. Presently I also heard another sound that made my heart throb; a man was moaning as if in great pain.

Then another cried, with an oath, "They 've got me! O Tom, haul out that spear!" A scream followed and then silence.

Some one very near me, who as yet was unaware of my presence, said, "He 's dead."

"Look out!" cried another. "See! There behind you!"

I was startled and instinctively dodged back. There was a crashing report in my face; the flame of a musket singed my brows and hair, and powder stung my skin. Then, as the man clubbed his gun, I dashed under his guard, scarcely aware of the pain in my shoulder, and locking my right heel behind his left, threw him hard to the deck, where we slipped and slid in a warm slippery stream that was trickling across the planks.

Back and forth we rolled, neither of us daring to give the other a moment's breathing-space in which to draw knife or pistol; and all the time the fight went on over our heads. I now heard Roger crying to the rest of us to stand by. I heard what I supposed to be his pistol replying smartly to the fire from Falk's party, and wondered where in that scene of violence he had got powder and an opportunity to load. But for the most part I was rolling and struggling on the slippery deck.

When some one lighted a torch and the flame flared up and revealed the grim scene, I saw that Falk and his remaining men were trying at the same time to stand off the enemy and to scramble over the bulwark, and I realized that they must have drawn up the pinnace. But I had only the briefest glimpse of what was happening, for I was in deadly terror every minute lest my antagonist thrust a knife between my ribs. I could hear him gasping now as he strove to close his hands on my throat, and for a moment I thought he had me; but I twisted away, got half on my knees with him under me, sprang to my feet, then slipped once more on the slow stream across the planks, and fell heavily.

In that moment I had seen by torchlight that the pinnace was clear of the ship and that the men with their guns and spikes were holding off the natives. I had seen, too, a spear flash across the space of open water and cut down one of the men. But already my adversary was at me again, and with his two calloused hands he once more was gripping my throat. I exerted all my strength to keep from being throttled. I tried to scream, but could only gurgle. His head danced before me and seemed to swing in circles. I felt myself losing strength. I rallied desperately, only to be thrown.

Then, suddenly, I realized that he had let me go and

had sat down beside me breathing heavily. It was the man from Boston whose nose had been broken. He eyed me curiously as if an idea had come upon him by surprise.

"I did n't go to fight so hard, mate," he gasped, "but you did act so kind of vicious that I just had to."

"You what?" I exclaimed, not believing my ears.

"It 's the only way I had to come over to your side," he said with a whimper. "Falk would ' a' killed me if I 'd just up an' come, though I wanted to, honest I did."

I put my hand on my throbbing shoulder, and stared at him incredulously.

"You don't need to look at me like that," he sniveled. "Did n't I stand by Bill Hayden to the last along with you? Ain't I human? Ain't I got as much appreciation as any man of what it means to have a murderin' pair of officers like Captain Falk and Mr. Kipping? You don't suppose, do you, that I 'd stay by 'em without I had to?"

I was somewhat impressed by his argument, and he, perceiving it, continued vehemently, "I *had* to fight with you. They 'd ' a' killed you, too, if I had n't."

There was truth in that. Unquestionably they would have shot me down without hesitation if we two had not grappled in such a lively tussle that they could not hit one without hitting the other.

We got up and leaned on the bulwark and looked down at the boat, which rode easily on the slow, oily swell. There in the stern-sheets the torchlight now revealed Falk.

"I 'm lawful master of this vessel," he called back, looking up at the men who lined the side. "I 'll see you hanged from the yard-arm yet, you white-livered wharf-rats, and you, too, you cabin-window popinjay!" — I knew that he meant me.— "There 'll come a day, by God! There 'll come a day!"

The men in the boat gave way, and it disappeared in the darkness and mist, its sides bristling with weapons. But still Falk's voice came back to us shrilly, "I 'll see you yet a-hanging by your necks," until at last we could only hear him cursing.

CHAPTER XXIII

WHAT WE FOUND IN THE CABIN

Now some one called, "Ben! Ben Lathrop! Where are you?"

"Here I am," I cried as loudly as I could.

"Well, Ben, what 's this? Are you wounded?"

It was Roger, and when he saw with whom I was talking he smiled.

"Well, Bennie," he cried, "so we 've got a prisoner, have we?"

"No, sir," whimpered the man from Boston, "not a prisoner. I come over, I did."

"You what?"

"I come over — to your side, sir."

"How about it, Ben?"

"Why, so he says. We were having a pretty hard wrestling match, but he says it was to cover up his escape from the other party."

"How was I to get away, sir, if I did n't have a subterfoog," the prisoner interposed eagerly. I *had* to wrastle. If I had n't have, they 'd 'a' shot me down as sure as duff on Sunday."

For my own part I was not yet convinced of his good faith. He had gripped my throat quite too vindictively. To this very day, when I close my eyes I can feel his hard fingers clenched about my windpipe and his knees forcing my arms down on the bloody deck. He had let me go, too, only when we both knew that Captain Falk and his men had put off from the ship. It seemed very much as if he were trying to make the best of a bad bargain. But

if, on the other hand, he was entirely sincere in his pro-
testations, it might well be true that he did not dare come
over openly to our side.   The problem had so many faces
that it fairly made me dizzy, so I abandoned it and tore
open my clothes to examine the flesh wound on my
shoulder.

"Ay," I thought, when I saw where the musket-ball
had cut me at close range, "that was a friendly shot, was
it not?"

Roger himself was not yet willing to let the matter fall
so readily.   His sharp questions stirred the man from
Boston to one uneasy denial after another.

"But I tell you, sir, I come over as quick as I could."

Again Roger spoke caustically.

"But I tell you, sir, I did.   And what's more, I can
tell you a lot of things you'd like to know. Perhaps
you'd like to know —"   He stopped short.

Roger regarded him as if in doubt, but presently he said
in a low voice, "All right!   Say nothing of this to the
others.   I'll see you later."

Captain Falk and his crew, meanwhile, had moved
away almost unmolested.   Their pikes and guns had held
off the few natives who made a show of pursuing them,
and the great majority of our allies were running riot
on the ship, which was a sad sight when we turned to
take account of the situation.

Three natives were killed and two were wounded, not
to mention my injured shoulder among our own casual-
ties; and two members of the other party in the crew
were sprawled in grotesque attitudes on the deck.   Counting the one who was hit by a spear and who had fallen
out of the boat, it meant that Falk had lost three dead,
and if blood on the deck was any sign, others must have
been badly slashed.   In other words, our party was,

numerically, almost the equal of his. Considering the man from Boston as on our side, we were seven to their eight. The lantern that we now lighted revealed more of the gruesome spectacle, and it made me feel sick to see that both the man from Boston and I were covered from head to foot with the gore in which we had been rolling; but to the natives the sight was a stupendous triumph; and the cook, when I next saw him, was walking down the deck, looking at the face of one dead man after another.

By and by he came to me where, overcome by a wave of nausea, I had sat down on the deck with my back against the bulwark. "Dey ain't none of 'em Kipping," he said grimly. Then he saw my bleeding shoulder and instantly got down beside me. "You jest let dis yeh ol' nigger took a hand," he cried. "Ah 's gwine fix you all up. You jest come along o' me!" And helping me to my feet, he led me to the galley, where once more he was supreme and lawful master.

In no time at all he had a kettle of water on the stove, in which the coals of a good fire still lingered, and with a clean cloth he washed my wound so gently that I scarcely could believe his great, coarse hands were actually at work on me. "Dah you is," he murmured, bending over the red, shallow gash that the bullet had cut, "dah you is. Don' you fret. Ah 's gwine git you all tied up clean an' han'some, yass, sah."

The yells and cries of every description alarmed and agitated us both. It was far from reassuring to know that that mob of natives was ranging the ship at will.

"Ef you was to ask me," Frank muttered, rolling his eyes till the whites gleamed starkly, "Ah 's gwine tell you dis yeh ship is sottin', so to speak, on a bar'l of gunpowder. Yass, sah!"

An islander uttered a shrill catcall just outside the galley and thrust his head and half his naked body in the door. He vanished again almost instantly, but Frank jumped and upset the kettle. "Yass, sah, you creepy ol' sarpint," he gasped. "Yass, sah, we 's sottin' on a bar'l of gunpowder."

I am convinced, as I look back on that night from the pinnacle of more than half a century, that not one man in ten thousand has ever spent one like it. Allied with a horde whose language we could not speak, we had boarded our own ship and now — mutineers, pirates, or loyal mariners, according to your point of view — we shared her possession with a mob of howling heathens whose goodwill depended on the whim of the moment, and who might at any minute, by slaughtering us out of hand, get for their own godless purposes the ship and all that was in her.

The cook cautiously fingered the keen edge of his cleaver as we looked out and saw that dawn was brightening in the east.

"Dat Falk, he say he gwine git us yet," the cook muttered. "Maybe so — maybe not. Maybe we ain't gwine last as long as dat."

"All hands aft!"

Frank and I looked at each other. The galley was as safe and comfortable as any place aboard ship and we were reluctant to leave it.

"*All hands aft!*" came the call again.

"Ah reckon," Frank said thoughtfully, "me and you better be gwine. When Mistah Hamlin he holler like dat, he want us."

Light had come with amazing swiftness, and already we could see the deck from stem to stern without help of the torches, which still flamed and sent thin streamers of smoke drifting into the mist.

As we emerged from the galley, I noticed that the after-hatch was half open. That in itself did not surprise me; stranger things than that had come to pass in the last hour or two; but when some one cautiously emerged from the hold, with a quick, sly glance at those on the quarter-deck, I 'll confess that I was surprised. It was the man from Boston.

Smiling broadly and turning his black rat-like eyes this way and that, the chief of our wild allies, who held a naked kris from which drops of blood were falling, stood beside Roger. Blodgett was at the wheel, nervously fingering the spokes; Neddie Benson stood behind him, obviously ill at ease, and Davie Paine, who had got from the cabin what few of his things were left there, to take them forward, was a little at one side. But the natives were swarming everywhere, aloft and alow, and we knew only too well that no small movable object would escape their thieving fingers.

"Ef on'y dem yeh heathen don't took to butcherin'!" the cook muttered.

The prophetic words were scarcely spoken when what we most feared came to pass. One of the islanders, by accident or design, bumped into Blodgett,— always erratic, never to be relied on in a crisis,— who, turning without a thought of the consequences, struck the man with his fist a blow that floored him, and flashed out his knife.

That single spark threatened an explosion that would annihilate us. Spears enclosed us from all sides; krises leaped at our throats.

"Come on, lads! Stand together," Blodgett shrieked.

With a yell of terror the cook sprang to join the others, and bellowing in panic, swung his cleaver wildly.

The man from Boston and Neddie Benson shrank back

against the taffrail as a multitude of moving brown figures seemed to swarm about us. Then I saw Roger leap forward, his arms high in air, his hands extended.

"Get back!" he cried, glancing at us over his shoulders.

As all stopped and stared at him, he coolly turned to the chief and handed him his pistol, butt foremost. Was Roger mad, I wondered? He was the sanest man of all our crew. The chief gravely took the proffered weapon and looked at Blodgett, whose face was contorted with fear, and at the Malay, who by now was sitting up on deck blinking about him in a dazed way. Then he smiled and raised his hand and the points of the weapons fell.

In truth I was nearly mad myself, for now it all struck me as funny and I laughed until I cried, and all the others looked at me, and soon the natives began to point and laugh themselves. I suppose I was hysterical, but it created a diversion and helped to save the day; and Neddie Benson and the man from Boston, whom Roger had sent below, returned soon with bolts of cloth and knives and pistols and threw them in a heap on the quarter-deck.

Some word that I suppose meant gifts, went from lip to lip and our allies eagerly crowded around us.

"Get behind me, men," Roger said in an undertone. "Whatever happens, guard the companionway. I think we're safe, but since by grace of Providence we're all here together, we'll take no chances that we can avoid."

The first rays of sunlight shone on the heap of bright stuffs and polished metal, but the sun itself was no brighter than the face of the chief when Roger draped over him a length of bright cloth and presented him with a handsome knife. He threw back his head, laughing aloud, and strutted across the deck. Turning in grave farewell, he grasped his booty with one arm and, after a few sharp words to his men, swung himself down by the chains with the other. To man after man we gave gaudy cloths or knives or, when all the knives were given away, a cutlass or a gun; and when at last the only canoes in sight were speeding toward shore like comets with tails of red flannel and purple calico, we breathed deeply our relief.

"Now, men," said Roger, "we have a hard morning's work in front of us. Cook, break out a cask of beef and a cask of bread, and get us something to eat. Davie, you stand watch and keep your eye out either for a native canoe or for any sign of Falk or his party. The rest of you — all except Lathrop — wash down the deck and sew those bodies up in a piece of old sail with plenty of ballast. Ben, you and I have a little job in front of us. Come into the cabin with me."

I gladly followed him. He was as composed as if battle and death were all in the routine of a day at sea, and I was full of admiration for his coolness and courage.

The cabin was in complete disorder, but comparatively few things had been stolen. Apparently not many of the natives had found their way thither.

"Fortunately," Roger said, unlocking Captain Whidden's chest of which he had the key, "they 've left the spare quadrant. We have instruments to navigate with, so, when all 's said and done, I suppose we 're lucky."

He closed the chest and locked it again; then he took from his pocket a second key. "Benny, my lad," he said, "let 's have a look at that one hundred thousand dollars in gold."

Going into the captain's stateroom, we shut the door and knelt beside the iron safe. The key turned with difficulty.

"It needs oil," Roger muttered, as he worked over it. "It turns as hard as if some one has been tinkering with it."   By using both hands he forced it round and opened the door.

The safe was empty.

VI

IN WHICH WE REACH THE PORT OF OUR DESTINATION

CHAPTER XXIV

FALK PROPOSES A TRUCE

As we faced each other in amazed silence, we could hear the men working on deck and the sea rippling against the hull of the ship. I felt that strange sensation of mingled reality and unreality which comes sometimes in dreams, and I rather think that Roger felt it, too, for we turned simultaneously to look again into the iron safe. But again only its painted walls met our eyes.

The gold actually was gone.

Roger started up. "Now how did Falk manage that?" he cried. "I swear he had n't time to open the safe. We took them absolutely by surprise — I could swear we did."

I suggested that he might have hidden it somewhere else.

"Not he," said Roger.

"Would Kipping steal from Captain Falk?"

"From Captain Falk!" Roger exclaimed. "If his mother were starving, he 'd steal her last crust. How about the bunk?"

We took the bunk apart and ripped open the mattress. We sounded the woodwork above and below. With knives we slit the cushion of Captain Whidden's great armchair, and pulled out the curled hair that stuffed it. We ransacked box, bag, cuddy, and stove; we forced our way into every corner of the cabin and the staterooms. But we found no trace of the lost money.

It seemed like sacrilege to disturb little things that once had belonged to that upright gentleman, Captain

Joseph Whidden. His pipe, his memorandum-book, and his pearl-handled penknife recalled him to my mind as I had seen him so many times of old, sitting in my father's drawing-room, with his hands folded on his knee and his firm mouth bent in a whimsical smile. I thought of my parents, of my sister and Roger, of all the old far-away life of Salem; I must have stood dreaming thus a long time when my eyes fell on Nathan Falk's blue coat, which he had thrown carelessly on the cabin table and had left there, and with a burst of anger I came back to affairs of the moment.

"They 've got it away, Benny," said Roger, soberly. "How or when I don't know, but there 's no question that it 's gone from the cabin. Come, let 's clear away the disorder."

As well as we could we put back the numerous things we had thrown about, and such litter as we could not replace we swept up. But wisps of hair still lay on the tables and the chairs, and feathers floated in the air like thistle-down. We had little time for housewifery.

We found the others gathered round the galley, eating a hearty meal of salt beef, ship's bread, and coffee, at which we were right glad to join them. Roger had a way with the men that kept them from taking liberties, yet that enabled him to mingle with them on terms far more familiar than those of a ship's officer. I watched him as he sat down by Davie Paine, and grinned at the cook, and asked Neddie Benson how his courage was and laughed heartily at Blodgett who had spilled a cup of coffee down his shirt-front — yet in such a way that Blodgett was pleased by his friendliness rather than offended by his amusement. I suppose it was what we call "personality." Certainly Roger was a born leader. After our many difficulties we felt so jolly and so much at home,— all,

that is, except the man from Boston, who sat apart from
the rest and stared soberly across the long, slow seas,—
that our little party on deck was merrier by far than many
a Salem merrymaking before or since.

I knew that Roger was deeply troubled by the loss of
the money and I marveled at his self-control.

Presently I saw something moving off the eastern point
of the island. Thinking little of it, I watched it idly
until suddenly it burst upon me that it was a ship's
boat. With a start I woke from my dream and shouted,
"Sail ho! Off the starboard bow!"

In an instant our men were on their feet, staring at the
newcomer. In all the monotonous expanse of shining,
silent ocean only the boat and the island and the tiny
sails of a junk which lay hull down miles away, were to
be seen. But the boat, which now had rounded the point,
was approaching steadily.

"Ben, lay below to the cabin and fetch up muskets,
powder, and balls," Roger cried sharply. "Lend a hand,
Davie, and bring back all the pikes and cutlasses you can
carry. You, cook, clear away the stern-chasers and
stand by to load them the minute the powder's up the
companionway. Blodgett, you do the same by the long
gun. You, Neddie, bear a hand with me to trice up the
netting!"

Spilling food, cups, pans, and kids in confusion on the
deck, we sprang to do as we were bid. In the sternsheets
of the approaching boat we could make out at a distance
the slim form of Captain Nathan Falk.

The rain had stopped long since, and the hot sun
shining from a cloudless sky was rapidly burning off the
last vestige of the night mist as Captain Falk's boat
came slowly toward us under a white flag. A ground-
swell gave it a leisurely motion and the men approached

so cautiously that their oars seemed scarcely more than
to dip in and out of the water.

With double-charged cannon, with loaded muskets
ready at hand, and with pikes and cutlasses laid out on
deck, one for each man, where we could snatch them up
as soon as we had spent our first fire, we grinned from
behind the nettings at our erstwhile shipmates. Tables
had turned with a vengeance since we had rowed away
from the ship so short a time before. They now were a
sad-looking lot of men, some of them with bandages on
their limbs or round their heads, all of them disheveled,
weary, and unkempt. But they approached with an air
of dignity, which Falk tried to keep up by calling with a
grand fling of his hand and his head, "Mr. Hamlin, we
come to parley under a flag of truce."

I think we really were impressed for a moment. His
face was pale, and he had a blood-stained rag tied round
his forehead, so that he looked very much as if he were
a wounded hero returning after a brave fight to arrange
terms of an honorable peace. But the cook, who heartily
disapproved of admitting the boat within gunshot,
shattered any such illusion that we may have entertained.

"Mah golly!" he exclaimed in a voice audible to every
man in both parties, "ef dey ain't done h'ist up cap'n's
unde'-clothes foh a flag of truce!"

The remark came upon us so suddenly and we were
all so keyed up that, although it seems flat enough to tell
about it now, then it struck us as irresistibly funny and
we laughed until tears started from our eyes. I heard
Blodgett's cat-yowl of glee, Davie Paine's deep guffaw,
Neddie Benson's shrill cackle of delight. But when, to
clear my eyes, I wiped away my tears, the men in the
other boat were glaring at us in glum and angry silence.

"Ah, it's funny is it?" said Falk, and his voice made

me think of the times when he had abused Bill Hayden. "Laugh, curse you, laugh! Well, that's all right. There's no law against laughing. I've got a proposition to put up to you. You've had your little fling and a costly one it's like to be. You've mutinied and unlawfully confined the master of the ship, and for that you're liable for a fine of one thousand dollars and five years in prison. You've usurped the command of a vessel on the high seas unlawfully and by force, and for that you're liable to a fine of *two* thousand dollars and *ten* years in prison. Think about that, some o' you men that have n't a hundred dollars in the world. The law 'll strip and break you. But if that ain't enough, we 've got evidence to convict you in every court of the United States of America of being pirates, felons, and robbers, and the punishment for that is death. Think of that, you men."

Falk lowered his head until his red scarf, which he had knotted about his throat, made the ghastly pallor of his face seem even more chalky than it was, and thrust his chin forward and leveled at us the index finger of his right hand. The slowly rolling boat was so near us now that as we waited to see what he would say next we could see his hand tremble.

"Now, men," he continued, "you 've had your little fling, and that's the price you 'll have to pay the piper. I 'll get you, never you fear. Ah, by the good Lord's help, I 'll see you swinging from a frigate's yard-arm yet, unless" — he stopped and glared at us significantly — "unless you do like I 'm going to tell you.

"You 've had your fling and there's a bad day of reckoning coming to you, don't you forget it. But if you drop all this nonsense now, and go forward where you belong and work the ship like good seamen and swear on the Book to have no more mutinous talk, I 'll forgive you everything and see that no one prosecutes you for all you 've done so far. How about it? Nothing could be handsomer than that."

"Oh, you always was a smooth-tongued scoundrel," Blodgett, just behind me, murmured under his breath.

The men in the two parties looked at each other in silence for a moment, and if ever I had distrusted Captain Falk, I distrusted him four times more when I saw the mild, sleek smile on Kipping's face. It was reassuring to see the gleam in black Frank's eyes as he fingered the edge of his cleaver.

I turned eagerly to Roger, upon whom we waited unanimously for a reply.

"Yes, that 's very handsome of you," he said reflectively. "But how do we know you 'll do all that you promise?"

Falk's white face momentarily lighted. I thought that for an instant his eyes shone like a tiger's. But he answered quietly, "Ain't my word good?"

"Why, a *gentleman's* word is always good security."

There was just enough accent on the word "gentleman" to puzzle me. The remark sounded innocent enough, certainly, and yet the stress — if stress was intended — made it biting sarcasm. Obviously the men in the boat were equally in doubt whether to take offense or to accept the statement in good faith.

"Well, you have my word," said Falk at last.

"Yes, we have your word. But there 's one other thing to be settled. How about the owners' money?"

For a moment Falk seemed disconcerted, and I, thinking now that Roger was merely badgering him, smiled with satisfaction. But Falk answered the question after only brief hesitation, and Roger's next words plunged me deep in a sea of doubt.

"Why, I shall guard the owners' money with all possible care, Mr. Hamlin, and expend it in their best interests," said Falk.

"If that 's the case," said Roger, "come alongside."

CHAPTER XXV

INCLUDING A CROSS-EXAMINATION

FALK tried, I was certain, to conceal a smile of joy at
Roger's simplicity, and I saw that others in the boat were
averting their faces. Also I saw that they were shifting
their weapons to have them more readily available.

Our own men, on the contrary, were remonstrating
audibly, and to my lasting shame I joined them.

A queer expression appeared on Roger's face and he
looked at us as if incredulous. I suddenly perceived that
our rebellious attitude hurt him bitterly. He had led us
so bravely through all our recent difficulties! And now,
when success seemed assured, we manifested in return
doubt and disloyalty! I literally hung my head. The
others were abashed and silent, but I knew that my own
defection was more contemptible by far than theirs, and
had Roger reproached me sharply, I might have felt better for it. Instead, he spoke without haste or anger in a
voice pitched so low that Falk could not possibly overhear him.

"We simply *have* to hold together, men. All to the
gangway, now, and stand by for orders."

That was all he said, but it was enough. Thoroughly
ashamed of ourselves, we followed him to the gangway
whither the boat was coming slowly.

Roger assumed an air of neutral welcome as he reached
for the bow of the pinnace; but to us behind him he
whispered sharply, "Stand ready, all hands, with muskets
and pikes."

"Now, then, Captain Falk," he cried, "hand over the money first.   We 'll stow it safe on board."

"Come, come," Falk replied.   "Belay that talk."   He was standing ready to climb on deck.

"The money first," said Roger coolly.

Suddenly he tried to hook the bow of the pinnace, but missed it as the pinnace dipped in the trough.

The rest of us, waiting breathlessly, for the first time comprehended Roger's strategy.

Falk looked up at him angrily.   "That 'll get you nowhere," he retorted.   "Come, stand away, or so help me, I 'll see you hanged anyhow."

Roger smiled at him coldly.   "The word of a gentleman?   The money first, Captain Falk."

"Well, if you are so stupid that you have n't discovered the truth yet, I have n't the money."

"Where is the money?"

"In the safe in the cabin, as you very well know," replied Falk.

"You lie!"   Roger responded.

With a ripping oath, Captain Falk whipped out his pistol.

"You lie!"   Roger cried again, hotly.   "Put down that pistol or I 'll blow you to hell.   Stand by, boys.   We 'll show them!"

Though we were fewer than they, we had them at a tremendous disadvantage, for we were protected by the bulwarks and could pour our musket-fire into the open boat at will, and in a battle of cutlasses and pikes our advantage would be even greater.

"Don't a flag of truce give us no protection?"   Kipping asked in that accursedly mild voice — I could not hear it without thinking of poor Bill Hayden, and to the others, they told me later, it brought the same bitter memory.

"How long since Cap'n Falk's ol' unde'shirt done be a p'tection?" muttered the cook grimly.

"Yes, laugh! Laugh, you black baboon! Laugh, you silly little fool, Lathrop!" Falk yelled. "I 'll have you laughing another tune one of these days. Give way, men! We 'll have out their haslets yet."

A hundred feet from the ship, the men rested on their oars, and Falk put on a very different manner. "Roger Hamlin," he cried, "you ain't going to send us away, are you?"

I was astounded. As long as I had known Falk, I had never realized how many different faces the man could assume at the shortest notice. But Roger seemed not at all surprised. "Yes," he said, shortly, "we 're going to send you away, you black-hearted scoundrel."

"Good God! We 'll perish!"

Although obvious retorts were many, Roger made no reply.

Now Kipping spoke up mildly and innocently:—

"What 'll we do? We can't land — the Malays was waiting for us on shore with knives, all ready to cut our throats. We can't go to sea like this. What 'll we do?"

"Supposing," cried old Blodgett, sarcastically, "supposing you row back to Salem. It 's only three thousand miles or more. You 'll find it a pleasant voyage, I 'm sure, and you 'd ought to run into enough Ladronesers and Malays to make it interesting along the way."

"Ain't we human?" Kipping whined, as if trying to wring pity from even Blodgett. "Ain't you going at least to give us a keg o' water and some bread?"

"If you 're not out of gunshot in five minutes," Roger cried, "I 'll train the long gun and blow you clean out of water."

Without more ado they rowed slowly away, growing

smaller and smaller, until at last they passed out of sight round the point.

"Ah me," sighed Neddie Benson, "I 'm glad they 're gone. It 's funny Falk ain't quite a light man nor yet a real dark man."

"*Gone!* " Davie repeated ominously. "*I* wish they was gone." He looked up at the furled sails. "They ain't — and neither is we."

"There 's work to be done," said Roger, "and we must be about it. Leave the nets as they are. Stack the muskets in the waist, pile the pikes handy by the deck-house, and all lay aft. We 'd best have a few words together before we begin."

A moment later, as I was busy with the pikes, Roger came to me and murmured, "There 's something wrong afoot. The after-hatch has been pried off."

I noticed the hatch once more the next time I passed it, and I remembered seeing the man from Boston emerge from the hold. But there was so much else to be attended to that it was a long, long time before I thought of it again.

When we had done as Roger told us, we gathered round him where he waited, leaning against the cabin, with his hands in his pockets.

"We 're all in the same boat together, men," he began. "We knew what the chances were when we took them. If you wish to have it so, in the eyes of the 'law we 're pirates and mutineers, and since Falk seems to have got away with what money there was on board, things may go hard with us. *But* —" he spoke the word with stern emphasis —"*but* we 've acted for the best, and I think there 's no one here wants to try to square things up by putting Falk in command again. How about it?"

"Square things up, is it?" cried Blodgett. "The

dirty villain would have us hanged at the nearest gallows
for all his buttery words."

"Exactly!" Roger threw back his head. "And when
we get to Salem, I can promise you there's no man here
but will be better off for doing as he's done so far."

"But whar's all dat money gone?" the cook demanded
unexpectedly.

"I don't know," said Roger.

"What! Ain' dat yeh money heah?"

"No."

At that moment my eye chanced to fall on the man from
Boston, who was looking off at the island as if he had no
interest whatever in our conversation. The circumstances
under which he had stayed with us were so strange and
his present preoccupation was so carefully assumed, that
I was suddenly exceedingly suspicious of him, although
when I came to examine the matter closely, I could find
no very definite grounds for it.

Blodgett was watching him, too, and I think that
Roger followed our gaze for suddenly he cried, "You
there!" in a voice that brought the man from Boston to
his feet like the snap of a whip.

"Yes, sir! Yes, sir!" he replied briskly.

"What are you doing here, anyway?" Roger demanded.

The fellow, who had begun to assume as many airs and
as much self-confidence as if he had been one of our own
party from the very first, was sadly disconcerted. "Why
I come over to your side first chance I had," he replied
with an aggrieved air.

"What were you doing in the cabin when the natives
were running all over the ship?"

The five of us, startled by the quick, sharp questions,
looked keenly at the man from Boston. But he, re-
covering his self-possession, replied coolly enough, "I

was just a-keeping watch so they would n't steal — I
kept them from running off with the quadrant."

"Keeping watch so *nobody 'd* steal, I suppose," said
Roger.

"Yes, sir! Yes, sir! That 's it exactly."

Suddenly my mind leaped back to the night when Bill
Hayden had died, and the man from Boston had made
that cryptic remark, to which I called attention long
since. "He said he could tell something, Roger," I
burst out. But Roger silenced me with a glance.

Turning on the fellow again, he said, "If I find that
you are lying to me, I 'll shoot you where you stand.
What do you know about who killed Captain Whidden?"

For once the fellow was taken completely off his guard.
He glanced around as if he wished to run away, but there
was no escape. He saw only hostile faces.

"What do you know about who killed Captain Whidden?"

"Mr. Kipping killed him," the fellow gasped, startled
out of whatever reticence he may have intended to
maintain. "Yes, sir! Yes, sir!"

"Do you expect me to believe that Kipping shot the
captain? If you lie to me —" Roger drew his pistol.
By eyes and voice he held the man in a hypnosis of terror.

"He did! I swear he did. Don't shoot me, sir!
I 'm telling you the very gospel truth. He cursed awful
and said — don't point that pistol at me, sir! I swear
I 'll tell the truth! — 'Mr. Thomas is as good as done for,'
he said. 'There 's only one man between us and a
hundred thousand dollars in gold.' And Falk — Kipping
was talking to Falk low-like and did n't know I was anywhere about — and Falk says, 'No, that 's too much.'
Then he says, wild-like, 'Shoot — go on and shoot.'
Then Kipping laughs and says, 'So you 've got a little

gumption, have you?' and he shot Captain Whidden and killed him. Don't point that pistol at *me*, sir! I did n't do it."

Roger had managed the situation well. His sudden and entirely unexpected attack had got from the man a story that a month of ordinary cross-examinations might not have elicited; for although the fellow had volunteered to tell all he knew, his manner convinced me that under other circumstances he would have told no more than he had to. Also he had admitted being in the cabin while the natives were roaming over the ship!

CHAPTER XXVI

AN ATTEMPT TO PLAY ON OUR SYMPATHY

FOR the time being we let the matter drop and, launching a quarter-boat for work around the ship, turned our attention to straightening out the rigging and the running gear so that we could get under way at the earliest possible moment. Twice natives came aboard, and a number of canoes now and then appeared in the distance; but we were left on the whole pretty much to our own devices, and we had great hopes of tripping anchor in a few hours at the latest.

Roger meanwhile got out the quadrant and saw that it was adjusted to take an observation at the first opportunity; for there was no doubt that by faulty navigation or, more probably, by malicious intent, Falk had brought us far astray from the usual routes across the China Sea.

Occasionally bands of natives would come out from shore in their canoes and circle the ship, but we gave them no further encouragement to come aboard, and in the course of the morning Roger divided us anew into anchor watches. All in all we worked as hard, I think, as I ever have worked, but we were so well contented with the outcome of our adventures that there was almost no grumbling at all.

When at last I went below I was dead tired. Every nerve and weary muscle throbbed and ached, and flinging myself on my bunk, I fell instantly into the deepest sleep. When I woke with the echo of the call, "All hands on deck," still lingering in my ears, it seemed as if I scarcely had closed my eyes; but while I hesitated

between sleeping and waking, the call sounded again
with a peremptory ring that brought me to my feet in
spite of my fatigue.

"All hands on deck! Tumble up! Tumble up!" It
was the third summons.

When we staggered forth, blinded by the glaring sunlight, the other watch already had snatched up muskets
and pikes and all were staring to the northeast. Thence,
moving very slowly indeed, once more came the boat.

Falk was sitting down now; his chin rested on his
hands and his face was ghastly pale; the bandage round
his head appeared bloodier than ever and dirtier. The
men, too, were white and woe-begone, and Kipping was
scowling disagreeably.

It seemed shameful to take arms against human beings
in such a piteous plight, but we stood with our muskets
cocked and waited for them to speak first.

"Have n't you men hearts?" Falk cried when he had
come within earshot. "Are you going to sit there aboard
ship with plenty of food and drink and see your shipmates a-dying of starvation and thirst?"

The men rested on their oars while he called to us;
but when we did not answer, he motioned with his hand
and they again rowed toward us with short, feeble strokes.

"All we ask is food and water," Falk said, when he had
come so near that we could see the lines on the faces of
the men and the worn, hunted look in their eyes.

They had laid their weapons on the bottom of the boat,
and there was nothing warlike about them now to remind
us of the bloody fight they had waged against us. With
a boy's short memory of the past and short sight for the
future, I was ready to take the poor fellows aboard and
to forgive them everything; and though it undoubtedly
was foolish of me, I am not ashamed of my generous

weakness. They seemed so utterly miserable! But fortunately wiser counsels prevailed.

"You ain't *really* going to leave us to perish of hunger and thirst, are you?" Falk cried. "We can't go ashore, even to get water. Those cursed heathen are laying to butcher us. Guns pointed at friends and shipmates is no kind of a 'welcome home.'"

"Give us the money, then —" Roger began.

The cook interrupted him in an undertone that was plainly audible though probably not intended for all ears. "Yeee-ah! Heah dat yeh man discribblate! He don't like guns pointed at shipmates, hey? How about guns pointed at a cap'n when he ain't lookin'? Hey?"

Falk obviously overheard the cook's muttered sally and was disconcerted by it; and the murmur of assent with which our men received it convinced me that it went a long way to reinforce their determination to withstand the other party at any cost whatsoever.

After hesitating perceptibly, Falk decided to ignore it. "All we want 's bread and water," he whined.

"Give us the money, then," Roger repeated, "and we 'll see that you don't starve." His voice was calm and incisive. He absolutely controlled the situation.

Falk threw up his hands in a gesture of despair. "But we ain't got the money. So help me God, we ain't got a cent of it."

"Hand over the money," Roger repeated, "and we 'll give you food and water." He pointed at the quarter-boat, which swung at the end of a long painter. "Come no nearer. Put the money in that boat and we 'll haul it up."

"*We ain't got the money*, I tell you. I swear on my immortal soul, we ain't got it." Falk seemed to be on the point of weeping. He was so weak and white!

When Roger did not reply, I turned to look at him. There was a thoughtful expression on his face, and following the direction of his eyes, my own gaze rested on the face of the man from Boston. He was smiling. But when he saw us looking at him, he stopped and changed color.

"I believe you," Roger declared suddenly. "You 'll have to keep your distance or I 'll blow your boat to pieces; but if you obey orders, I 'll help you out as far as a few days' supply of food will go. Cook, haul in that boat and put half a hundredweight of ship's bread and four buckets of water in it. That 'll keep 'em for a while."

"You ain't gwine to feed dat yeh Kipping, sah, is you?"

"Yes."

The cook turned in silence to do Roger's bidding.

Twice the man from Boston started forward as if to speak. The motion was so slight that it almost escaped me, but the second time I was sure that I really had detected such an impulse, and at the same moment I perceived that Falk, whose fingers were twitching nervously, was shooting an angry glance at him. This by-play to a considerable extent distracted my attention; but when the fellow finally did get up courage to speak, I saw that the eyes of every man in Falk's boat were on him and that Kipping had clenched both fists.

"Stop!" the man from Boston cried. "Stop!" He stepped toward Roger with one hand raised.

Roger soberly turned on him. "Be still," he said.

"But, sir —"

"Be still!"

"But, sir, there ain't no —"

Certainly as far as we could see, the man's feverish persistence was arrant insubordination. What Roger would have done we had no time to learn, for Blodgett, bursting with zeal for our common cause, grasped him by the throat and choked his words into a gurgle. A queer expression of spite and hatred passed over the man's face, and when he squirmed away from Blodgett's grip I saw that he was muttering to himself as he rubbed his bruised neck. But the others were paying him no attention and he presently folded his arms with an air that continued to trouble me and stood apart from the rest.

And Falk and Kipping and all their men now were grinning broadly!

The water slopped over the edges of the buckets and wet some of the bread as the cook pushed the boat out toward Falk; but the men in the pinnace watched it eagerly, and when it floated to the end of the painter, they clutched for it so hastily that they almost upset the precious buckets.

When they had got it, they looked at each other and laughed and slapped their legs and laughed again in an uproarious, almost maudlin mirth that we could not understand.

We covered them with our muskets lest they try to seize the boat, which I firmly believe they had contemplated before they realized how closely we were watching them, and we smiled to see them cram their mouths with bread and pass the buckets from hand to hand. When they had finished their inexplicable laughter, they ate like animals and drew new strength and courage from their food. Though Falk was still white under his bloody bandage, his voice was stronger.

"I 'll remember this," he said. "Maybe I 'll give you a day or two of grace before you swing. Oh, you can laugh at me now, you white-livered sons of sea-cooks, but the day 's coming when you 'll sing another song to pay your piper."

He looked round and laughed at his own men, and

again they all laughed as if he had said something clever, and he and Kipping exchanged glances.

"They ain't found the gold," he caustically remarked to Kipping. "We 'll see what we shall see."

"Ay, we 'll see," Kipping returned, mildly. "We 'll see. It 'll be fun to see it, too, won't it, sir?"

It was all very silly, and we, of course, had nothing to say in return; so we watched them, with our muskets peeping over the bulwark and with the long gun and the stern-chasers cleared in case of trouble, and in undertones we kept up an exchange of comments.

After whispering among themselves, the men in the boat once more began to row toward us. Singularly enough they showed no sign of the exhaustion that a little before had seemed so painful. It slowly dawned upon me that their air of misery had been nothing more than a cheap trick to play upon our compassion. We watched them suspiciously, but they now assumed a frank manner, which they evidently hoped would put us off our guard.

"Now you men listen to me," said Falk. "After all, what 's the use of behaving this way? You 're just getting yourselves into trouble with the law. We can send you to the gallows for this little spree, and what 's more we 're going to do it — unless, that is, unless you come round sensible and call it all off. Now what do you say? Why don't you be reasonable? You take us on board and we 'll use you right and hush all this up as best we can. What do you say?"

"What do we say?" said Roger, "We say that bread and water have gone to your head. You were singing another tune a while back."

"Oh well, we *were* a little down in the mouth then. But we 're feeling a sight better now. Come, ain't our plan reasonable?"

All the time they were rowing slowly nearer to the ship.
"Mistah Falk, O Mistah Falk!"

"Well?" Falk received the cook's interruption with an
ill temper that made the darkey's eyes roll with joy.

"Whar you git dat bootiful head-piece?"

A flush darkened Falk's pale face under the bandage,
and with what dignity he could muster, he ignored our
snickers.

"What do you say?" he cried to Roger. "Evidently
you have n't found the money yet."

To us Roger said in an undertone, "Hold your fire."
To Falk he replied clearly, "You black-hearted villain,
if you show your face in a Christian port you 'll go to the
gallows for abetting the cold-blooded murder of an able
officer and an honorable gentleman, Captain Joseph
Whidden. Quid that over a while and stow your tales
of piracy and mutiny. Back water, you! Keep off!"

Here was no subtle insinuation. Falk was stopped in
his tracks by the flat statement. He had a dazed,
frightened look. But Kipping, who had kept himself in
the background up to this point, now assumed command.

"Them 's bad words," he said mildly, coldly. "Bad
words. *But* —" he slightly raised his voice — "we ain't
a-goin' to eat 'em. Not we." All at once he let out a
yell that rang shrilly far over the water. "At 'em, men!
At 'em! Pull, you sons of the devil, pull! Out pikes and
cutlasses! Take 'em by storm! Slash the netting and
go over the side."

"Hold your fire,"— Roger repeated,— "one minute —
till I give the word."

My heart was pounding at my ribs. I was breathing
in fast gulps. With my thumb on the hammer of the
musket, I gave one glance to the priming, and half raised
it to my shoulder.

From the bottom of the boat Falk's men had snatched up the weapons that hitherto they had kept out of sight. I had no time then to wonder why they did not shoot; afterwards we agreed that they probably were so short of powder and balls that they dared not expend any except in gravest emergency. Kipping was standing as they rowed, and so fiercely now did they ply their oars, casting to the winds every pretence of weakness, that the boat rocked from side to side.

"At 'em!" Kipping snarled. "We'll show 'em! We'll show 'em!"

"Hold your fire, men," said Roger the third time. "I'll wing that bird." And aiming deliberately, he shot.

The report of his musket rang out sharply and was followed by a groan. Kipping clutched his thigh with both hands and fell. The men stopped rowing and the boat, gradually losing way, veered in a half circle and lay broadside toward us. In the midst of the confusion aboard it, I saw Kipping sitting up and cursing in a way that chilled my blood. "Oh," he moaned, "I'll get you yet! I'll get you yet!" Then some one in the boat returned a single shot that buried itself in our bulwark.

"Yeeeehaha! Got Kipping!" the cook cackled. "He got Kipping!"

"Now then," cried Roger, "bear off. We've had enough of you. If ever again you come within gunshot of this ship, we'll shoot so much lead into you that the weight will sink you. It's only a leg wound, Kipping. I was careful where I aimed."

In a disorderly way the men began to pull out of range, but still we could hear Kipping shrieking a stream of oaths and maledictions, and now Falk stood up and shook his fist at us and yelled with as much semblance of dignity as he could muster, "I'll see you yet, all seven of

you, I 'll see you a-swinging one after another from the
same yard-arm!" Then, to our amazement, one of them
whispered to the others behind his hand, and they all
began to laugh again as if they had played some famous
joke on us.

Instead of going toward the island, they rowed out into
the ocean. We could not understand it. Surely they
would not try to cross the China Sea in an open boat!
Were they so afraid of the natives?

Still we could hear Kipping, faintly now, bawling wrath
and blasphemy. We could see Captain Falk shaking his
fist at us, and very clearly we could hear his faint voice
calling, "I 'll sack that ship, so help me! We 'll see then
what 's become of the money."

Where in heaven's name could they be going? Suddenly the answer came to us. Beyond them in the
farthest offing were the tiny sails of the almost becalmed
junk. They were rowing toward it. Eight mariners
from a Christian land!

In that broad expanse of land and sea and sky, the only
moving object was the boat bearing Captain Falk and
his men, which minute after minute labored across the
gently tossing sea.

Already the monsoon was weakening. The winds were
variable, and for the time being scarce a breath of air
was stirring.

From the masthead we watched the boat grow smaller
and smaller until it seemed no bigger than the point of a
pin. The men were rowing with short, slow strokes.
They may have gone eight or ten miles before darkness
closed in upon them and blotted them out, and they must
have got very near to the junk.

The moon, rising soon after sunset, flooded the world
with a pale light that made the sea shine like silver and

made the island appear like a dark, low shadow. But of the boat and the junk it revealed nothing.

The cook and Blodgett and I were talking idly on the fore hatch when faintly, but so distinctly that we could not mistake it, we heard far off the report of a gun.

"Listen!" cried Blodgett.

It came again and then again.

The cook laid his hand on my shoulder. "Boy," he gasped out, "don' you heah dat yeh screechin'?"

"No," said I.

"Listen!"

We sat for a long time silent, and presently we heard one more very distant gunshot.

Neither Blodgett nor I had heard anything else, but the cook insisted that he had heard clearly the sound of some one far off shrieking and wailing in the night. "Ah heah dat yeh noise, yass, sah. Ah ain't got none of dem yamalgamations what heahs what ain't."

He was so big and black and primitive, and his great ears spread so far out from his head, that he reminded me of some wild beast. Certainly he had a wild beast's keen ears.

But now Blodgett raised his hand. "Here's wind," he said.

And wind it was, a fresh breeze that seemed to gather up the waning strength of the light airs that had been playing at hide and seek with our ropes and canvas.

At daybreak, cutting the cable and abandoning the working bower, we got under way on the remainder of our voyage to China, bearing in a generally northwesterly course to avoid the dangerous waters lying directly between us and the port of our destination.

As we hauled at halyard and sheet and brace, and sprang quickly about at Roger's bidding, I found no leisure to watch the dawn, nor did I think of aught save the duties of the moment, which in some ways was a blessed relief; but I presently became aware that David Paine, who seemed able to work without thought, had stopped and was staring intently across the heavy seas that went rolling past us. Then, suddenly, he cried in his deep voice, "Sail ho!"

Hazily, in the silver light that intervened between moonset and sunrise, we saw a junk with high poop and swinging batten sails bearing across our course. She took the seas clumsily, her sails banging as she pitched, and we gathered at the rail to watch her pass.

"See there, men!" old Blodgett cried.

He pointed his finger at the strange vessel. We drew closer and stared incredulously.

On the poop of the junk, beside the cumbersome rudder windlass, leaning nonchalantly against the great carved rail, were Captain Nathan Falk and Chief Mate Kipping. That the slow craft could not cross our bows, they saw as well as we. Indeed, I question if they cared a farthing whether they sighted us that day or not. But they and their men, who gathered forward to stare sullenly as we drew near, shook fists and once more shouted curses. I could see them distinctly, Falk and Kipping and the carpenter and the steward and the sail-maker and the rest — angry, familiar faces.

When we had swept by them, running before the wind, some one called after us in a small, far-off voice, "We'll see you yet in Sunda Strait."

There was a commotion on the deck of the junk and Blodgett declared that Falk had hit a man.

Were they changing their tune for some reason that they did not want us to suspect? *Did they really wish to cut us off on our return?*

Speculating about the fate of the yellow mariners who once had manned those clumsy sails, and about what scenes of bloody cruelty there must have been when those eight mad desperadoes attacked the ancient Chinese vessel, we sailed away and left them in their pirated junk. But I imagined, even when the old junk was hull down beyond the horizon, that I could hear an angry voice calling after us.

CHAPTER XXVII

WE REACH WHAMPOA, BUT NOT THE END OF OUR TROUBLES

WE were only seven men to work that ship, and after all these years I marvel at our temerity. Time and again the cry "All hands" would come down the hatch and summon the three of us from below to make sail, or reef, or furl, or man the braces. Weary and almost blind with sleep, we would stagger on deck and pull and haul, or would swarm aloft and strive to cope with the sails. The cook, and even Roger, served tricks at the wheel, turn and turn about with the rest of us; and for three terrible weeks we forced ourselves to the sheets and halyards, day and night, when we scarcely could hold our eyes open or bend our stiffened fingers.

A Divine Providence must have watched over us during the voyage and have preserved us from danger; for though at that season bad storms are by no means unknown, the weather remained settled and fine. With clear water under our keel we passed shoal and reef and low-lying island. Now we saw a Tonquinese trader running before the wind, a curious craft, with one mast and a single sail bent to a yard at the head and stiffened by bamboo sprits running from luff to leech; now a dingy nondescript junk; now in the offing a fleet of proas, which caused us grave concern. But in all our passage only one event was really worth noting.

When we were safely beyond London Reefs and the Fiery Cross, we laid our course north by east to pass west of Macclesfield Bank. All was going as well as we had dared expect, so willing was every man of our little company, except possibly the man from Boston, whom I suspected of a tendency to shirk, when late one evening the cook came aft with a very long face.

"Well," said Roger, his eyes a-twinkle. "What 's wrong in the galley, doctor?"

"Yass, sah, yass, sah! S'pose, sah, you don't know dah 's almost no mo' wateh foh to drink, sah."

"What 's that you say?"

"Yass, sah, yass, sah, we done share up with dat yeh Kipping and dah ain't no mo' to speak of at all, sah."

It was true. The casks below decks were empty. In the casks already broken out there was enough for short rations to last until we made port, so our predicament as yet was by no means desperate; but we remembered the laughter of Falk and his men, and we were convinced that they knew the trick they played when they persuaded us to divide the ship's bread and water. By what mishap or mismanagement the supply of food had fallen short — there had been abundant opportunity for either — we were never to learn; but concerning the water-supply and Falk's duplicity, we were very soon enlightened.

"Our friend from Boston," Roger said slowly, when the cook had gone, "seems to have played us double. We 'll have him below, Ben, and give him a chance to explain."

I liked the fellow less than ever when he came into the cabin. He had a certain triumphant air that consorted ill with his trick of evading one's eyes. He came nervously, I thought; but to my surprise Roger's caustic accusal seemed rather to put him at ease than to disconcert him further.

"And so," Roger concluded, after stating the case in no mincing terms, "you knew us to be short of water, yet you deliberately neglected to warn us."

"Did n't I try to speak, sir? Did n't you cut me off, sir?"

Roger looked at him gravely. Although the fellow flinched, he was telling the truth. In justice we had to admit that Roger had given him no hearing.

"Ay, and that skinny old money-chaser tried to throttle me," he continued. "Falk lay off that island only because we needed water. Ay, we all knew we needed it — Falk and all of us. But them murderin' natives was after our heart's blood whenever we goes ashore, just because Chips and Kipping drills a few bullet-holes in some of 'em. I knew what Falk was after when he asks you for water, sir. The scuttle-butts with water in 'em was on deck handy, and most of them below was empty where you wa' n't likely to trouble 'em for a while yet. He see how 't would work out. Was n't I going to tell you, even though he killed me for it, until you cut me off and that 'un choked me? It helps take the soreness — it — I tried to tell you, sir."

In petty spite, the fellow had committed himself, along with the rest of us, to privation at the very least. Yet he had a defense of a kind, contemptible though it was, and Roger let him go.

It was a weary voyage; but all things have an end, and in ten days we had left Helen Shoal astern. Now we saw many junks and small native craft, which we viewed with uncomfortable suspicion, for though our cannon were double-charged and though loaded muskets were stacked around the mizzenmast, we were very, very few to stand off an attack by those yellow demons who swarmed the Eastern seas in the time of my boyhood and who, for all I know, swarm them still.

There came at last a day when we went aloft and saw

with red eyes that ached for sleep hills above the horizon and a ship in the offing with all sails set. A splendid sight she was, for our own flag flew from the ensign halyards, and less than three weeks before, any man of us would have given his right hand to see that ship and that flag within hail; but now it was the sight of land that thrilled us to the heart. Hungry, thirsty, worn out with fatigue, we joyously stared at those low, distant hills.

"Oh, mah golly, oh, mah golly!" the cook cried, in ecstasy, "jest once Ah gits mah foots on dry land Ah's gwine be de happies' nigger eveh bo'n. Ah ain' neveh gwine to sea agin, no sah, not neveh."

"Ay, land's good," Davie Paine muttered, "but the sea holds a man."

Blodgett said naught. What dreams of wealth were stirring in his head, I never knew. He was so very pale! He more than any one else, I think, was exhausted by the hardships of the voyage.

Roger, gaunt and silent, stood with his arms crossed on the rail. He had eaten almost nothing; he had slept scarcely at all. With unceasing courage he had done his duty by day and by night, and I realized as I saw him standing there, sternly indomitable, that his was the fibre of heroes. I was proud of him — and when I thought of my sister, I was glad. Then it was that I remembered my father's words when, as we walked toward Captain Whidden's house, we heard our gate shut and he knew without looking back who had entered.

We came into the Canton River, or the Chu-Kiang as it is called, by the Bocca-Tigris, and with the help of some sailing directions that Captain Whidden had left in writing we passed safely through the first part of the channel between Tiger Island and Towling Flat. Thence, keeping the watch-tower on Chuen-pee Fort well away from the North Fort of Anung-hoy, we worked up toward Towling Island in seven or eight fathoms.

A thousand little boats and sampans clustered round us, and we were annoyed and a little frightened by the gesticulations of the Chinese who manned them, until it dawned on us that they wished to serve as pilots. By signs we drove a bargain — a silver dollar and two fingers; three fingers; five fingers — and got for seven silver dollars the services of several men in four sampans, who took their places along the channel just ahead of us and sounded the depth with bamboo poles, until by their guidance we crossed the second bar on the flood tide, which providentially came at the very hour when we most needed it, and proceeded safely on up the river.

That night, too tired and weak to stand, we let the best bower go by the run in Whampoa Roads, and threw ourselves on the deck. By and by — hours later it seemed — we heard the sound of oars.

"Island Princess ahoy!" came the hearty hail.

"Ahoy," some one replied.

"What's wrong? Come, look alive! What does this mean?"

I now sat up and saw that Roger was standing in the stern just as he had stood before, his feet spread far apart, his arms folded, his chin out-thrust. "Do you, sir," he said slowly, "happen to have a bottle of wine with you?"

I heard the men talking together, but I could not tell what they were saying. Next, I saw a head appear above the bulwark and realized that they were coming aboard.

"Bless my soul! What's happened? Where's Captain Whidden? Bless my soul! Who are *you?*" The speaker was big, well dressed, comfortably well fed. He stared at the six of us sprawled out grotesquely on the deck, where we had thrown ourselves when the ship swung at her anchor. He looked up at the loose, half-furled sails. He turned to Roger, who stood gaunt and silent before him. "Bless my soul! *Who are you?*"

"I," said Roger, "am Mr. Hamlin, supercargo of this ship."

"But where — what in heaven's name has taken place? Where 's Captain Whidden?"

"Captain Whidden," said Roger, "is dead."

"But when — but what —"

"*Who are you?*" Roger fired the words at him like a thunderclap.

"I — I — I am Mr. Johnston, agent for Thomas Webster and Sons," the man stammered.

"Sir," cried Roger, "if you are agent for Thomas Webster and Sons, fetch us food and water and get watchmen to guard this ship while we sleep. Then, sir, I 'll tell you such a story as you 'll not often hear."

The well-fed, comfortable man regarded him with a kind of frown. The situation was so extraordinary that he simply could not comprehend it. For a moment he hesitated, then, stepping to the side, he called down some order, which I did not understand, but which evidently sent the boat hurrying back to the landing. As he paced the deck, he repeated over and over in a curiously helpless way, "Bless my soul! Bless my soul!"

All this time I was aware of Roger still standing defiantly on the quarter-deck. I know that I fell asleep, and that when I woke he was still there. Shortly afterwards some one raised my head and gave me something hot to drink and some one else repeated my name, and I saw that Roger was no longer in sight. Then, as I was carried below, I vaguely heard some one repeating over and over, "Bless my soul! It is awful! Why won't that young man explain things? Bless my soul!" When I opened my eyes sunlight was creeping through the hatch.

"Is this not Mr. Lathrop?" a stranger asked, when I stepped out in the open air and virtually for the first time, so weary had I been the night before, saw the pointed hills, the broad river, and the great fleet of ships lying at anchor.

"Yes," said I, surprised at the man's respectful manner. Immediately I was aware that he was no sailor.

"I thought as much. Mr. Hamlin says, will you go to the cabin. I was just going to call you. Mr. Johnston has come aboard again and there's some kind of a conference. Mr. Johnston does get so wrought up! If you 'll hurry right along —"

As I turned, the strange landsman kept in step with me. "Mr. Johnston is so wrought up!" he repeated interminably. "So wrought up! I never saw him so upset before."

When I entered the cabin, Roger sat in the captain's chair, with Mr. Johnston on his right and a strange gentleman on his left. Opposite Roger was a vacant seat, but I did not venture to sit down until the others indicated that they wished me to do so.

"This is a strange story I 've been hearing, Mr. Lathrop," said Mr. Johnston. His manner instantly revealed that my family connection carried weight with him. "I thought it best you should join us. One never knows when a witness will be needed. It 's one of the most disturbing situations I 've met in all my experience."

The stranger gravely nodded.

"Certainly it is without precedent in my own experience," said Roger.

Mr. Johnston tapped the table nervously. "Captain and chief mate killed by a member of the crew; second mate — later, acting captain — accused of abetting the murder. You must admit, sir, that you make that charge on decidedly inadequate evidence. And one hundred thousand dollars in gold gone, heaven knows where! Bless my soul, what shall I do?''

"Do?" cried Roger. "Help us to make arrangements to unload the cargo, to ship a new crew, and to get a return cargo. It seems to me obvious enough what you 'shall do'!"

"But, Mr. Hamlin, the situation is extraordinary. There are legal problems involved. There is no captain — bless my soul! I never heard of such a thing."

"I 've brought this ship across the China Sea with only six hands. I assure you that I shall have no difficulty in taking her back to Salem when a new crew is aboard." Roger's eyes twinkled as of old. "Here 's your captain — I 'll do. Lathrop, here, will do good work as supercargo, I 'm sure. I 'm told there 's the crew of a wrecked brig in port. They 'll fill up our forecastle and maybe furnish me with a mate or two. You 'll have to give us papers of a kind."

"Lathrop as supercargo? He 's too young. He 's only a lad."

"We can get no one else off-hand who has so good an education," said Roger. "He can write a fair copy, cipher, and keep books. I 'll warrant, Mr. Johnston, that not even you can catch him napping with a problem in tare and tret. Above all, the Websters know him well and will be glad to see him climb."

"Hm! I 'm doubtful — well, very well. As you say. But one hundred thousand dollars in gold — bless my soul! I was told nothing about that; the letters barely mention it." Mr. Johnston beat a mad tattoo on the arm of his chair.

"That, sir, is my affair and my responsibility. I will answer to the owners."

"Bless my soul! I'm afraid I'll be compounding piracy, murder, and heaven knows what other crimes; but we shall see — we shall see." Mr. Johnston got up and paced the cabin nervously. "Well, what's done's done. Nothing to do but make the best of a bad bargain. Woolens are high now, praise the Lord, and there's a lively demand for ginseng. Well, I've already had good offers. I'll show you the figures, Captain Hamlin, if you'll come to the factory. And you, too, Mr. Lathrop. If you dare n't leave the ship, I'll send ashore for them. I'm confident we can fill out your crew, and I suppose I'll have to give you some kind of a statement to authorize your retaining command — What if I am compounding a felony? Bless my soul! And one hundred thousand dollars!"

I was glad enough to see Mr. Johnston rowed away from the ship. Roger, accompanying him, returned late in the evening with half a dozen new men and a Mr. Cledd, formerly mate of the brig Essay, which had been wrecked a few weeks before in a typhoon off Hainan. He was a pleasant fellow of about Roger's age, and had a frank manner that we all liked. The new men, all of whom had served under him on the Essay, reported him to be a smart officer, a little severe perhaps, but perfectly fair in his dealings with the crew; so we were almost as glad to have him in the place of Kipping, as we were to have Roger in the place of Captain Falk. We had settled down in the forecastle to talk things over when presently word came that Davie Paine and I were wanted aft.

"Ben," said Roger to me, cordially, "you can move your things into the cabin. You are to be supercargo." He tapped his pencil on the table and turned to Davie with a kindly smile. "You, Davie, can have your old berth of second mate, if you wish it. I 'll not degrade a faithful man. You 'd better move aft to-day, for the new crew is coming aboard to-morrow."

Davie scratched his head and shifted his feet uneasily. "'Thank you, sir," he said at last. "It 's good of you and I 'm sure I appreciate it, but I ain't no great shakes of a scholar and I — well, if it 's all the same to you, sir, I 'll stay for'ard with the men, sir."

I was surprised to find how hard it was to leave the forecastle. The others were all so friend y and so glad of my good fortune, that they brought a lump to my throat and tears to my eyes. It seemed as if I were taking leave forever, instead of only moving the length of the ship; and, indeed, as I had long since learned, the distance from forecastle to cabin is not to be measured by feet and inches.

"I knew 't would come," Neddie Benson remarked. "You was a gentleman's son. But we 've had good times together — ay, and hard times, too." He shook his head dolefully.

All who were left of the old crew gathered round me while I closed my chest, and Blodgett and Davie Paine seized the beckets before I knew what they were about and carried it to my stateroom.

As I passed the galley the cook stopped me. "You ain't gwine far, sah, praise de Lo'd!" he said. "Dah 's a hot time ahead and we gotta stand one by anotheh. Ah 's gwine keep my eye on dat yeh man f'om Boston. Yass, sah! Ah 's gwine keep mah eye on him."

Now what did the cook mean by that, I wondered. But no answer suggested itself to me, and when I entered the cabin I heard things that drove the cook and the man from Boston far out of my mind.

"Kipping!" Mr. Cledd, the new chief mate was saying. "Not _William_ Kipping?"

Roger got down the attested copy of the articles and pointed at the neatly written name: "William Kipping."

Mr. Cledd looked very grave indeed. "I've heard of Falk — he's a vicious scoundrel in some ways, although too weak to be dangerous of his own devices. But I _know_ Kipping."

"Tell me about him,' said Roger.

"Kipping is the meanest, doggonedest, low-down wharf-runner that ever robbed poor Jack of his wages. That's Kipping. Furthermore, he never signed a ship's articles unless he thought there was considerable money in it somewhere. I tell you, Captain Hamlin, he's an angry, disappointed man at this very minute. If you want to know what I think, he's out somewhere on those seas yonder —_just — waiting_. We've not seen the last of Kipping."

Roger got up, and walking over to the chest of ammunition, thoughtfully regarded it.

"No, sir!" Mr. Cledd reiterated, "if Kipping's Kipping, we've not seen the last of him."

VII

OLD SCORES AND NEW
AND A DOUBTFUL WELCOME

CHAPTER XXVIII

A MYSTERY IS SOLVED, AND A THIEF GETS AWAY

INNUMERABLE sampans were plying up and down the river, some with masts and some without, and great junks with carved sterns lay side by side so closely that their sails formed a patchwork as many-colored as Joseph's coat. There were West River small craft with arched deck-houses, which had beaten their way precariously far up and down the coast; tall, narrow sails from the north, and web-peaked sails on curved yards from the south; Hainan and Kwangtung trawlers working up-stream with staysails set, and a few storm-tossed craft with great holes gaping between their battens. All were nameless when I saw them for the first time, and strange; but in the days that followed I learned them rope and spar.

Vessels from almost every western nation were there, too — bluff-bowed Dutch craft with square-headed crews, brigantines from the Levant, and ships from Spain, England, and America.

The captains of three other American ships in port came aboard to inquire about the state of the seas between the Si-Kiang and the Cape of Good Hope and shook their heads gravely at what we told them. One, an old friend of Captain Whidden, said that he knew my own father. "It's shameful that such things should be — simply shameful," he declared, when he had heard the story of our fight with the Arab ship. "What with Arabs and Malays on the high seas, Ladronesers in port — ay, and British men-of-war everywhere!"

He went briskly over the side, settled himself in the stern-sheets of his boat, and gave us on the quarter-deck a wave of his hand; then his men rowed him smartly away down-stream.

"Ay, it is shameful," Roger repeated. He soberly watched the other disappear among the shipping, then he turned to Mr. Cledd. "I shall go ashore for the day," he said. "I have business that will take considerable time, and I think that Mr. Lathrop had better come, too, and bring his books."

As we left the ship we saw Mr. Cledd observing closely all that went forward, and Roger gravely nodded when I remarked that our new mate knew his business.

At the end of some three weeks of hard work we had cleared the hold, painted and overhauled the ship inside and out, and were ready to begin loading at daylight on a Monday morning. However great was Mr. Johnston's proclivity to get "wrought up," he had proved himself an excellent man of business by the way he had conducted our affairs ashore when once he put his hand to them; and we, too, had accomplished much, both in getting out the cargo and in putting the ship in repair. We had stripped her to her girt-lines, calked her, decks and all, from her hold up, and painted her inside and out. She was a sight to be proud of, when, rigged once more, she swung at her anchorage.

That evening, as Roger and Mr. Cledd, the new second mate, and I were sitting in the cabin and talking of our plans and prospects, we heard a step on the companionway.

"Who's that?" Mr. Cledd asked in an undertone. "I thought steward had gone for the night."

Roger motioned him to remain silent. We all turned.

To our amazement it was the cook who suddenly appeared before us, rolling his eyes wildly under his deep frown.

"'Scuse me, gen'lems! 'Scuse me, Cap'n Hamlin! 'Scuse me, Mistah Cledd! 'Scuse me, ev'ybody! Ah knows Ah done did n't had ought to, but Ah says, Frank, you ol' nigger, you jest up 'n' go. Don't you let dat feller git away with all dat yeh money."

"What 's that?" Roger cried sharply.

"Yass, sah! Yass, sah! Him f'om Boston! He 's got de chisel and de hammer and de saw."

We all stared.

"Come, come, doctor," said Roger. "What 's this cock-and-bull story?"

"Yass, sah, he 's got de chisel and de hammer and de saw. Ah was a-watchin', yass, sah. He don't fool dis yeh ol' nigger. Ah see him sneakin' round when Chips he ain't looking."

For a moment Roger frowned, then in a low, calm voice he said, "Mr. Cledd, you 'll take command on deck. Have a few men with you. Better see that your pistols are well primed. You two, come with me. Now, then, Frank, lead the way."

From the deck we could see the lanterns of all the ships lying at anchor, the hills and the land-lights and a boat or two moving on the river. We hurried close at the negro's heels to the main hatch.

"Look dah!" The negro rested the blunt tip of one of his great fingers on the deck.

Some sharp tool had dropped beside the hatch and had cut a straight, thin line where it fell.

"Chisel done dat."

We were communicating in whispers now, and with a finger at his lips the cook gave us a warning glance. He then laid hold of the rope that was made fast to a shears overhead, swung out, and slid down to the very keelson. Silently, one at a time, we followed. The only sound was our sibilant breathing and the very faint shuffle of feet. Now we could see, almost midway between the hatches, the dim light of a candle and a man at work. While we watched, the man cautiously struck several blows. Was he scuttling the ship? Then, as Roger and the cook tiptoed forward, I suddenly tripped over a piece of plank and sprawled headlong.

As I fell, I saw Roger and the cook leap ahead, then the man doused the light. There was a sound of scuffling, a crash, a splutter of angry words. A moment later I heard the click of flint on steel, a tiny blaze sprang from the tinder, and the candle again sent up its bright flame.

"Come, Ben, hold the light," Roger called. He and Frank had the man from Boston down on the limber board and were holding him fast. The fight, though fierce while it lasted, already was over.

The second mate now handed me the candle, and bent over and examined the hole the man had cut in the ceiling. "Is the scoundrel trying to sink us?" he asked hotly.

Roger smiled. "I suspect there's more than that behind this little project," he replied.

The man from Boston groaned. "Don't — don't twist my arm," he begged.

"Heee-ha-ha!" laughed the cook. "Guess Ah knows whar dat money is."

"Open up the hole, Ben," said Roger.

I saw now that there was a chalk-line, as true as the needle, from somewhere above us in the darkness, drawn along the skin of the hold perpendicular to the keelson, and that the man from Boston had begun to cut at the bilge where the line crossed it.

He blinked at me angrily as I sawed through the planks. But when with chisel and saw I had removed a square yard of planking and revealed only the bilge-water that had backed up from the pump well, he brightened. Had the Island Princess not been as tight as you could wish, we should have had a wetter time of it than we had. Our feet were wet as it was, and the man from Boston was sadly drabbled.

"There's nothing there?" said Roger, interrogatively. "Hm! Put your hand in and feel around."

I reluctantly obeyed. Finding nothing at first, I thrust my arm deeper, then higher up beyond the curve. My fingers touched something hard that slipped away from them. Regardless of the foul water, I thrust my arm in still farther, and, securing my hold on a cord, drew out a leather bag. It was black and slimy, and so heavy that I had to use both hands to lift it, and it clinked when I set it down.

"I thought so," said Roger. "There'll be more of them in there. Fish them out, Bennie."

While Roger and the cook sat on the man from Boston and forced him down into the evil-smelling bilge-water, the second mate and I felt around under the skin of the hold and drew out bag after bag, until the candle-light showed eighteen lying side by side.

"There ought to be two more," said Roger.

"I can't find another one, sir," the second mate replied.

I now hit upon an idea. "Here," said I, "here's what will do the work." I had picked up a six-foot pole and the others eagerly seized upon my suggestion.

I worked the pole into the space between the inner and outer planking while the man from Boston blinked at me angrily, and fished about with it until I discovered and pried within reach two more leather bags.

"Well done!" Roger cried. "Cook, suppose you take this fellow in tow,— we 've a good strong set of irons waiting for him,— and I 'll help carry these bags over under the hatch."

Calling up to Mr. Cledd, Roger then instructed him to throw down a tarpaulin, which he did, and this we made fast about the twenty bags. Having taken several turns of a rope's end round the whole, Roger, carrying the other end, climbed hand-over-hand the rope by which we had lowered ourselves, and I followed at his heels; then we rigged a tackle and, with several men to help us, hauled up the bundle.

"Cap'n Hamlin, sah," the cook called, "how 's we gwine send up dis yeh scound'l?"

"Let him come," said Roger. "We 'll see to him. Prick his calves with a knife if he 's slow about it."

We heard the cook say in a lower voice, "G'wan, you ol' scalliwaggle"; then, "Heah he is, cap'n, heah he come! Watch out foh him. He 's nimble — yass, sah, he 's nimble."

The rope swayed in the darkness below the hatch, then the fellow's head and shoulders appeared; but, as we reached to seize him, he evaded our outstretched fingers by a quick wriggle, flung himself safely to the deck on the far side of the hatch, and leaping to the bulwark, dove into the river with scarcely a splash.

Some one fired a musket at the water; the flash illuminated the side of the ship, and an echo rolled solemnly back from the shore. Three or four men pointed and called, "There he goes — there — there! See him swimming!" For a moment I myself saw him, a dark spot at the apex of a V-shaped ripple, then he disappeared. It was the last we ever knew of the man from Boston.

CHAPTER XXIX

HOMEWARD BOUND

WE had the gold, though, twenty leather bags of it; and we carried it to the cabin and packed it into the safe, which it just filled.

"Now," said Roger, "we *have* a story to tell Mr. Johnston."

"So we have!" exclaimed Mr. Cledd, who had heard as yet but a small part of this eventful history. "Will you tell me, though, how that beggar ever knew those bags were just there?"

"Certainly." Roger's eyes twinkled as of old. "He put them there. When the islanders were everywhere aboard ship, and the rest of us were so much taken up with them and with the fight we 'd just been through that we did n't know what was on foot,— it was still so dark that he could work unnoticed,— he sneaked below and opened the safe, which he had the craft to lock again behind him, and hauled the money forward to the hatch, a few bags at a time. Eventually he found a chance to crawl over the cargo, start a plank in the ceiling, drop the bags down inside the jacket one by one, and mark the place. Then, holding his peace until the cargo was out of the hold, he drew a chalk line straight down from his mark to the lower deck, took bearings from the hatch, and continued the line from the beam-clamp to the bilge, and cut on the curve. There, of course, was where the money had fallen. He worked hard — and failed."

Then I remembered the hatch that had been pried off when the natives were ranging over the boat.

Early next morning Roger, Mr. Cledd, and I, placing the money between us in the boat and arming ourselves and our men, each with a brace of pistols, went ashore. That brief trip seems a mere trifle as I write of it here and now, so far in distance and in time from the river at Whampoa, but I truly think it was as perilous a voyage as any I have made; for pirates, or Ladronesers as they were called, could not be distinguished from ordinary boatmen, and enough true stories of robbery and murder on that river passed current among seafaring men in my boyhood to make the everlasting fortune of one of those fellows who have nothing better to do than sit down and spin out a yarn of hair-raising adventures. But we showed our cocked pistols and passed unmolested through the press, and came at last safe to the landing.

Laboring under the weight of gold, we went by short stages up to the factory, where Mr. Johnston in his dressing-gown met us, blessing his soul and altogether upset.

"Never in my life," he cried, clasping his hands, "have I seen such men as you. And now, pray, what brings you here?"

"We have come with one hundred thousand dollars," said Roger, "to be paid to the Chinese gentleman of whom you and I have spoken together."

Mr. Johnston looked at the lumpy bundles wrapped now in canvas and for once rose to an emergency. "Come in," he said. "I'll dispatch a messenger immediately. Come in and I'll join you at breakfast."

We ate our breakfast that morning with a fortune in gold coin under the table; and when the boat came down the river, bringing a quiet man whom Mr. Johnston introduced as the very person we were seeking, and who himself in quaint pidgin English corroborated the statement that he it was who had sent to Thomas Webster the five teakwood chests, we paid him the money and received in return his receipt beautifully written with small flourishes of the brush.

"That's done," said Roger, when all was over, "in spite of as rascally a crew as ever sailed a Salem ship. I am, I fear, a pirate, a mutineer, and various other unsavory things; but I declare, Mr. Cledd, in addition to them all, I am an honest man."

The coolies already had begun to pass chests of tea into the hold when we came aboard; and under the eye of the second mate, who was proving himself in every respect a competent officer,— in his own place the equal, perhaps, of Mr. Cledd in his,— all hands were industriously working. The days passed swiftly. Work aboard ship and business ashore crowded every hour; and so our stay on the river drew to an end.

Before that time, however, Blodgett hesitantly sought me out one night. "Mr. Lathrop," he said with a bit of constraint, "I and Davie and Neddie and cook was a-thinkin' we'd like to do something for poor Bill Hayden's little girl. Of course we ain't got no great to give, but we've taken up a little purse of money, and we wondered would n't you, seein' you was a good friend to old Bill, like to come in with us?"

That I was glad of the chance, I assured him. "And Captain Hamlin will come in, too," I added. "Oh, I'm certain he will."

Blodgett seemed pleased. "Thinks I, he's likely to, but it ain't fit I should ask the captain."

Promising to present the plea as if it were my own, I sent Blodgett away reassured, and eventually we all raised a sum that bought such a royal doll as probably no merchant in Newburyport ever gave his small daughter, and enough silk to make the little maid, when she should reach the age for it, as handsome a gown as ever woman wore. Nor was that the end. The night before we sailed from China, Blodgett came to me secretly, after a mysterious absence, and pressed a small package into my hand. "Don't tell," he said. "It's little enough. If we'd stopped off on some o' them islands I might ha' done better. Thinks I last night, I'd like to send her a bit of a gift all by myself as a kind of a keepsake, you know, sir, seeing I never had a little lass o' my own. So I slips away from the others and borrows a boat that was handy to the shore and drops down stream quiet-like till I comes in sight of one of them temples where there's gongs ringing and all manner of queer goings-on. Says I,— not aloud, you understand,— 'Here, my lad, 's the very place you're looking for, just a-waiting for you!' So I sneaks up soft and easy,— it were a rare dark night,— and looks in, and what do I see by the light o' them there crazy lanterns? There was one o' them heathen idols! Yes, sir, a heathen idol as handy as you please. 'Aha!' says I,— not aloud, you understand, sir,— 'Aha! I'll wager you've got a fine pair o' rubies in your old eye-sockets, you blessed idol.' And with that I takes a squint at the lay o' the land and sees my chance, and in I walks. The old priest, he gives a squawk, but I cracks him with a brass pot full of incense, which scatters and nigh chokes me, and I grabs the ear-rings and runs before they catches me, for all there's a million of 'em a-yammering at my heels. I never had a chance at the eyes — worse luck! But I fared well, when all's said and done. It was a dark night, thank heaven, and the boat was handy. The rings is jade. She'll like 'em some day."

I restrained my chuckles until he had gone, and added the stolen treasures to the rest of the gifts. What else could I do? Certainly it was beyond my power to restore them to the rightful owners.

The last chest of tea and the last roll of silk were swung into the hold, the hatches were battened down, and all was cleared for sailing as soon as wind and tide should favor us.

That morning Mr. Johnston came aboard, more brisk and pompous than ever, and having critically inspected the ship, met us in the cabin for a final word. My new duties as supercargo had kept me busy and my papers were scattered over the table; but when I started to gather them up and withdraw, he motioned me to stay.

"Never in all my experience has such a problem as this arisen," he exclaimed, rubbing his chin lugubriously. "Bless my soul! Who ever heard of such a thing? Captain and chief mate murdered — crew mutinied — bless my soul! Well, Captain Hamlin — I suppose you 've noticed before, that I give you the title of master? — well, Captain Hamlin, I fear I 'm compounding felony, but after all that 's a matter to be settled in the courts. I 'm confident that I cannot be held criminally responsible for not understanding a nice point in admiralty. Whatever else happens, the ship must go home to Salem, and you, sir, are the logical man to take her home. Well, sir, although in a way you represent the owners more directly than I do, still your authority is vicariously acquired and I 've that here which 'll protect you against interruption in the course of the voyage by any lawful process. I doubt, from all I 've heard, if Falk will go to law; but here 's a paper —" he drew it out of his pocket and laid it on the table — "signed, sealed and witnessed, stating that I, Walter Johnston, agent in China for Thomas Webster and Sons, do hereby recognize you as master of the ship Island Princess, and do invest you, as far as my authority goes, with whatever privileges and responsibilities are attached to the office. All questions, legal and otherwise, ensuing from this investure, must be settled on your arrival at the United States of America. That, sir, is the best I can do for you, and I assure you that I hope sincerely you may not be hanged as a pirate, but that I am by no means certain of it."

Thus he left-handedly concluded his remarks, and murmuring under his breath, "Bless my soul," as if in final protest against everything without precedent, folded his fat hands over his expansive waist-band.

"I thank you, Mr. Johnston," Roger replied gravely, though he could not completely hide the amusement in his eyes. "I 'm sure it is handsome of you to do so much for us, and I certainly hope no act of piracy or violence, of which we may have been guilty, will compromise you in the slightest degree."

"Thank *you*, Captain Hamlin. I hope so myself."

If I had met Roger's glance, I must have laughed outright. The man was so unconscious of any double edge to Roger's words, and so complacent, that our meeting was all but farce, when he bethought himself of another subject of which he had intended to speak.

"Bless my soul!" he exclaimed. "I well nigh forgot. Shall you — but of course you will not! — go home by way of Sunda Strait?"

Mr. Cledd, who hitherto had sat with a slight smile on his lean Yankee face, now looked at Roger with keener interest.

"Yes," said Roger, "I shall go home by way of Sunda Strait."

"Now surely, Captain Hamlin, that would be folly; there are other courses."

"But none so direct."

"A long way round is often the shortest way home Why, bless my soul, that would be to back your sails in the face of Providence."

Roger leaned forward. "Why should I *not* go home by way of Sunda Strait?"

"Why, my dear sir, if any one were — er-er — to wish you harm,— and if your own story is to be believed, there are those who *do* wish you harm,— Sunda Strait, of all places in the world, is the easiest to cut you off."

"Mr. Johnston, that is nonsense," said Roger. "Such things don't happen. I *will* go home by way of Sunda Strait."

"But, Captain Hamlin,—" the good man rubbed his hands more nervously than ever,— "but, Captain Hamlin, bless my soul, I consider it highly inadvisable."

Roger smiled. "Sir, I will not back down. By Sunda Strait we came. By Sunda Strait we 'll return. If any man wishes to see us there —" He finished the sentence with another smile.

Mr. Cledd spoke up sharply. "Ay, and if a certain man we all know of should appear, I 'm thinking he 'd be unpleasantly surprised to find *me* aboard."

Mr. Johnston rubbed his hands and tapped the table and rubbed his hands again. So comfortable did he appear, and so well-fed, that he seemed quite out of place in that severely plain cabin, beside Roger and Mr. Cledd. That he had a certain mercantile shrewdness I was ready to admit; but the others were men fearless and quick to act.

"Bless my soul!" he said at last, beating a tattoo on the table with his soft fingers. "Bless my soul!"

CHAPTER XXX

THROUGH SUNDA STRAIT

LADEN deep with tea and silk, we dropped down the Chu-Kiang, past Macao and the Ladrone Islands, and out through the Great West Channel. Since the northeast monsoon now had set in and the winds were constant, we soon passed the tide-rips of St. Esprit, and sighting only a few small islands covered with brush and mangroves, where the seas broke in long lines of silver under an occasional cocoanut palm, we left astern in due time the treacherous water of the Paracel Reefs.

Each day was much like every other until we had put the China Sea behind us. We touched at the mouth of the Saigon, but found no promise of trade, and weighed anchor again with the intention of visiting Singapore. Among other curious things, we saw a number of pink porpoises and some that were mottled pink and white and brown. Porpoises not infrequently are spotted by disease; but those that we saw appeared to be in excellent health, and although we remarked on their odd appearance, we believed their strange colors to be entirely natural. A fleet of galleys, too, which we saw in the offing, helped break the monotony of our life. There must have been fifty of them, with flags a-flutter and arms bristling. Although we did not approach them near enough to learn more about them, it seemed probable that they were conveying some great mandarin or chief on affairs of state.

"That man Blodgett is telling stories of one kind or another," Mr. Cledd remarked one afternoon, after watching a little group that had gathered by the fore-castle-hatch during the first dog-watch. "The fortune-teller fellow, too, Benson, is stirring up the men."

As I looked across the water at the small island of palms where the waves were rolling with a sullen roar, which carried far on the evening air, I saw a native boat lying off the land, and dimly through the mists I saw the sail of an old junk. I watched the junk uneasily. Small wonder that the men were apprehensive, I thought.

After leaving Singapore, we passed the familiar shores of eastern Sumatra, Banka Island and Banka Strait, and the mouths of the Palambang, but in an inverted order, which made them seem as strange as if we never before had sighted them. Then one night, heading west against the tide, we anchored in a rolling swell, with Kodang Island to the northeast and Sindo Island to the north. On the one hand were the Zutphen Islands; on the other was Hog Point; and almost abeam of us the Sumatran coast rose to the steep bluff that across some miles of sea faces the Java shore. We lay in Sunda Strait.

I came on deck after a while and saw the men stirring about.

"They 're uneasy," said Mr. Cledd.

"I 'm not surprised," I replied.

The trees on the high summit of the island off which we lay were silhouetted clearly against the sky. What spying eyes might not look down upon us from those wooded heights? What lawless craft might not lurk beyond its abrupt headlands?

"No, I don't wonder, either," said Mr. Cledd, thought-fully.

At daybreak we again weighed anchor and set sail. Three or four times a far-away vessel set my heart leaping, but each in turn passed and we saw it no more. A

score of native proas manœuvring at a distance singly
or by twos caused Roger to call up the watch and prepare
for any eventuality; but they vanished as silently as they
had appeared. At nightfall we once more hove to, having
made but little progress, and lay at anchor until dawn.

In the darkness that night the cook came up to me in
the waist whither I had wandered, unable to sleep.
"Mistah Lathrop," he muttered, "Ah don't like dis yeh
nosing and prying roun' islands whar a ship's got to
lay up all night jes' like an ol' hen with a mess of chickens."

We watched phosphorescent waves play around the
anchor cable. The spell of uneasiness weighed heavily on
us both.

The next evening, still beating our way against adverse
winds, we rounded Java Head, which seemed so low by
moonlight that I scarcely could believe it was the famous
promontory beyond which lay the open sea. I went
to my stateroom, expecting once again to sleep soundly
all night long. Certainly it seemed now that all our
troubles must be over. Yet I could not compose myself.
After a time I came on deck, and found topsails and
royals set and Mr. Cledd in command.

"All goes well, Mr. Lathrop," he said with a smile,
"but that darky cook seems not to believe it. He's
prowling about like an old owl."

"Which is he?" I asked; for several of the men were
pacing the deck and at the moment I could not distin-
guish between them.

"They do seem to be astir. That nearest man walks
like Blodgett. Has the negro scared them all?"

When, just after Mr. Cledd had spoken, Blodgett came
aft, we were surprised; but he approached us with an air
of suppressed excitement, which averted any reprimand
Mr. Cledd may have had in mind.

"If you please, sir," he said, "there's a sail to windward"

"To windward? You're mistaken. You ought to call out if you see a sail, but it's just as well you did n't this time."

Mr. Cledd turned his back on Blodgett after looking hard up the wind.

"If you please, sir, I've got good eyes." Blodgett's manner was such that no one could be seriously offended by his persistence.

"My eyes are good, too," Mr. Cledd replied rather sharply. "I see no sail."

Nor did I.

Blodgett leaned on the rail and stared into the darkness like a cat. "If you please, sir," he said, "I beg your pardon, but I *can* see a sail."

Now, for the first time I thought that I myself saw something moving. "I see a bank of fog blowing westward," I remarked, "but I don't think it's a sail."

After a moment, Mr. Cledd spoke up frankly. "I 'll take back what I 've just said. I see it too. It's only a junk, but I suppose we 'd better call the captain."

"Only a junk!" Blodgett repeated sharply. "When last we saw 'em, a junk was all they had."

"What's that?" Mr. Cledd demanded.

"Ay, ay, sir, they was sailing away *in a junk*, sir."

Mr. Cledd stepped to the companionway. "Captain Hamlin," he called.

The junk was running free when we first sighted her, but just as she was passing astern of us, she began to come slowly about. I could see a great number of men swaying in unison against the helm that controlled the gigantic rudder. Others were bracing the curious old sails.

"I wish she were near enough for us to watch them handle the sails on the after masts," I said.

She had a pair of mizzen-masts, one on the larboard side, one on the starboard, and I was puzzled to know how they were used.

"She 'll pass close aboard on this next tack," Mr. Cledd replied. "I think we 'll be able to see." He had paused to watch her manœuvres.

"Here 's the doctor," Blodgett murmured.

Black Frank was coming aft with a quick humpy walk. "'Scuse me, sah, 'scuse me!" he said. "But I 's skeered that we —"

Mr. Cledd now had gone to the companion. "Captain Hamlin," he called again, "there 's a junk passing close aboard."

I heard Roger's step on the companion-way. It later transpired that he had not heard the first summons.

"Mah golly! Look dah!" the cook exclaimed.

The junk was looming up dangerously.

Mr. Cledd caught my arm. "Run forward quick — quick — call up all hands," he cried. Then raising the trumpet, "Half a dozen of you men loose the cannon."

Leaping to the spar deck, I ran to do his bidding, for the junk now was bearing swiftly down upon us. On my way to the forecastle-hatch I noted the stacked pikes and loaded muskets by the mainmast, and picked out the most likely cover from which to fire on possible boarders. That my voice was shaking with excitement, I did not realize until I had sent my summons trembling down into the darkness.

I heard the men leaping from their bunks; I heard Roger giving sharp commands from the quarter-deck; I heard voices on the junk. By accident or by malice, she inevitably was going to collide with the Island Princess.

As we came up into the wind with sails a-shiver, I scurried back to the stack of muskets.

Neddie Benson was puffing away just behind me. "I didn't ought to 'ave come," he moaned. "I had my warning. Oh, it serves me right — I might 'a' married the lady."

"Bah, that's no way for a *man* to talk," cried Davie Paine.

It all was so unreal that I felt as if I were looking at a picture. It did not seem as if it could be Ben Lathrop who was standing shoulder to shoulder with Neddie Benson and old Davie. There was running and calling on all sides and aloft. Blocks were creaking as the men hauled at braces and halyards; and when the ship rolled I saw that the men on the yard-arms were shaking the courses from the gaskets. Although our crew was really too small to work the ship and fight at the same time, it was evident that Roger intended so far as possible to do both.

But meanwhile the junk had worn ship and she still held her position to windward. Suddenly there came from her deck the flash of a musket and a loud report. Then another and another. Then Roger's voice sounded sharply above the sudden clamor and our own long gun replied.

Flame from its muzzle burst in the faces of the men at the bow of the junk, and the ball, mainly by chance, I suppose, hit her foremast and brought down mast and sail. Then the junk came about and bumped into us abreast, with a terrific crash that stove in the larboard bulwark and showered us with fragments of carved and gilded wood broken from her towering bow.

CHAPTER XXXI

PIKES, CUTLASSES, AND GUNS

As I hastily poured powder into the pan of my musket, a man sprang to our deck and dashed at Davie Paine, who thrust out a pike and impaled him as if he were a fowl on a spit, then reached for a musket. Another came and another; I saw them leap down singly. One of our new men whom we had signed at Canton raised his cutlass and sliced down the third man to board us; then they came on in an overwhelming stream.

Seeing that it would be suicide to attempt to maintain our ground, and that we already were cut off from the party on the quarter-deck, we retreated forward, fighting off the enemy as we went, and ten or a dozen of us took our stand on the forecastle.

Kipping and Falk and the beach-combers they had gathered together had conducted their campaign well. Some half of us were forward, half aft, so that we could not fire on the boarders without danger of hitting our own men. Davie Paine clubbed his musket and felled a strange white man, and Neddie Benson went down with a bullet through his thigh; then the pirates surged forward and almost around us. Before we realized what was happening, we had been forced back away from Neddie and had retreated to the knightheads. We saw a beast of a yellow ruffian stab Neddie with a kris, then one of our own men saw a chance to dart back under the very feet of our enemies and lay hold of Neddie's collar and drag him groaning up to us.

They came at us hotly, and we fought them off with

pikes and cutlasses; but we were breathing hard now and our arms ached and our feet slipped. The circle of steel blades was steadily drawing closer.

That the end of our voyage had come, I was convinced, but I truly was not afraid to die. It was no credit to me; simply in the heat of action I found no time for fear. Parry and slash! Slash and parry! Blood was in my eyes. A cut burned across my right hand. My musket had fallen underfoot and I wielded a rusty blade that some one else had dropped. Fortunately the flesh wound I got from the musket-ball in our other battle had healed cleanly, and no lameness handicapped me.

We had no idea what was going on aft, and for my own part I supposed that Roger and the rest were in straits as sore as our own; but suddenly a tremendous report almost deafened us, and when our opponents turned to see what had happened we got an instant's breathing-space.

"It's the stern-chasers," Davie gasped. "They've faced 'em round!"

The light of a torch flared up and I saw shadowy shapes darting this way and that.

There were two cannon; but only one shot had been fired.

Suddenly Davie seized me by the shoulder. "See! See there!" he cried hoarsely in my ear.

I turned and followed his finger with my eyes. High on the stern of the junk, black against the starlit sky, I saw the unmistakable figure of Kipping. He was laughing — mildly. The outline of his body and the posture and motion of his head and shoulders all showed it. Then he leaped to the deck and we lost sight of him. Where he had mustered that horde of slant-eyed pirates, we never stopped to wonder. We had no time for idle questions.

I know that I, for one, finding time during the lull in the fighting to appraise our chances, expected to die there and then. A vastly greater force was attacking us, and we were divided as well as outnumbered. But if we were to die, we were determined to die fighting; so with our backs to the bulwark and with whatever weapons we had been able to snatch up in our hands, we defended ourselves as best we could and had no more respite to think of what was going on aft.

Only one stern gun, you remember, had been fired. Now the second spoke.

There was a yell of anguish as the ball cut through the midst of the pirates, a tremendous crash that followed almost instantly the report of the cannon, a sort of brooding hush, then a thunderous reverberation compared with which all other noises of the night had been as nothing.

Tongues of flame sprang skyward and a ghastly light shot far out on the sea. The junk heaved back, settled, turned slowly over and seemed to spread out into a great mass of wreckage. Pieces of timber and plank and spar came tumbling down and a few men scrambled to our decks. We could hear others crying out in the water, as they swam here and there or grasped at planks and beams to keep themselves afloat.

The cannon ball had penetrated the side of the junk and had exploded a great store of gunpowder.

Part of the wreckage of the junk was burning, and the flames threw a red glare over the strange scene aboard the ship, where the odds had been so suddenly altered. Our assailants, who but a moment before had had us at their mercy, now were confounded by the terrific blow they had received; instead of fighting the more bravely because no retreat was left them, they were confused and did not know which way to turn.

Davie Paine, sometimes so slow-witted, seemed now to grasp the situation with extraordinary quickness. "Come on, lads," he bellowed, "we've got 'em by the run."

Again clubbing his musket, he leaped into the gangway so ferociously that the pirates scrambled over the side, brown men and white, preferring to take their chances in the sea. As he charged on, I lost sight of him in the maelstrom of struggling figures. On my left a Lascar was fighting for his life against one of our new crew. On every side men were splashing and shouting and cursing.

Now, high above the uproar, I heard a voice, at once familiar and strange. For a moment I could not place it; it had a wild note that baffled me. Then I saw black Frank, cleaver in hand, come bounding out of the darkness. His arms and legs, like the legs of some huge tarantula, flew out at all angles as he ran, and in fierce gutturals he was yelling over and over again:—

"Whar's dat Kipping?"

He peered this way and that.

"Whar's dat Kipping?"

Out of the corner of my eye I saw some one stir by the deck-house, and the negro, seeing him at the same moment, leaped at my own conclusion.

In doubt whither to flee, too much of a coward at heart either to throw himself overboard or to face his enemy if there was any chance of escape, the unhappy Kipping hesitated one second too long. With a mighty lunge the negro caught him by the throat, and for a moment the two swayed back and forth in the open space between us and our enemies.

I thought of the night when they had fought together in the galley door. Momentarily Kipping seemed actually to hold his own against the mad negro; but his strength was of despair and almost at once we saw that it was failing.

"Stop!" Kipping cried. "I'll yield! Stop — stop! Don't kill me!"

For a moment the negro hesitated. He seemed bewildered; his very passion seemed to waver. Then I saw that Kipping, all the while holding the negro's wrist with his left hand, was fumbling for his sheath-knife with his right. With basest treachery he was about to knife his assailant at the very instant when he himself was crying for quarter. My shout of warning was lost in the general uproar; but the negro, though taken off his guard, had himself perceived Kipping's intentions.

By a sudden jerk he shook Kipping's hand off his wrist and raised high his sharp weapon.

From the shadow of the deck-house one of Kipping's own adherents sprang to his rescue, but Davie Paine — blundering old Davie! — knocked him flat.

For an instant the cook's weapon shone bright in the glare of the torches. Kipping snatched vainly at the black wrist above him, then jerked his knife clean out of the sheath — but too late.

"Ah got you now, you pow'ful fighter, you! Ah got you now, you dirty scut!" the cook yelled, and with one blow of his cleaver he split Kipping's skull to the chin.

When at last we braced the yards and drew away from the shattered fragments of the junk, which were drifting out to sea, we found that of the lawless company that so confidently had expected to murder us all, only five living men, one of whom was Captain Nathan Falk, were left aboard. They were a glum and angry little band of prisoners.

Lights and voices ashore indicated that some of our assailants had saved themselves, and by their cries and confused orders we knew that they in turn were rescuing others.   Of their dead we had no record, but the number must have been large.

Of us six who had defied Falk in that time long ago, which we had come to regard almost as ancient history, only Neddie Benson had fallen.   Although we had laughed time and again at the charming plump lady who had prophesied such terrible events, it had proved in bitter earnest a sad last voyage for Neddie.

From the low and distant land there continued to come what seemed to be only faint whispers of sound, yet we knew that they really were the cries of men fighting for their lives where the sea beat against the shore.

"Ah wonder," said the cook, grimly, "how dem yeh scalliwaggles gwine git along come Judgment when Gab'el blows his ho'n and Peter rattles his keys and all de wicked is a-wailin' and a-weepin' and a-gnashin' and can't git in nohow. Yass, sah. Ah guess dis yeh ol' nigger, he's gwine sit on de pearly gate and twiddle his toes at 'em."

He folded his arms and stood in the lantern light, with a dreamy expression on his grotesque face such as I had seen there once or twice before.   When he glanced at me with that strange affection shining from his great eyes, he seemed like some big, benign dog.   Never had I seen a calmer man.   It seemed impossible that passion ever had contorted those homely black features.

But the others were discussing the fate of our prisoners. I heard Roger say, "Let me look at them, Mr. Cledd. I'll know them — some of them anyway. Ah, Captain Falk? And the carpenter? Well, well, well! We had n't dared hope for the pleasure of your company on the return voyage.   In fact, we'd quite given it up. I may add that we'd reconciled ourselves to the loss of it."

I now edged toward them, followed by the cook.

"Ay, Mr. Hamlin, it's all very well for you to talk like that," Falk replied in a trembling voice from which all arrogance had not yet vanished. "I'm lawful master of this here vessel, as you very well know. You're nothing but a mutineer and a pirate. Go ahead and kill me! Why don't you? You know I can tell a story that will send you to the gallows. What have I done, but try to get back the owners' property and defend it? To think that I could have knocked you and that addle-pated Ben Lathrop on the head any day I wished! And I wished it, too, but Kipping he said —"

Falk stopped suddenly.

"So Kipping had a finger in the pie, did he?" said Roger. "Well, Mr. Falk, what did Kipping say?"

Falk bit his lip sullenly and remained silent.

There really was something pathetic in the man's plight. He had been ambitious, and ambition alone, which often is a virtue, had gone far to contribute to his downfall. In many ways he was so weak! A quality that in other men might have led to almost anything good, in him had bred resentment and trickery and at last downright crime. He stood there now, ruined in his profession, the leader of a defeated band of criminals and vagabonds. Yet if he had succeeded in capturing the ship and putting the rest of us to death, he could have sailed her home to Salem, and by spreading his own version of the mutiny have gained great credit, and probably promotion, for himself.

"Well, Chips," said Roger, "I hope you, at least, are pleased with your prospects."

The carpenter likewise made no reply.

"Hm, Mr. Cledd, they haven't a great deal to say, have they?"

"Aha," the negro murmured just behind me, "dey's got fine prospec's, dey has. Dey's gwine dance, dey is, yass, sah, on de end of a rope, and after dey 's done dance a while dey 'a gwine be leetle che'ubs, dey is, and flap dey wings and sing sweet on a golden harp.   Yass, sah."

The carpenter shot an angry glance at the cook, but no one else paid him any attention.

A fire was flaming now on the distant shore.   The seas rushed and gurgled along the side of the ship.   Our lights dipped with the rigging as the ship rolled and tossed, now lifting her dripping sides high out of water, now plunging them again deep into the trough.

"Mr. Cledd, I think we can spare those five men a boat," Roger said, after a time.

"You're not going to let them go!" Mr. Cledd exclaimed.

"Yes."

Mr. Cledd raised his eyebrows, but silently acceded.

I thought that an expression of relief crossed Falk's face, yet dismay was mingled with it.   Those were dark, inhospitable lands to leeward.   The carpenter opened his mouth as if to speak, closed it without a word, and vacantly stared at Roger.   The rest of us exchanged glances of surprise.

When we had hove to, they lowered the boat, fumbling at the falls while they did so, as if they were afraid to leave the ship.   The seas caught the boat and bumped it against the side, but Falk still lingered, even when Roger indicated by a gesture that he was to go.

"Ay," he cried, "it 's over the side and away.   You 're sending us to our death, Mr. Hamlin."

"To your death?" said Roger.   "Sir, do you wish to return with us to Salem?"

Falk glared sullenly, but made no reply.

"Sir," Roger repeated sharply, "do you wish to return with us to Salem?"

Still there was no response.

"Ah, I thought not. Stay here, if you wish. I shall have you put in irons; I should not be justified in any other course. But in Salem we 'll lay our two stories before the owners — ay, and before the law. Then, sir, if you are in the right and I am in the wrong, your triumph will repay you many times over for the discomforts of a few months in irons. No? Will you not come?"

Still Falk did not reply.

"Sir," Roger sternly cried, "if I were to take you back a prisoner to Salem, you 'd go to the gallows by way of the courts. Here you can steer your own course — though in all probability the port will be the same."

Without another word Falk went over the side, and down by the chains to the boat that was bumping below. But before we cast off the painter, he looked up at us in the light of a lantern that some one held over the bulwark and cried bitterly, "I hope, Mr. Hamlin, you 're satisfied now. I 'm rightful master of that vessel in spite of all your high-handed tricks."

For the first time I noticed the marks of wounds that he had got in the fight off the island. His face was white and his eyes were at once fierce and hunted.

"You 're mistaken," Roger replied. "I have papers from the firm's agent that appoint me as master." Then he laughed softly and added, "But any time you wish to carry our little dispute to the courts, you 'll find me ready and willing to meet you there. Too ready, Mr. Falk, for your own good. No, Mr. Falk, it 's better for you that you leave us here. Go your own gait. May you fare better than you deserve!"

We cast off the painter, and they rowed into the dark toward the shore of Java. They were men of broken fortunes, whose only hope for life lay in a land infested with cut-throat desperadoes. I thought of Kipping who lay dead on our deck.   It seemed to me after all that Falk had got the worse punishment; he had aspired to better things; weak though he was, there had been the possibility of much good in his future.   Now his career was shattered; never again could he go home to his own country.

Yet when all was said and done, it was more merciful to set him adrift than to bring him home to trial.   Though he must suffer, he would suffer alone.   The punishment that he so fully deserved would not be made more bitter by his knowing that all who knew him knew of his ruined life.

"Poor Falk!" I thought, and was amazed at myself for thinking almost kindly of him.

CHAPTER XXXII

"SO ENDS"

THROUGH the watches that followed I passed as if everything were unreal; they were like a succession of nightmares, and to this day they are no more than shadows on my memory. Working in silence, the men laid the dead on clean canvas and washed down the decks; cut away wreckage, cleared the running rigging, and replaced with new sails those that had been cut or burned in battle. Then came the new day with its new duties; and a sad day it was for those of us who had stood together through so many hardships, when Neddie Benson went over the side with a prayer to speed him. We were homeward bound with all sail set, but things that actually had happened already seemed incredible, and concerning the future we could only speculate.

We had gone a long way on our journey toward the Cape of Good Hope before our new carpenter had repaired the broken bulwark and the various other damages the ship had suffered, and before the rigging was thoroughly restored. Weeks passed, their monotony broken only by the sight of an occasional sail; days piled on end, morning and night, night and morning, until weeks had become months. In the fullness of time we rounded Good Hope, and now swiftly with fair winds, now slowly with foul, we worked up to the equator, then home across the North Atlantic.

On the afternoon of a bright day in the fall, more than a year after we first had set sail, we passed Baker Island and stood up Salem Harbor.

Bleak and bare though they were, the rough, rocky shores were home. To those of us who hailed from Salem, every roof and tree gave welcome after an absence of eighteen months. Already, we knew, reports of our approach would have spread far and wide. Probably a dozen good old captains, sweeping the sea, each with his glass on his "captain's walk," had sighted our topsails while we were hull down and had cried out that Joseph Whidden was home again. Such was the penetration of seafaring men in those good old days when they recognized a ship and its master while as yet they could spy nothing more than topgallantsails.

We could see the people gathering along the shore and lining the wharf and calling and cheering and waving hands. We thought of our comrades whom we had left in far seas; we longed and feared to ask a thousand questions about those at home, of whom we had thought so tenderly and so often.

Already boats were putting out to greet us; and now, in the foremost of them, one of the younger Websters stood up. "Mr. Hamlin, ahoy!" he called, seeing Roger on the quarter-deck. "Where is Captain Whidden?"

Roger did not answer until the boat had come fairly close under the rail, and meanwhile young Webster stood looking up at him as if more than half expecting bad news.

Only when the boat was so near that each could see the other's expression and hear every inflection of the other's voice, did Roger reply.

"He is dead."

"We heard a story," young Webster cried in great excitement, coming briskly aboard. "One Captain Craigie, brig Eve late from Bencoolen, brought it. An appalling tale of murder and mutiny. As he had it, the men mutinied against Mr. Thomas and against Mr. Falk when he assumed command. They seized the ship and killed Mr. Thomas and marooned Mr. Falk, who, while Captain Craigie was thereabouts, hustled a crew of fire-eating Malays and white adventurers and bought a dozen barrels of powder and set sail with a fleet of junks to retake the ship. But that, of course, is stuff and nonsense. Where 's Falk?"

"Falk," said Roger with a wry smile, "decided to spend the rest of his days at the Straits."

"Oh!" Young Webster looked hard at Roger and then looked around the deck. All was ship-shape, but there were many strange faces.

"Oh," he said again. "And you —" He stopped short.

"And I?" Roger repeated.

Again young Webster looked around the ship. He bit his lip. "What is *your* story, Mr. Hamlin?" he said sharply.

"Is your father here, Mr. Webster?" Roger asked.

"No," the young man replied stiffly, "he is at Newburyport, but I have no doubt whatsoever that he will return at once when he hears you have arrived. This seems to be a strange situation, Mr. Hamlin. Who is in command here?"

"I am, sir."

"Oh!" After a time he added, "I heard rumors, but I refused to credit them."

"What do you mean by that, sir?" Roger asked.

"Oh, nothing much, sir. You evaded my question. What is *your* story?"

"*My* story?" Roger looked him squarely in the eye. In Roger's own eyes there was the glint of his old humorous twinkle, and I knew that the young man's bustling self-importance amused him.

"My story?" Roger repeated. "Why, such a story as I have to tell, I'll tell your father when I report to him."

Young Webster reddened. "Oh!" he said with a sarcastic turn of his voice. "Stuff and nonsense! It may be — or it may not." And with that he stationed himself by the rail and said no more.

When at last we had come to anchor and young Webster had gone hastily ashore and we had exchanged greetings at a distance with a number of acquaintances, Roger and Mr. Cledd and I sat down — perhaps more promptly than need be — over our accounts in the great cabin. I felt bitterly disappointed that none of my own people had come to welcome me; but realizing how silly it was to think that they surely must know of our arrival, I jumped at Roger's suggestion that we gather up our various documents and then leave Mr. Cledd in charge — he was not a Salem man — and hurry home as fast as we could go.

As we bent to our work, Mr. Cledd remarked with a dry smile, "I'm thinking, sir, there's going to be more of a sting to this pirate-and-mutiny business than I'd believed. That smug, sarcastic young man means trouble or I've no eye for weather."

"He's the worst of all the Websters," Roger replied thoughtfully. "And I'll confess that Captain Craigie's story knocks the wind out of *my* canvas. Who'd have looked for a garbled story of our misfortunes to outsail us? However,—" he shook his head and brushed away all such anxieties,— "time will tell. Now, gentlemen, to our accounts."

Before we had more than got well started, I heard a voice on deck that brought me to my feet.

There was a step on the companionway, and then,

"Father!" I cried, and leaped up with an eagerness that, boy-like, I thought I concealed with painstaking dignity when I shook his hand.

"Come, come, come, you young rascals!" my father cried. "What's the meaning of this? First hour in the home port and you are as busy at your books as if you were old students like myself. Come, put by your big books and your ledgers, lads. Roger, much as I hate to have to break bad news, your family are all in Boston, so — more joy to us! — there's nothing left but you shall come straight home with Benny here. Unless, that is —" my father's eyes twinkled just as Roger's sometimes did — "unless you've more urgent business elsewhere."

"I thank you, sir," said Roger, "but I have *no* more urgent business, and I shall be — well, delighted does n't half express it."

His manner was collected enough, but at my father's smile he reddened and his own eyes danced.

"Pack away your books and come along, then. There's some one will be glad to see you besides Benny's mother. Leave work till morning. I'll wager come sun-up you'll be glad enough to get to your tasks if you've had a little home life meanwhile. Come, lads, come."

Almost before we fully could realize what it meant, we were walking up to the door of my own home, and there was my mother standing on the threshold, and my sister, her face as pink now as it had been white on the day long ago when she had heard that Roger was to sail as super-cargo.

Many times more embarrassed than Roger, whom I never had suspected of such shamelessness, I promptly turned my back on him and my sister; where upon my father laughed aloud and drew me into the house. From the hall I saw the dining-table laid with our grandest silver, and, over all, the towering candle-sticks that were brought forth only on state occasions.

"And now, lads," said my father, when we sat before such a meal as only returning prodigals can know, "what's this tale of mutiny and piracy with which the town's been buzzing these two weeks past? Trash, of course."

"Why, sir, I think we've done the right thing," said Roger, "and yet I can't say that it's trash."

When my father had heard the story he said so little that he frightened me; and my mother and sister exchanged anxious glances.

"Of course," Roger added, "we are convinced absolutely, and if that fellow had n't got away at Whampoa, we'd have proof of Kipping's part in it —"

"But he got away," my father interposed, "and I question if his word is good for much, in any event. Poor Joseph Whidden! We were boys together."

He shortly left the table, and a shadow seemed to have fallen over us. We ate in silence, and after supper Roger and my sister went into the garden together. What, I wondered, was to become of us now?

That night I dreamed of courts and judges and goodness knows what penalties of the law, and woke, and dreamed again, and slept uneasily until the unaccustomed sound of some one pounding on our street door waked me in the early morning.

After a time a servant answered the loudly repeated summons. Low voices followed, then I heard my father open his own door and go out into the hall.

"Is that you, Tom Webster?" he called.

"It is. I'm told you've two of my men here in hiding. Rout 'em out. What brand of discipline do you call this? All hands laying a-bed at four in the morning. I've been up all night. Called by messenger just as I turned

in at that confounded tavern, charged full price for a
night's lodging,— curse that skinflint Hodges! — and
took a coach that brought me to Salem as fast as it could
clip over the road. I'm too fat to straddle a horse.
Come, where's Hamlin and that young scamp of yours?"

I scrambled out of bed and was dressing as fast as I
could, when I heard Roger also in the hall.

"Aha! Here he is," Mr. Webster cried. "Fine sea-
captain you are, you young mutineer, laying abed at
cockcrow! Come, stir a leg there. I've been aboard
ship this morning, after a ride that was like to shake my
liver into my boots. Where's Ben Lathrop? Come,
come, you fine-young-gentleman supercargo."

Crying, "Here I am," I pulled on my boots and joined
the others in the lower hall, and the three of us, Mr.
Webster, Roger, and I, hurried down the street in time
to the old man's testy exclamations, which burst out fer-
vently and often profanely whenever his lame foot struck
the ground harder than usual. "Pirates—mutineers—
young cubs — laying abed — cockcrow —" and so on,
until we were in a boat and out on the harbor, where
the Island Princess towered above the morning mist.

"Lathrop 'll row us," the old man snapped out. "Good
for him — stretch his muscles."

Coming aboard the ship, we hailed the watch and went
directly to the cabin.

"Now," the old man cried, "bring out your log-book
and your papers."

He slowly scanned the pages of the log and looked at
our accounts with a searching gaze that noted every
figure, dot and comma. After a time he said, "Tell me
everything."

It was indeed a strange story that Roger told, and I
thought that I read incredulity in the old man's eyes;

but he did not interrupt the narrative from beginning to end. When it was done, he spread his great hands on the table and shot question after question, first at one of us, then at the other, indicating by his glance which he wished to answer him.

"When first did you suspect Falk? — What proof had you? — Did Captain Whidden know anything from the start? — How do you know that Falk was laying for Mr. Thomas? — Do you know the penalty for mutiny? — Do you know the penalty for piracy? — Hand out your receipts for all money paid over at Canton.— Who in thunder gave you command of my ship? — Do you appreciate the seriousness of overthrowing the lawful captain? — How in thunder did you force that paper out of Johnston?"

His vehemence and anger seemed to grow as he went on, and for twenty minutes he snapped out his questions till it seemed as if we were facing a running fire of musketry. His square, smooth-shaven chin was thrust out between his bushy side-whiskers, and his eyes shot fiercely, first at Roger, then at me.

A small swinging lantern lighted the scene. Its rays made the corners seem dark and remote. They fell on the rough features of the old merchant mariner who owned the ship and who so largely controlled our fortunes, making him seem more irascible than ever, and faded out in the early morning light that came in through the deadlights.

At last he placed his hands each on the opposite shoulder, planted his elbows on the table, and fiercely glared at us while he demanded, "Have you two young men stopped yet to think how it 'll seem to be hanged?"

The lantern swung slowly during the silence that followed. The shadows swayed haltingly from side to side.

"No," cried Roger hotly, "we have not, Captain Webster. We've been too busy looking after *your* interests."

The scar where the case-knife had slashed his cheek so long ago stood starkly out from the dull red of his face.

At that the old man threw back his head and burst into a great guffaw of laughter. He laughed until the lantern trembled, until his chair leaned so far back that I feared he was about to fall,— or hoped he was,— until it seemed as if the echoes must come booming back from the farthest shore.

"Lads, lads!" he cried, "you're good lads. You're the delight of an old man's heart! You've done fine! Roger Hamlin, I've a new ship to be finished this summer. You shall be master, if you'll be so kind, for an old man that wishes you well, and"— here he slyly winked at me — "on the day you take a wife, there'll come to your bride a kiss and a thousand dollars in gold from Thomas Webster. As for Ben, here, he's done fine as supercargo of the old Island Princess,— them are good accounts, boy,— and I'll recommend he sails in the new ship with you."

He stopped short then and looked away as if through the bulkhead and over the sea as far, perhaps, as Sunda Strait, and the long line of Sunda Islands bending like a curved blade to guard the mysteries of the East against such young adventurers as we.

After a time he said in a very different voice, "I was warned of one man in the crew, just after you sailed." His fingers beat a dull tattoo on the polished table. "It was too late then to help matters, so I said never a word — not even to my own sons. But —" the old man's voice hardened — "if Nathan Falk ever again sets foot on American soil he'll hang higher than ever Haman hung, if I have to build the gallows with my own two hands, Mr. Hamlin — ay, he or any man of his crew. The law and I'll work together to that end, Mr. Hamlin."

So for a long time we sat and talked of one thing and another.

When at last we went on deck, Mr. Cledd spoke to Roger of something that had happened early in the watch. I approached them idly, overheard a phrase or two and joined them.

"It was the cook," Mr. Cledd was saying. "He was trying to sneak aboard in the dark. I don't think he had been drinking. I can't understand it. He had a big bag of dried apples and said that was all he went for. I don't like to discipline a man so late in the voyage."

"Let it pass," Roger replied. "Cook's done good work for us."

I did n't understand then what it meant; but later in the day I heard some one say softly, "Mistah Lathrop, Ah done got an apple pie, yass, sah. Young gen'lems dey jest got to have pie. You jest come long with dis yeh ol' nigger."

There were tears in my eyes when I saw the great pie that the old African had baked. I urged him to share it with me, and though for a time he refused, at last he hesitantly consented. "Ah dunno," he remarked, "Ah dunno as Ah had ought to. Pies, dey's foh young gen'lems and officers, but dis yeh is a kind of ambigoo-cous pie — yass, sah, seeing you say so, Ah will."

Never did eating bread and salt together pledge a stronger or more enduring friendship. To this very day I have the tenderest regard for the old man with whom I had passed so many desperate hours.

That old Blodgett and Davie Paine should take our gifts to "the tiny wee girl" at Newburyport we all agreed, when they asked the privilege. "It ain't but a wee bit to do for a good ship-mate," Blodgett remarked with a deprecatory wave of his hand. "I'd do more 'n that for the memory of old Bill Hayden." And just before he left for the journey he cautiously confided to me, "I 've got a few more little tricks I picked up at that 'ere temple. It don't do to talk about such trinkets,— not that I'm superstitious,— but she 'll never tell if she don't know where they come from. Ah, Mr. Lathrop, it 's sad to lose a fortune, and that 's what we done when we let all them heathen islands go without a good Christian expedition to destroy the idols and relieve them of their ill-gotten gains."

The two departed side by side, with their bundles swung over their shoulders. They and the cook had received double wages to reward their loyal service, and they carried handsome presents for the little girl of whom we had heard so much; but it was a sad mission for which they had offered themselves. No gift on all the green earth could take the place of poor, faithful old Bill, the father who was never coming home.

That night, when Roger and I again went together to my own father's house, eager to tell the news of our good fortune, we found my mother and my sister in the garden waiting for us. I was not wise enough then to understand that the tears in my mother's eyes were for a young boy and a young girl whom she had had but yesterday, but of whom now only memories remained — memories, and a youth and a woman grown. Nor could I read the future and see the ships of the firm of Hamlin and Lathrop sailing every sea. I only thought to myself, as I saw Roger stand straight and tall beside my sister, with the white scar on his face, that *there* was a brother of whom I could be proud.

THE END

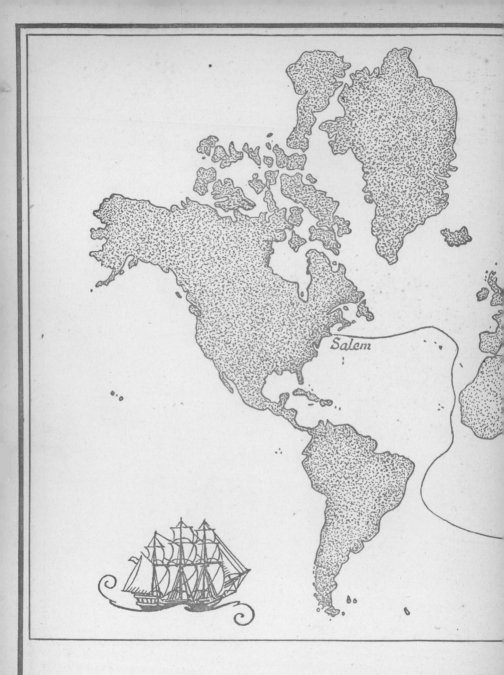

Salem

THE COURSE OF T